BUT THE MORNING WILL COME

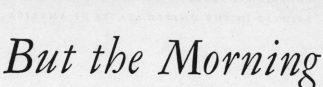

But the Morning Will Come

A Novel

BY

CID RICKETTS SUMNER

THE BOBBS-MERRILL COMPANY, INC.
Publishers
INDIANAPOLIS   NEW YORK

First Edition

BUT THE MORNING WILL COME

THESE *are the years of waiting, the in-between years when
one looks back, trying to understand, when one looks forward, building up strength. For what is to come is ever made
out of what has been. There was a time when I thought
otherwise, when I said, "Here is my life, separate, unique
and all my own to do with as I please." Now I know better.
I know that out of the past we who are the unfortunate have
inherited a debt of evil, to be paid in pain and humiliation.
Those others, the lucky ones, live on the good that has come
down to them, an unearned increment. Our good must be
wrought by us, for ourselves and for those that come after.*

*Our waiting and our apprehension involve but a handful
of people, yet the conditions out of which they have grown
are of large concern. So it must all be set down and looked
at and understood. Meanwhile there are for us the deep
dread and the slow gathering of courage—a delicate balanc-
ing of the two, with only our resolution to tip the scales.*

*And, strangely enough, there is also our happiness. Some
may find it possible to take happiness as their right and due,
with careless acceptance, but we are keenly aware of ours, as
one on the edge of danger savors his bread and cheese with
heightened relish. Ours is sharp, almost to pain, as our eyes
meet above a child's head, as we pause at work in the field
and look across the corn, seeing the heat waves dance above
the tasseled green, as we listen at night to winter rain strik-*

ing the hewn shingles of the roof and running down the gutter to make the cistern a music box of one refrain.

The thing we wait for, the release and the challenge, hang on an old woman's breath. Until it leave her, the promise shall be kept. For a promise is binding even though given to one unloved, out of pity and forbearance.

BUT THE MORNING WILL COME

BUT THE MORNING WILL COME

· 1 ·

WHY is one day set apart from the rest when you look back into your life? What makes one day stand out vivid and arresting as if a wind blew in from the vast subconscious reaches, riffling through the old year's calendar to pin back one page before the mind's eye?

This morning was no different from many another early spring morning since I married Philip and came to live at Cedar Bluff. As usual he finished breakfast quickly and left the dining room to get ready for town. Miss Kate was going with him, as she often did, to one of her innumerable club meetings, so she too excused herself. I poured my second cup of coffee, took another of Minerva's hot buttered biscuits and went out through the hall to enjoy them along with the morning.

I crossed the wide front gallery and paused on the open square where the steps divided in two long curving flights. The house at Cedar Bluff had been built under the French influence and the first floor was high above ground, making a cool understory, now little used. The steps at my right led to a path that ran between altheas to the side yard where the car waited now for Philip. Yellow Anse, lanky and shambling, was flicking a lazy cloth over its hood. I took the steps on the other side and went out under the cedars, across the yard to where the land dropped away abruptly to the river. The path I followed was one my own feet had made, a faint path always, as though the Churston earth yielded unwillingly to alien tread. Cup in hand, I stood on the brink of the bluff beside an old cedar stump and looked down the green-pricked tangle to the water, looked out across the wide Mississippi.

I was always going for a look at the river. Its great sweep of water moving lazily in winter or tumbling along as now in a rush to reach the Gulf satisfied something uncertain within me. It was

1

more than a reminder of the early settlers with flatboats heaped high with household goods, of Indians in tipsy canoes, of the first steamboats, the showboats and handsome packets. It was the future as well as the past. It would be here when I was gone and forgotten, as others had been forgotten. Changeless and ever-changing, it seemed to set my little moment in time.

The river was high now, filled up with brown water from far-off places. I could hear the current murmuring to itself as it nibbled away at the bank. Eventually the whole place would be eaten away. "But not in our time," Philip always said. What came after was not his concern. He expected the Churston family to die with him.

"But it won't," I said aloud to the morning, speaking it out boldly where none could hear. I took a hungry bite of biscuit, leaning over so the melted butter would not drip down on my clean brown percale, thinking how the government dredger could make a straight channel over on the Louisiana side. Then this great bend would be bereft of current and power. In time, with shifting sand bars, there might be only a lake here, moon-shaped and still, where other Churstons would paddle and fish and say how this was once a part of the main stream. I might tell Philip, beginning with the river. "Philip," I might say, "you'd better see about getting a channel cut through so Cedar Bluff will be safe for posterity."

"Why, Bentley!" He had a way of saying my name quick and sharp when I puzzled him. "What do you mean, posterity?"

I licked the melted butter from my fingers, smiling to myself, treasuring my secret. Then I heard him, in the house, calling up the stairs, "Are you ready, Aunt Kate?" I drained the last of my coffee, relishing its flavor and the delicacy of the thin china cup. Our cups at home—my mother's and mine—had been thick and heavy, straight ten-cent-store. Everything we had was like that, cheap as could be had. The Churston things were different.

Turning, I looked back. The cedars, planted long ago by Philip's great-grandfather, looked as if they had been there for-ever and meant to stay as long again. They were secret now as

2

always, their heavy green weighted down and swathed in moss. If one looked down on them from a plane, they would shape a spade. Here at the bluff was the handle. The shaft led straight toward the house and the blade was a hollow square that held it. They were black this morning, as if night had overslept among them. The moss, still wet and darkened by last night's rain, dripped with a whispering sound on leaf and grass and scraggly shrubs that were just showing a tentative green. The house itself was but a story and a half high above the ground floor, without dormers, steep-roofed, and the chimneys at each side were pricked up high and straight, like listening ears.

Philip came out on the gallery, hat in hand. He looked taller than ever there at the top of the high steps, his thin-beaked nose sharp in profile as he turned toward the side yard where Anse with slow-motion strokes was still wiping the car. Philip looked at his watch, tapped the floor with one foot. He did not like to be kept waiting. His hair was black against the white wall of the house. He had brushed it down flat and smooth but one lock was always trying to curl. There was something comical about it— and sweet. I loved the way Philip got cross at that lock, and praised my hair for hanging long and straight to my shoulders as it did now, showing off its straightness as some would flaunt their curls. He even liked its pale-brown color—I would rather have had it black or red or any decided shade.

Seeing him there erect and tall, with that air of being some-body—of being a Churston—I felt pride that I was his wife. I wanted to be a Churston, too, in all my ways. Yet surely it was my own self which had been Bentley Carr, towngrown but a tom-boy, that sent me now running toward him, hair flying, calling out to him so gaily that old Humble, who had followed Philip to the gallery, wagged his tail and opened his sad hound mouth in a sympathetic woof.

I set the cup down on the edge of the gallery and came breath-less to Philip's side. I smoothed down the rebellious lock and then brought my hands down to his shoulders, for I loved their firm compact feel. "Oh, Philip," I began—and caught back the

3

words just in time. I had almost said, "I hope the baby will look just like you." Heavens, this was not the right moment, just as he was leaving for town!

His arms came round me in his fierce quick way. "You won't be lonely?" He was always afraid I would be lonely. Before I could answer, his thin cool lips brushed my cheek and he was saying, "There, dear. We'll be starting. The plantation road may be muddy after last night's rain."

My arms fell to my sides and I stepped back. I knew without looking around that Miss Kate on her tiny rubber heels had come out on the gallery. It was a wonder how anyone as heavy, as big all over, as Miss Kate could move so lightly. She was in the doorway now, drawing on her white gloves, forcing her tiny, limp hands into a size too small because she was vain of them, as she was of her feet. Under the wide-brimmed hat, her face, layered over with powder, was as white as the gardenias that ringed the crown. Little flakes of powder were drifting down from the folds of her chin to settle among the green and blue beads that decorated the front of her black silk dress. As she brushed at them, her prominent gray-green eyes fastened on the cup I had left on the floor. Her mouth, tiny in the vast white expanse of her face, opened in a dismayed circle. "Oh, you will be careful dear? That set—you know it is my treasured one!" Her voice was deep and exclamatory, as if she had too much breath for her words.

I looked at the cup, avoiding the determined sweetness of her face. I would have liked it better if she had just said, "Damn it, Bentley, what are you doing with my best cup?" Miss Kate was iced with sweetness, and the icing, like the powder that plastered her cheeks and neck, was so thick that one could not be sure what was underneath. "I'll be careful," I said, and added, "It's the one Minerva broke the saucer to."

Philip was already half down the steps. "It doesn't matter," he said, not looking back.

Miss Kate followed him with short, noiseless steps, holding her small white purse out, away from her side. Her firmly corseted figure had a solid look that made everything around her seem nebulous and airy, as if she could walk right through it if she

4

took the notion. "But Philippe—" she gave his name a French twist in honor of some of the ancestors she prized so highly— "Philippe, dear, it does matter. Everything matters."

Philip closed the car door behind her, went round to the other side, and Anse, giving his cloth a final flourish, sent a cloud of dust over him. Philip spoke sharply. "Look what you're doing, Anse. Haven't you got any sense?"

Anse stepped back, grinning in the foolish way he had, saying, "Yassuh, nossuh—that's right, suh."

Philip shook the dust from his coat and began with quiet intensity to tell him what a damn fool he was. I turned away, trying not to hear. I could never get used to Philip's manner with the servants: Old Sam, Anse, even Minerva he ordered about, reprimanded or blasted to hell as the notion took him. "But they would not understand anything else," he said once when I protested. "It rolls right off their backs. Just leave them to me to manage." I said no more. I had heard other men speak in the same way and yet with a difference too, with a sort of easygoing tolerance and good nature which took the sting out of their words. With Philip, the sting was there. I was sure of it, even though I knew little about Negroes, really. We had had no servants at home, only old Maria who washed for us, and I loved her.

Philip got in the car now, slammed the door and raked the gears. Miss Kate was an incongruous figure in the long open car. Philip, dark and distinguished-looking, his hat set at the proper angle, went better with it. He had got the car when, rejected for active service because of his heart, he had gone to work in the munition plant at Briggsville for the duration of the war. It was only a few years ago, yet it seemed a long time since he had first driven me about in it, my hair flying in the wind and Philip gay and reckless as he had never been since. There was something about wartimes that made anybody reckless, even Philip.

I watched the car jounce over the cedar roots, skid on the muddy turn and disappear beyond the pecan grove. Then I stood a little while trying to recapture the mood of early morning. When Anse's shuffling step had passed beyond my hearing, everything was still, the house silent and empty, old Humble asleep

5

against the wall. In the yard, not a leaf stirred or a wisp of moss. My step sounded ghostly and hollow as, after picking up the cup, I moved through the open front door, under the many-paned fanlight.

I was gathering myself together again, becoming my whole self, not just Philip's wife. Was it always like that? I wondered. Did a woman always have to shape herself to the one she loved? Did a woman in love always have to be a little worm, curling to fit—or less than a worm, an amoeba, maybe, flowing this way and that? I laughed at the notion. Love was wonderful, anyway.

I liked the feel of the empty house. It became mine, somehow, when Miss Kate left it. The stairs pleased me, rising as they did in a graceful, unsupported curve to a landing where an arched door led to the upper ell porch. On my right and left the double sliding doors to parlor and music room were closed, and along the walls, above the horsehair sofa and following the stair upward, the Churston portraits hung, gold-framed and fixed in their rigid pose. All Churstons. The other side of the family had not run to that kind of vanity. "I'd chuck you all out, if I had my way," I said aloud. "Throw everything away and start over." With that my spirits rose. I had the whole day to myself and plenty to do.

A few moments later, in sneakers and blue jeans and an old white shirt of Philip's, its tail flapping, I was on the open platform that extended from the ell porch to cover the well. I worked the pump handle briskly up and down. Overhead the cloudless sky was a pale, hazy blue, the black shingles of the ell roof sloped up to empty space, and the black cedar tops that showed above them, pointed without meaning. All the color in the world was caught in the courtyard formed by the main body of the house, the ell and the runway to the kitchen. There the azaleas—red, white, pink, magenta—trapped on these three sides spilled out to where the cedars dammed them back. Color like heat waves danced in the air, reflected by the white walls of the house.

Philip had had the house painted just before he brought me here as a bride. I wished that someone had told him any bride would rather have plumbing or electricity. But Miss Kate liked

6

the house to stay as it had always been—even to her own inconvenience. Until this spring she had always had her club luncheon here at the time of the azalea's blooming. But this year she had announced with no explanation that she was entertaining in town, joint hostess with Mrs. Bellows Woodworth. Was it because I was not eligible to the club, and there was an awkwardness about having the meeting here? For Miss Kate's sake I wished I had had ancestors distinguished before the Revolution.

Yet, if my ancestors and I were not good enough, my descendants would be. And that made me think of a new way to tell Philip what I had to tell him. Leaning on the pump handle, I laughed as I imagined myself saying, "Philip, in November perhaps I shall present you with a little Colonial Dame."

Minerva, dark and gaunt, faded skirts flapping about her long legs, came across the runway, the lamp chimneys set on her fingers like hurricane shades on black candles. "Some folks feelin' mighty fine this mornin', Miss Bent." She let the words out grudgingly, as always. Then when she had set the dripping chimneys in a row on the ell table where the lamps stood for filling, she added, "Sound good, hearin' a body laugh round here."

That struck me. Nobody really laughed here at Cedar Bluff. Philip smiled at my nonsense sometimes, but Miss Kate—would anything in the world make Miss Kate laugh?

The water was gushing forth now, filling the pail, running over into the trough that fed the ditches around the azaleas. I gave one last strong downward push and caught my breath, letting the pump handle fly. Somehow I had twisted a muscle. I was always forgetting to be careful. Minerva as usual missed nothing. "Hadn't ought to be pumpin' like that. Liable damage yourself."

As the sharp twinge passed, I flung around to face her, a question in my eyes. It couldn't be—nobody knew yet. But Negroes— they had a sort of second sight about some things. Like old Maria that morning five years ago when I met her in the kitchen and tried to get out the incredible words, Maria saying, "It's your ma," knowing without being told. I could not have lived through those next lonely months without Maria.

Now, looking across the well platform to Minerva, seeing her face dark against the white wall of the ell, I knew that she knew. I felt my lips tremble, then I let go and grinned in answer to her rare snaggle-toothed smile. She came across the ell gallery, turning solemn now, the light reflected on one knobby cheekbone above the dark hollow of her cheek. Her voice was a whisper, though there was none in the house to hear, her bony black fingers tightened on the lamp chimney in her hands. "It's a good thing, Miss Bent. Don't let nobody tell you different." Her black eyes narrowed. "You have that child, I tell you. You have him."

I stared back at her, speechless, my breath quickening under her dark gaze. Then, sharp in the silence came the crack of glass. The chimney shattered in her grasp, fell to the floor, the broken pieces breaking anew. Minerva looked down, stepped back. She crossed herself, her lips moved without sound. Then she turned toward the runway mumbling, ". . . Ain't me . . . done broke itself, that's what."

After a moment I bent and picked up the pail of water and moved slowly through the door to the back hall. The way she had spoken was enough to give a body the creeps. But who was going to want me to . . . to not have—why, it was ridiculous. Just Minerva's funny way. She was a strange Negro, not at all the old-mammy type people talked about so much. Half the time she did not speak when spoken to. She even answered Miss Kate back sometimes. I heard her one day when Miss Kate said, "Here, Minerva, I saved you some gumbo to take home for your supper." Minerva said, "Won't the dawg eat it?" She never even said thank you if one did something for her, just grunted. Oh, it was silly to be all shivery over the way she had acted just now. She probably knew Philip did not want children, that was all. Lots of men did not want children, especially men who were older, like Philip, and had got out of the idea of having a family. Once it was here, he would love the baby. He would probably be one of those utterly foolish, indulgent fathers.

I thrust Minerva from my mind, stopping at the turn of the stairs to cast a housewifely glance over the lower hall. There was dust along the tops of the portraits, a cobweb starting across the fanlight and I just could not understand where all the dust came from. For here there was no city street, no town traffic as there had been at home. Even the gravel road did not begin till one had passed the plantation gate, and the main highway was all of a mile to the east of that. "Dust just creates," old Maria used to say. But I was not going to dust today. I had more interesting things to do.

Upstairs I passed Miss Kate's half-open door and wondered as always at the complete disorder of her room. I had grown up in a shabby old house on the wrong side of town with all the spare, bare rooms let out to roomers. I didn't set myself or my family up to be anybody, but our house was always neat. Miss Kate—how could she keep her things like this! The bureau was littered with bottles, handkerchiefs, powder puffs, powder boxes with the lids off; two bureau drawers were partly open with garments trailing out. One shoe was in the middle of the unmade bed, her everyday corsets hung over the back of a rocker by the fireplace and her nightgown was on the floor, just as she had stepped out of it. Yet Miss Kate would come out of that room even on days when she was not going to town, looking neat and tidy, her faded, straw-colored hair that showed no streak of gray drawn back smoothly to a great bun at the back of her neck. But I could never understand Miss Kate.

I turned in at the opposite door, entering a room identical in size and shape and furnishings. Upstairs here in the main part of the house there was only the wide hall and these two rooms. This was mine and Philip's and here everything was in order. Of course Philip himself was painfully neat, and besides he had another room on the basement floor where he kept his old clothes, his papers and account books. I took a pride in keeping things tidy. Perhaps a trace of malice was mixed with my pride, for my neatness was a reproof to Miss Kate's careless ways.

I took a key from the marble top of the bureau where Philip had left it, straightened a corner of the spread as I passed the old four-poster and went on to a door which I had never seen open. The lock creaked, the hinges cried out and as it swung back a veil of gray spider web stretched and tore. Warm musty air rushed out to meet me. Three steps led down into the room—as I

9

should have known, for the ell was lower than the main part of the house.

Even when I had opened porch door and window, the stale air lingered in the room as if, after thirty undisturbed years, it were reluctant to stir. I sat on the top step and looked the place over. Philip had said I could spread out here for the summer if I liked. Of course I should have told him then that I wanted it for a nursery. But once more I had put off telling him.

This had been Philip's mother's sitting room and it was surprisingly bare. There were a few wicker chairs, an oak chiffonier that had lost one leg and leaned dejectedly against the wall. There were a shabby table and a low open book case, and over by the window a small rocker lay on its side. On the window sill beside it there was a sewing basket with some scraps of lace and a spool of yellowed white thread with a threaded needle laid across the top of it. Philip's mother must have been sewing when they came and took her away.

I could not take my eyes from that spool of thread. All at once the tragedy of her life was real, sharp and poignant as it had never been before. She too had come here as a bride. She had borne two sons and then—— "She turned against us . . . a nervous breakdown," Philip had told me. "It became impossible to keep her here, to give her the proper care." That was all he had ever said, except that she lived on, and that he scarcely remembered her. He never spoke of his father. I knew only what Miss Kate had told me—that he was a recluse, a scholar, and that he had died of pneumonia many years ago. My thoughts came back to Philip's mother. What was she like now, shut away all these years in the state hospital near Jackson? The portrait in the library showed her as a young girl with a delicate, sensitive face, an innocent, a defenseless air. In that dark, dull room the pure gold of her hair was like a flame, lighting up the corner where the portrait hung.

I drew a sigh, got up and went for mop and broom and dustcloth. I thought I would have the walls whitewashed, maybe, for the old boards were almost bare of the original paint, and I could dye cheesecloth for the window curtains. I did not mind pinching pennies, though I had to keep reassuring Philip on that score. He was always worrying about money, worrying because his munition-plant savings were so quickly gone—for the car, for painting the house and for our wedding trip to the Coast.

"You are sure you won't be lonely?" That was his other worry.

"Why, I love it here," I had told him over and over. I did, too. It had seemed glamorous and romantic to me. Maybe every Southerner is touched by the landowning fever and has illusions about plantation life—a kind of hang-over from handed-down stories of ante bellum days and from reading too much moonlight-and-magnolia fiction. The kind that has no more relation to reality than my childhood impression of Philip fitted the man he really was. For I remembered him out of long ago.

The Churston pew was up in the front of the church, in the middle. My mother and I sat off to one side where the pews followed the curve of the chancel. The whole congregation was there for me to look at during the long sermons. It would have been hard to miss one of Miss Kate's size and dignity, crowned with a big picture hat such as she still wore. There was a streak of purple light that came through a stained-glass window to fall across her shoulders like a royal scarf. I thought she had a royal look.

In those far-off days Philip had seemed almost as old as Miss Kate, a grown young man who could not be expected to see a skinny little girl with pigtails and a sharp, eager small face. Nor could Miss Kate see my mother. There was a great gulf fixed between the important families of the county and a widow seamstress who lived on the shabby side of town, and Miss Kate was not one of the ladies who came to our house for fittings and thought it well worth while to pass through the second-class business district to get sewing cheaply done. On the far side of Miss Kate someone else used to sit in the Churston pew—Philip's younger brother Hollis, with hair of pure gold. Fair as an angel, I used to think, looking across at him. To this day I cannot hear the word suicide without remembering him.

I shook a broomful of cobwebs and baby spiders out the window, thinking how curious it was the way one's first associations

11

clung to a word. Island, for instance. I remembered the first time I ever heard of an island. There was a tiny one in the pond on the Curry Road where my mother and I used to walk on Sunday afternoons and she had told me what it was. On our street there was an old beech tree with a knobby growth on its trunk. Excrescence—she had pronounced each syllable carefully till I could repeat it. So the word suicide——

I heard it first on the sidewalk in front of the church. I know the very spot where Mrs. McCall stopped my mother, tossing back the long widow's veil she wore, though it was no longer the fashion to wear mourning veils. She and her sister Mrs. Mall—there was always something fascinating about the way their names rhymed—were both widows and wore black dresses my mother had made for them, and on Sundays these long black veils, as if they would reproach the Lord for the untimely removal of their husbands. Usually they came in late, after the first hymn, when everyone was seated again. Only this morning in their eagerness to spread the news they were early.

"Oh, Mrs. Carr!" they cried together, gathering close like black buzzards to a feast. Mrs. Mall said, "Did you hear about the younger Churston boy?"

Mrs. McCall pecked the morsel with relish. "Last night. Committed suicide." The word made a hissing sound.

The Churston pew was empty that morning with a haunting emptiness. After church, crossing the little park on our way home, I asked, "What does it mean . . . he committed . . . that thing?" It seemed too terrible to speak the word right out into the clear bright morning.

My mother waited a moment before answering. I can still remember the look of the gravel path and one small stone I kicked with the toe of my shoe, forgetting that Sunday shoes must not be scuffed. When she had answered, all I said was, "He had such pretty curly hair."

"Too curly," my mother said, comforting me perhaps for my own straight locks.

The books and shelves were wiped clean of dust now and I had put away the scraps of lace, the threaded, rusty needle and the spool. I stood back from the window and measured it with my eye. Six yards would be enough, and the dye would cost only fifteen cents.

Minerva came with my lunch on a tray, as she often did when Philip and Miss Kate were away. I took it to the upper ell porch where I could sit and stretch my legs while I ate. "It's going to be the nursery," I told Minerva when I saw her looking into the room. She only grunted and went on. I wondered if she would help me whitewash the walls. My mother and I had done the back bedroom at home. Though it was really too much for her. I wished now, as I had a thousand times, that I had noticed how gray her color was that last year. But I was about to get through high school and for the first time I was thinking of parties, wanting to be invited to more of them than I was invited to, relentless in my begging for new clothes, hoping they would somehow make a difference. Yet I had not really cared too much—life was fun and what the heck, I would say.

Then, afterward, there was no money left, for the house still had the mortgage that was taken out to cover the expense of my father's illness when I was a baby. There was no hope of college. I had to go to work at once—at the new munition plant, and that was a lucky thing, for there Philip and I met.

Minerva came again, bringing wet mop and soap. "Reckon I mought scrub the floor for you," she said gruffly, as if ashamed.

"That will be wonderful," I sighed. "I'll sit and cool off till it dries." I grinned at her, feeling the secret bond between us in spite of her glum manner. "Don't you tell," I said.

"Humph! Knows a sight of things I ain't tellin' nobody." She slammed the mop down and got to work.

I wiped the sweat from my forehead, pushing my hair back of my ears. It was really hot today—though after those summers at the munition plant I had resolved never again to complain of heat. The building I had worked in was an oven, even for the swing shift. There were explosions, too, though it took the biggest one of all to make Philip notice me out of all the women who were in the department he supervised. It came late one hot August night.

13

One moment, seated at the assembly line, I had been reaching out for a spoonful of powder to put in the partly filled shell before me. The woman next me was squawking, "Bodies, bodies," and the cry was being tossed across the room, relayed by varying voices till it should reach the boy who brought supplies. Bodies to kill bodies, I was thinking. Bodies making bodies to kill bodies. The next instant it came—a flash, a roar and a sheet of flame that swept my arm and shoulder and threw me over backward. I lay on the floor quite indifferent to all around me. Vaguely I was conscious of movement, of screams, shouts and one crisp cool voice calling out orders. With detachment I studied the way the falling powder burned at the long workbench, how the flames dripped down like bright water spilled from a bowl of fire. Pretty, pretty fire. I was annoyed when someone came between to gather me up and bear me out of the brightness, across the uneven ground of the dark yard to lay me down on a narrow white bed in the first-aid room. I blinked at the nurse, and at another face bending over me—Philip's, smoke-stained and anxious. "I'm all right," I said. And I was. Only my hair was singed.

That night Philip drove me home to my rented room in town, not letting me take the bus as I usually did. He swore he had been wanting to do that for a long time, ever since he first saw me. After that he took me home every night. There had been nothing worried and cautious about him then. It was as if his sudden falling in love with me had created another emergency, like the explosion, to which he had risen with courage and decision. Yet, knowing him as I did now, after these years, I found it hard to reconcile that Philip with this one.

By midafternoon the room was clean, all but the window. I stood on the sill and wiped away the thick gray dust from the old-fashioned small panes. It was hot up there close to the ceiling. I had to stop to wipe the sweat from my face and when I got down for a cloth wet in cold ammonia water, I undid the top button of my blue jeans and tied my shirttail up, leaving a bare midriff to cool me.

The house was still. Minerva had gone home, not to come back till time to cook dinner. I had the place all to myself. But after the baby came, I thought, I would always have company. Scrubbing away, I let myself dream a little about him. There must be something special about a baby that was . . . unplanned. Some persistent roguishness, maybe. This amused me and I worked faster, humming a tuneless little song.

Suddenly, though there was no sound save the rub and squeak of my cloth against the pane, I knew that someone was near. Holding to the window facing with one hand, I looked around. Miss Kate was standing in the doorway. But what was the matter? Her mouth was open in a stupid little round, her face under its sweat-streaked powder seemed to be cracking. The washcloth slipped from my hand and fell to the floor with a little plop that was loud in the silence. I turned away, fumbling at the knot in my shirttail, wanting to cover myself against those knowing eyes. "You—you must have taken the bus," I said, not looking.

She let the words fall unnoticed as the drop of the washcloth. I felt her eyes still on me as she moved down the steps like something floating weightless on the air. "Does Philippe . . . know?" She whispered it on an indrawn breath, as if she would take back the words even as they were spoken.

I swallowed, a pitiful small choking sound. I clung to the window like a bird, snake-struck. Then dumbly I shook my head.

Miss Kate's lips closed in a thin line, her mouth no bigger than a fishhook. "Come down, please, dear." Her husky voice was back to normal now and she gathered her sweetness around her like a cloak.

I stood before her as if convicted of wrongdoing, waiting a sentence, my eyes on the wet cloth on the floor while she took her time. But why should I feel guilty and ashamed? Why was this any of Miss Kate's business? I flung back my head, straightened up and spoke before she could. "I would prefer to be the one to tell him, Miss Kate. If you don't mind." The words were mild enough but I put a sharp edge on each one.

They did not seem to cut into Miss Kate's consciousness. She could always ignore what she did not wish to see or hear. "How far along?" she asked.

After a pause that said it was none of her damn business, I

15

told her. She drew a quick breath. "Well now, listen, dear. You may not have noticed, but Philippe has not been looking at all well lately. We must spare him this worry. Monday I will take you to Dr. Whitlow. He will do everything that's necessary. Philippe need never know."

I had to wet my lips before I could speak. "You—you mean——"

Miss Kate turned away and her deep voice came back to me as she mounted the steps. "Of course, dear. It's the only thing to do.'

She was crossing my room on her soft whispering tread when I cried out, "No!"

She stopped, stood motionless while the sound of that one word seemed to beat against the walls before it broke into silence. "Then we shall have to wait and see what Philippe says."

I heard her door close. Then I left the room, I left the house, moving blindly toward the river, quickening my steps as I went. I could not breathe, I could not see, I was all atremble with fury. But my feet found their way along the path at the top of the bluff. Branches struck my face, tore at my sleeve; I did not feel them as I went faster and faster.

I did not slow my steps till I had passed the little iron-fenced enclosure that was the family burying ground. Dark-green magnolia trees shaded it, making it cool and quiet save for the crackle of the dead leaves under my feet. When I stopped, they went on crackling, as if ghostly feet were following after me. The Negroes said it was Philip's grandfather walking. But I was not thinking of that now. Miss Kate, I said to myself with bitterness—how could she? Miss Kate, so soft-spoken and sweet, gesturing with her boneless little hands that were too ladylike for anything but embroidery and crochet. Miss Kate, full of good works in the Ladies' Aid, in all the best clubs, proud and yet so sweet, people were always saying. I did not like her, never had. And she had never liked me. She resented me. She had not wanted Philip to marry at all, and if he had to marry she would have had him marry someone more *comme il faut*, as she would say. "I . . . I hate her." Now it was out, spoken aloud to tree and bush, to the little wild violets blooming under my feet.

Then I was ashamed. Philip's aunt. I must not let myself. I

16

walked on slowly, eyes on the ground, till the sound of voices stopped me. I looked around then and saw I had come too far inland, so that I was in the woods back of one of the Negro cabins, the one where Old Sam lived with his granddaughter Callie. Through the underbrush I saw her lying in the shade of a hackberry tree, her hands clasped under her head. Anse leaned against the tree trunk, bending his lanky body as he talked to her. I turned away quickly, yet the picture they made stayed with me, their soft voices followed me, so that I envied them their ease, their relaxed and carefree air. Callie never came to the house, though sometimes I met her when I walked out to the mailbox at the plantation gate. She would say, "How you today?" tossing her head, twitching her shoulders, swishing her plump little behind. She made me uncomfortable, as if she were really saying, "I'm as good as you are and I know it."

The afternoon sun slanting through pale-green leaves laid shadows across the tree trunks. I dipped into a small depression and came into a patch of bush honeysuckle, all rosy and fragrant. I broke a petal, put it between my lips and it was velvet-soft and sweet. The woods soothed me now as always and when I came out on the high bank of the river I was able to shake away the thought of Miss Kate. Philip was the one who counted. I would tell him tonight and everything would be all right.

I went down the slope to a sand bar—my sand bar, I called it. The brown rising river had diminished it and the outer willow stood in the water, one drooping branch going deep under the surface. It bobbed up and down, making a little whirlpool as if it had caught a fish. I kicked off my sneakers and the yellow sand was soft and warm to my bare feet. I cooled them in the rippling edge of the water, then I knelt and washed my face. I wanted to strip off my clothes and have a swim, but it was still rather early in the season, so I moved back to drop down alongside the old willow log. I stretched out on the sand, looking up into pale slender leaves against the blue sky.

No one else ever came here—by land. A few times I had seen a neighbor of ours on the river, paddling his dugout past the point, a fishing pole between his knees. Once he had come alongshore and we exchanged a few words—about the weather, about the string of fish he held up for me to see, their bright scales opalescent in the sun. When I had told Philip of seeing him, he said, "Jeff Wheeling. Lives down the road on the old place, in a house that used to be a Negro cabin. I don't know why he is trespassing on my land."

"But he was on the river."

Philip did not like to be corrected. Or maybe he just did not like Jeff Wheeling. "The man is a radical, full of wild ideas, though his family has lived here for generations. He went away, to college or something, and now he's back teaching school, down at the crossroads. There's some opposition to his re-election and quite right, too."

I wondered what Jeff's new ideas were, but I did not ask. Philip liked things to go on just as they always had gone. In fact, I thought now, flinging my hands up over my head, stretching, relaxing on the soft sand, it was a wonder that Philip, with his dislike of change, had married at all. For now he was going to get some changes whether he liked them or not. I rolled over on my stomach and closed my eyes.

The water lapped sweetly at the edge of the sand bar. The river breeze blew over me, lulling me to sleep, mild and soothing. After a while some alteration in the ripple of the water roused me. A faint sound of movement brought me wide-awake. I rolled over, got up on one elbow. A dugout was drawn up with its nose on the sand. A man in khaki trousers, bare to the waist, was bending to take a shirt from the bow. His bronzed back and shoulders were wet; water dripped from his hair. I knew him at once—Jeff Wheeling.

He had just drawn the shirt over his head when my sneakers there at the edge of the water caught his eye. He stared down at them, with such a comical look I had to laugh. He wheeled then, his eyes that were deep-set and blue widening and then crinkling up as he smiled. "I say, where did you come from?"

"I reckon I must have been asleep, here back of the log." I chuckled. "You looked at those shoes of mine as if you expected them to walk off by themselves."

18

"Thought I was seeing things." His fingers fumbled at the buttons of his shirt, his eyes holding mine.

"It's crooked."

He looked down, started over, buttoning it straight. He shook his head, like a big shaggy dog, got his shoes from the dugout and came over to the log to sit and put them on. It was only then that I saw he was lame, not badly, but enough to be noticeable, and I wondered if he had been in the war. "Nice spot—for a swim, or a nap," he said. His speech was slow, his movements were deliberate without being at all lazy. It was as if he took pleasure in every least thing he did.

I sat up, shook my hair back and watched his hands as he laced his shoes. I was always noticing hands, perhaps because I thought my own homely, too stubby-fingered for beauty. His were large and bony, like his face, like his whole body, and they moved with the same disarming awkwardness. I rested in their movement, and I did not feel that I must make any answer to what he said.

He straightened, fumbled in his shirt pocket for cigarettes, held them out to me. His fingers touched mine briefly as he gave me a light. They were firm and cool, they would smooth away a headache, they would hold fast what they took. I leaned back against the log and drew a long pull at the cigarette. It tasted good to me, though I had given up smoking. Philip did not like to see me smoke, perhaps because it was against doctor's orders for him. "How was the water?"

"It's getting warmer. Fishing was good, too."

"What did you catch?"

"A fair-sized cat—enough for supper for one hungry man."

"Don't you have any family?"

He shook his head. "Nor a cook either. But I can fry fish and make a hoecake. Of course I get my main meal at the school cafeteria."

After a minute I asked, "Is it just that you like to teach?"

He looked at me for a long moment with an expression I could not fathom. "Why is it people always expect one to apologize for being a teacher?"

"I . . . I didn't mean——"

19

"Not you. Most people."

"They don't know how important it is, maybe."

He nodded. "That's why I came back to teach."

I studied his rugged bronzed face, remembering what Philip had said about him. "Countrypeople are conservative, slow-moving and . . . and maybe a bit suspicious."

He leaned over, resting elbows on knees, his bright eyes fastening on me. "A kind of balance wheel for the wild ideas that hit the rest of the population. Only it won't do to let them lag too far behind." Then after a moment he added, "You've been hearing things."

I looked down at the sand, gathered up a handful and let it fall. "Y-yes, a few."

"You can't always believe what you hear. I've heard things, too, you know."

I flung back my head and tried to see how serious he was. "Wh-what do you mean?"

He laughed. "Don't look so startled. Nothing bad—only about how Phil Churston keeps his young wife hidden away at Cedar Bluff. Afraid to let anyone look at her, she's so beautiful."

"What nonsense!" I was cross and pleased at the same time.

"Not all of it."

"Yes, all. You know very well I'm no beauty." I laughed, remembering something from long ago. "When I was little I asked my mother if I would be a beautiful lady when I grew up. She said quite flatly, no. Though she added, to comfort me, that I had a bright quick look she liked better. So I've always known about me and beauty."

"Yeah?" It was nice the way he said it.

"And as for the rest of it—the hidden-away business—why, we go to church every Sunday of the world, and I go to town when . . . when I take the notion." There was just enough truth in the rumor that I spoke with more warmth than I intended.

"Don't you get lonely?"

"Of course not." But something in his clear steady gaze made me add, "Just sometimes. Who doesn't, sometimes?"

20

"Maybe you don't have enough to do, with Miss Kate running the house as, knowing Miss Kate, I'm sure she does."

Miss Kate—— I sprang up, seeing now that the sun was almost down. I snatched up my shoes, standing on one foot, then on the other to put them on. But there was a hard knot. "Damn," I said and broke the string. Oh, why had I stayed so long?

"You act like Cinderella at the first stroke of midnight," he said.

"But I'm not leaving any glass slippers around." I laughed and, without even saying good-by, ran across the sand and up the bluff.

21

· 2 ·

AFTER dinner Philip went straight to his desk in the library, moving the one reading lamp to stand at his elbow. Miss Kate, with a significant glance in my direction, went on to the music room adjoining. I sat down with the evening paper in my hands, not reading, just waiting till Philip should put away his pen and his accounts and be free to listen.

Miss Kate began to practice scales to the thin accompaniment of the old piano that tinkled off key. Or maybe it was Miss Kate who was off key. Her voice, husky and breathy, had a curious monotony of tone, as if even running up and down the scales it stayed in the same place. Every now and then there was a listening silence. Was she just turning a page of the exercise book or was she trying to hear if I was speaking? I rattled the newspaper so Philip could not hear the sudden pounding of my heart.

The yellow lamplight shone on his cheek, making it more sallow than usual; it showed up the touch of gray at his temple. Maybe he really was not well, as Miss Kate had said. Oh, dear Philip, I said deep inside myself, don't be sick. Be well and strong and don't mind, please don't mind what I'm going to tell you.

"Ah-ah-ah," Miss Kate sang. "Mi-mi-mi." Other evenings I could close my ears to it, but tonight, as I sat taut and keyed-up, the sound was amplified as if my head were a sounding box. I let the paper slip to the floor and covered my ears with my hands. Oh, why did I have to be so nervous and upset over something that was only natural and right and that I was really happy about?

I must get hold of myself. I put my hands in my lap again and tried to fix my mind on something else. I studied the room, making myself think what I would do to change it if I had money to spend. First of all, another window so it would be lighter, and gay yellow curtains instead of brown, brocaded bits of gloom. I

22

would keep Philip's desk, throw out the center table with its brown fringed cover, and I would get some easy chairs instead of the mission-oak monstrosities that had been bought when the original mahogany chairs and sofas went to pieces. I would rip out the carpet with its threadbare brown and blue cabbage roses, and I would have more than one good reading lamp so that Philip would not monopolize all the light when he sat at his desk.

Miss Kate was through with scales now. She began on her songs. There were four that she "kept up" so as to be prepared when called on to sing at one of her clubs. "My heart is like a singing bird," she breathed, rather than sang, one word melting into the next so I could never have understood but that I had heard them so often. "Whose nest is in a watershoot——" She stopped. I could almost hear her listening, trying to catch our voices. Oh, damn, damn, I thought, why did I keep thinking of her? As if she were one big eye, X-raying the wall to see me, as if she were one big ear cocked to the least sound.

She began again, "My heart is like a watershoot whose nest is in a singing bird . . ." At that, silent laughter seized me, shook me, bent me double. I kept telling myself it was not that funny, but I could not stop. Tears streamed down my cheeks and I could hold in no longer. Philip dropped his pen and ran to me.

"Why, Bentley! What on earth!" He caught me by my shoulders and shook me. "Stop it! Stop it! Here—Aunt Kate——"

That really stopped me. "No, no," I gasped, "don't call her. It's just the watershoot. Struck me all at once . . . don't . . ."

"Just lean back and relax. I'll get you a glass of water and——"

"No, no." I caught him by the coat and pulled him back. "J-just give me a handkerchief." I wiped my eyes, blew my nose, still holding him fast with one hand. Then I leaned back in the chair, limp and still trembling on the edge of laughter. "I'm just silly, that's all, Philip dear. Maybe I'm extra silly because I'm going to have a baby." I began to laugh. This was really funny, my coming out with it like this, after all my planning.

"Don't start again— What? What did you say?" His voice tightened.

There was a little silence between us, my laughter frozen. "Is

. . . is it so strange, so . . . horrible? After all——" I choked, seeing the stricken look on his face. "Oh, Philip, please want it. I do. I——"

He moved closer, yet a little behind me so I could not see his face. With one hand he slowly stroked my hair. "There, there, never mind," he said as if he were not thinking what he said. "Never mind. You couldn't help it."

"But I didn't want to . . . to help it. And you oughtn't to either." I shook away his hand and sprang to my feet. "Why do you have to mind so? What did you marry me for, anyway? What did you expect? Why can't you just be pleased and happy about it—the way I was till . . . till . . ."

He took me in his arms then, his cheek against my hair. "Of course. It's all right." He kept saying it over and over as if he had to convince himself, too. "It's just that you surprised me. Don't worry about it. It's all right."

"Is it? Really and truly?" I whispered against his coat.

"Of course, dear. It's only—well, the money." He drew a long breath. "I wanted to give you everything. I was a fool to—— I should never have brought you here, you, so young and lovely. It was only that I loved you. And I . . . I had to have something. . . ." His voice died away in a sort of groan.

But all my worry and hurt were gone, dissolved in the blessed fact that he loved me. I held him at arm's length, my hands on his shoulders, as I blinked away tears of relief. "Money, money—it doesn't matter. I don't want anything but just what you can give me. It doesn't take money to have a baby—not much anyway. I can get some. I'll smock dresses and sell them in Miss Ida's Shoppe as my mother did. I'll raise chickens——" The words came tumbling over one another. Oh, I was safe now, secure in his love.

When he kissed me tenderly and told me to go up to bed because he still had accounts to do, I went lightly up the stairs, not thinking once of Miss Kate or even knowing if she were still at her singing. Later, hearing the murmur of voices, I wondered what they were saying, but even that could not disturb me. Smiling to myself, I drifted off to sleep.

24

· 3 ·

THERE must always be some sadness mixed with the memory of
happy times. For, looking back, one sees what was hidden then,
knows how transient they were. Good times blur, like the spokes
of a wheel, fast turning. Perhaps that is how a thousand years
may be as yesterday and as a watch in the night.

The days that came now were swift days and fleeting. Spring
had gone all of a sudden into first summer, hot June summer.
Leaves that had been delicate and tentative were spread to the
sun, full-blown. Quick rainstorms blew up the river from the
Gulf; then the sun came out and all the lush, still earth steamed
in its fertility. In the fields the young corn had made a good
stand, the sweet-potato slips were thriving. There were life and
hope everywhere on the countryside and I was part of it.

It seemed as if Cedar Bluff plantation, after years of just scrap-
ing along, making little more than tax money, must prosper now;
it seemed as if that rare conjunction of good crops and good
markets had arrived at last. Yet Philip said no harvest was sure
until it was gathered. I began to see then that worry was a part
of him, from which he could never escape no matter how fair
the prospect. Yet his concern for me in these early weeks of the
summer was translated into a tenderness that was sweet beyond
anything I had ever known. The words of the marriage covenant
—to love and to cherish—so often spoken, so seldom remembered,
were real to me now.

Even Miss Kate was indulgent—of my happiness and of his care
for me. Not that she said much, but it was in the air, a kind of
benign tolerance, even a wistfulness in the way her eyes followed
me. She did not object when Philip brought me breakfast abed
on Sundays or came home early to take me for a little drive before supper. For my part, I could hear now without impatience
her endless talk of club meetings, her tales of famous ancestors

25

and her "ah-ah-ah" and her "mi-mi-mi." I did not mind her managing all the details of the house without consulting me. I did not wish to go to town or to see anyone. Everything I desired was here, ten miles from town, off the gravel road, shut in by the river and a ragged rail fence, sheltered under old cedar trees.

Once driving with Philip I had a glimpse of the old Wheeling place, saw the shabby small house, silver with age, set back from the road with a fan of green vines across its face, a woodpile on one side and a single water oak on the other. I remembered with wonder how eagerly I had talked with Jeff Wheeling at the sand bar and how for a brief moment I had seen my own life through a stranger's eyes and found it empty, precarious and lonely. Now I was safe and each day was filled with activity.

For I was determined to make enough money to pay for my hospital and doctor's bills. With some of my small savings from munition-plant days I had bought eggs for setting and I had had wonderful luck. The coops Anse had patched up for me sheltered a fine lot of baby chicks, downy, yellow and busily pecking from morning till night. I had sent off for government bulletins and studied them with eagerness. But I had no money to spend for brooders or to build fine runs. Minerva said, "Folks been raisin' chickens a long time without all them notions." So in the end I had just followed her advice, feeding them corn bread and curds and scraps from the table. Each morning I stole out of bed before Philip awoke, eager to see how they had come through the night.

My chicks were just losing their soft baby look and coming into the scraggly stage when the big storm came. All night wind shook the house and roared in the chimney; it banged the shutters and flung the rain in solid sheets against the side of the house. In the morning, at first light, running out through the courtyard to see how they had fared, I saw blank sky where it should not be. One of the largest cedars was laid low, its fan of red roots wrenched from the earth, indecently exposed, its branches muddied and its gray moss outflung like an old woman's hair.

The plank walk slipped under my feet, oozing sideways in the wet clay, but I caught my balance and ran on. Anse had helped me move the coops to fresh ground only the day before, and one of them was close by the cedar. It was unharmed, thank heaven! The wind had ripped loose a flap of tar roofing. That was all the damage I saw till I looked in through the opening. A mother hen was huddled in one corner and as she stirred a small sparse peeping came from under her wings. The floor of the coop was deep in mud that had washed in, and here and there as I leaned down, my face brushing the wet tar paper, I could see a yellow beak, a drenched feathery mass, an anguished claw thrust bitterly from the muck.

I ran from one coop to the other, gathering into my skirt the weak, the droopy. The mother hens, impassive, cruel as nature itself, were mindful only of the living. Overhead the sky was fair and blue, there was no wind, only the clear innocence of a summer day. How could it be so, heedless and without mercy!

In the kitchen, close to the warm wood stove, I lifted each pitiful small body and laid it in the box Minerva found for me. Some tottered and lay down. Others stayed precariously upright and some even pecked halfheartedly at the crumbs with which I tried to encourage them.

"Reckon you might save a few," Minerva said in her flat, grudging tone.

"Oh, don't say it like that," I cried. "So . . . so accepting, so resigned."

Minerva went on rolling out the breakfast biscuit. "What's daid's daid. Ain't nothin' gwine raise it."

"These aren't dead—not yet——" My voice broke. I had been counting on them so. I had spent hours figuring out how much money I would make, and while I sat sewing on some bright smocks to wear later, I had calculated how much ten more hens would cost and how many more fryers I could raise. Besides, I had loved them.

Maybe Minerva was sorry for me. She came and looked down into the box, her dark hands white with flour. But she only grunted, then got a cup and saucer and poured some black coffee. "Here," she said, setting it at the end of the kitchen table, "you better drink this."

I straightened up and moved slowly across the room to sit

there, one elbow on the table, forehead resting on my hand. The coffee did me good; the sick, hurt feeling passed. I let the dream go—my small childish dream of making a lot of money and astonishing Philip. Now I would have to earn what I could with my sewing. I could do it, for my mother had taught me well and I knew all the smocking designs she had used on little girls' dresses. I had just wanted to do something different.

Always when young, we rebel against the familiar, thinking our own lives must be more exciting and wonderful than our parents', not seeing that the likeness to their lives, to those of all humankind, is greater than any small variation we can invent, and that being born as we are, the pattern is mostly ready-set. I saw this now, and that I must accept it. I must sew as my mother had. "Minerva," I cried, springing up, "try to keep the chicks warm. Save what you can, will you, please? I have to go to town."

Minerva finished looking at the biscuit in the oven. She slammed the door. "Never let nothin' die yet, apurpose."

I met Philip in the hall. "I want to go with you to town—to get some cloth. Won't keep you waiting a minute." I dashed up the stairs two steps at a time. But at the turn his voice stopped me.

"Not today, Bentley. The plantation road will be impassable. I'll have to walk out and get the bus."

Miss Kate spoke from the upper hall. "Tomorrow's the day for you to go, dear. I forgot to tell you: I made an appointment for you with Dr. Whitlow. Twelve o'clock."

I stood motionless, caught, pinned between them. "Oh," I said, the enthusiasm draining from me. I looked up at Miss Kate. "I don't need a doctor. I never felt better in my life."

"Just a routine checkup, dear. I was talking to Mrs. Bellows Woodworth and she says it is the way they all do now and it is much better." She passed me on the landing, adding, "You find it out early, if anything is wrong."

I waited on the landing, my eyes on her broad back as she went quickly down the stairs, one small hand light as a powder puff sliding down the rail. If anything is wrong, if anything is wrong —the words seemed to swell and diminish with the sudden throbbing in my ears. It was as if the loss of my chicks, small thing that it really was, had opened a door, one I had not noticed before. Now, though it had not yet swung wide, other evils were free to enter. I shivered in the mild morning air.

"Coming, dear?" Miss Kate said, not looking round.

Philip finished breakfast quickly. "I'll be home early," he said, rising, stopping by my chair to lay his hand on my shoulder briefly. "I want to ride over the place and see if the storm did much damage."

I was glad then that I had not mentioned the loss I had had. If the crops were washed out, that would be a real disaster. I caught his coat and held him back from going. "Oh, Philip," I cried, seeing the deep, worried lines in his face, "you are the one who ought to be seeing a doctor for a checkup. I wish you would. You don't eat enough."

He bent and laid a light kiss on the top of my head, then went on without answering.

"He does look bad." Miss Kate helped herself to another biscuit and a spoonful of peach leather. "His heart—it's a chronic condition, really not dangerous as long as he takes care of himself. Of course right now he's concerned about you."

"He doesn't need to be. I'm fine."

"You're not eating this morning." Miss Kate never missed anything.

"N-no. The chicks—the little drowned ones. I keep remembering them."

"The storm, I suppose."

"Yes."

"Well, after all—" she patted her lips with her napkin in a way I particularly disliked—"it isn't quite the suitable thing for you to be doing." Her eyes turned to the window and her listening look made me listen, too.

I heard Philip outside, calling Anse, his voice sharp and angry. I went to the window, leaned out and saw him standing by the open door to the carriage house. Anse was shuffling toward him, tripping awkwardly in his haste. "Look at that. Just look at it."

29

Philip was pointing to the rear of the car. "Suppose I had been driving this morning. That tire was soft yesterday. I told you to change it as soon as I got home. Now look at it."

Anse mumbled something, standing with his arms hanging loose and long at his sides, shaking his head. Philip's words were like blows. My fingers tightened on the window sill. It was my fault Anse had not changed that tire. I had called him to help move the coops to fresh ground. "Philip!" I leaned out the window.

Miss Kate said, "Bentley! Wait, dear."

I turned. "What?"

"You must not interfere, you know."

"But why not? It's because of me. Anse was helping me——"

"Bentley dear—" Miss Kate smiled—"you cannot tell Philippe before a servant that he is wrong. What are you thinking of?"

"But if he is wrong——" I left the window, Philip's voice still sounding in my ears: ". . . and what's more I don't want you here after sundown. You don't live on my place and——"

Miss Kate said, "I advise you to leave the management of the Negroes to Philippe, dear. Now do have some more coffee."

"No . . . no, thank you, Miss Kate." Yet I drank it because she had gone right ahead and filled my cup. Then I left the room, went along the ell porch and out the runway to the kitchen.

Minerva was at the window, leaning out. "Anse, you fool," she was saying, "I told you not to be monkeyin' round with that Callie. What kind of trouble you want to get yourself into, man?"

Negroes were different when they spoke to each other, I thought, hearing her quick words and Anse's light laughter as I went on to the carton beside the stove. "Miss Kate is ready for you to clear the table, Minerva," I said.

She grunted, took up a tray and went. I lifted the old apron she had spread over my chicks and looked in. Three were dead, two were lying stiff-legged, far gone. I bent over them, grieving for their own small sakes, for the hopes they represented. Then I turned my mind to what I had to do. There was a remnant of blue chambray upstairs in my bureau drawer, enough for one little dress, and luckily I had the thread for smocking.

30

All morning I worked in my room, cutting, stitching the tiny stitches my mother had taught me. She seemed near to me always when I was sewing. I had never felt that she was in the graveyard on the outskirts of town where her body lay. I did not visit her grave, as some find comfort in doing. Why should I seek her where she was not? She came to me, a vivid, living presence, when I tucked in a sheet corner or did some such small thing, knowing as I did it that she had used that same quick movement of hand or that turn of wrist. Surely this is how the dead must live again, in moments brief as this, yet intimate and dear. So now, clipping my thread, I heard her in the quick snap of the scissors, in the small decisive clatter as I dropped them on the table, and I was comforted against the damage of the storm.

As usual, Miss Kate and I spent the day independently of each other. Minerva took her a tray—in her room if she was lying abed reading one of the murder mysteries Philip brought her from town, or in the library if she was up and crocheting. I went to the kitchen and made my own sandwich. We were two strangers staying at the same hotel, our lives as much apart as our thoughts and our manner of thinking. Only toward evening when it began to be time for Philip to come, only then did we meet, with common accord presenting to him a picture of amiability and companionship. Miss Kate never asked how I had spent the day. I could disappear for hours, swim alone in the swift river, row the skiff miles upstream and she never troubled to say, "Did you have a pleasant afternoon?" or "Well, dear, what have you been doing?" Nor did I inquire into her activities. It was a sort of freedom for me, perhaps for her as well, and I was grateful to her for it.

So this afternoon when my eyes were tired of fine stitches and my back ached from bending over my work, I got into shirt and slacks and went out to the river. The water was still high and, even this soon after the storm, it was reddish-brown, thick and heavy with the sediment it carried. I went down the bluff by the steps that had been cut long ago in the earth and now were partly washed out, making a perilous slope. Green leaves, whipped off by last night's wind, lay thick under my feet and saved my sneakers from mud. At the water's edge I untied the skiff, drew it up and tipped the water from it. It was old but good and stout and I was proud of my skill at the oars.

Going upstream as usual, I kept close to the shore under the shade of the bluff's projecting trees, moving out only to skirt a half-submerged trunk or a heap of driftwood lodged alongshore. The air was fresh and clean as if washed pure by the storm, and it was good to pull on the oars till the sweat broke out on my forehead. For all day, in spite of myself, I had mourned for my baby chicks, and the scene between Philip and Anse had weighed on me.

There were really three Philips, I thought, rowing on with steady stroke. There was the one I had known before we were married, the reckless, impulsive one. There was the gentle Philip who loved and cherished me, and there was this other one I had heard lashing out at Anse, a stranger, harsh and hurtful. Yet not quite a stranger, a small corner of my brain reminded me. There had been times when Philip was displeased with me. I do not mean that he spoke to me as he did to Anse. I almost would have preferred that. With me he was cold, withdrawn and formally polite. Without warning, without reason, he could change in an instant. Even on our honeymoon it had happened. On the veranda of the hotel at Biloxi a man in the chair next mine had fallen into casual conversation with us, telling stories of the islands in the Gulf. Of course I was interested, for it was all new to me. But Philip had taken it to be interest in the man himself. Ridiculous? Yes, but the truth was that Philip was horribly, unreasonably jealous. I had to be constantly on guard lest some glance, some word of mine, however harmless, should plunge him into one of those moods that so hurt and baffled me. I forgot, when they were past—until the next time, or until I heard Philip speak as he had this morning. Then it was as if the ground where I stood was quaking bog, as if the foundations of the house in which I lived were shaken.

I was far up the river now. The high bluff on my right was wild and densely wooded, with no sign of human habitation. The other shore, green and low-lying, was equally deserted and all the bright river was empty. I was alone in the world. Pulling **hard** against the current, I felt a sense of triumph over it, that I **could** drive the skiff ahead as I wished. For there is a fine exhilaration of spirit as well as body which comes of fighting something larger than one's self. I could not change the direction of the current— only the slow mighty force of nature could do that—but I **could** move in the desired direction.

Turning at last, I swung out, amidstream. From there I could float home, resting my oars, guiding myself with one hand on the rudder. I watched how the small waves broke and danced in the sunlight and their brightness lulled me, almost hypnotized me. I did not see the floating snag until it struck and almost swamped my skiff, set it spinning crazily. One oar got away from me, so I had to paddle awkwardly after it, reaching and missing and reaching it again. It was caught in one of those eccentric little currents in which the river abounds, one that moves counter to the main flow of the water and, seen from the shore, makes a little rosette of ripples on its bosom. I retrieved my oar at last and, trying to turn shoreward, found that I too was caught in that deceptively innocent eddy which moved downstream as it whirled. It was like a world turning on its axis and yet moving on its appointed course through the heavens. I was penned in by driftwood so I could not make a fair stroke of the oars.

I was breathless with the struggle when a voice hailed me from downstream. Jeff Wheeling shot his narrow dugout toward me, swinging his paddle with swift long strokes. "Take it easy. I'll get you." In a few moments he was near enough to toss me a rope. "Brace your feet and hang on. I'll have you out in a minute."

He kept to the edge of the eddy and with a few strong strokes drew me out of danger. "I've been caught like that, myself," he said. "These currents are tricky." When he had towed me close ashore, out of the main current, he held my skiff alongside his boat saying, "You ought to look where you're going, lady."

I laughed shakily. "I know. Half my chicks got drowned last night but I didn't mean to follow suit."

He gave me a keen look. "I'll take you in to the landing."

I let him take me most of the way, then I said, "Thanks **a lot.**

33

I'm all right now." For it was growing late and I did not want Philip coming out to the bluff to look for me and perhaps see us together. "Truly I am all right."

He caught the rope I tossed him and let me go. But he waited, holding his dugout against the current until I had come to the landing and climbed ashore. Then, with a wave of the hand, he turned and headed downstream. I watched till he was out of sight beyond the curve, then I tied up the skiff and slowly mounted the bluff.

Miss Kate sat rocking on the gallery, her crochet falling like a white apron across her dark skirt. She did not look up as I came to the top of the steps. She never looked at me when I was wearing blue jeans if she could help it, and I was glad of that now, for they were soaking wet to my knees. But I had to know. "Has Philip . . . Is he here yet?"

"Yes, dear." She bent to study a stitch. "He was asking for you, looking everywhere for you."

"Oh." I studied her impassive white face but it was blank. "Wh-where did he—— I mean, where is he?"

"He has ridden out to look over the fields. You'll have time to change your clothes before he comes in."

"Oh," I said again, and went slowly through the hall door. Had he looked out over the river? But even if he had, I would just tell him, tell him the truth, that Jeff Wheeling had probably saved my life, that—— Oh, why hadn't I rowed myself all the way home? Then there would not have been any chance of Philip's seeing him.

34

· 4 ·

THE drive in to town with Philip was always a treat to me. I went so seldom that the sights of the road could never be dull, and from the moment the plantation gate closed behind us I had a feeling of excitement and adventure. It was quite different from Sundays, going to church in midmorning when the dew was off the day and Miss Kate sat beside me, blocking my view with her large black hat, subduing me with her solid churchly air. Indeed it seemed to me that Miss Kate was always with us, except abed, and even then I sometimes had the feeling that her large ear was at the keyhole.

So this morning it seemed good to be off alone with Philip. He was quiet, for he did not like to talk when he was at the wheel. But I did not feel there was any other reason for his silence. He had found but little damage done to the crops by the storm and in his search for me the evening before he evidently had not passed near the river. My mind was full of plans for the day. When the shopping and the visit to the doctor were done with, I thought I would go to a movie. That would fill the time till Philip left his office at five. I sniffed the little moss rose I had pinned on the front of my blue linen jacket and said, "I feel as if I were going to a party."

Philip took his eyes from the road for a moment, turned them on me with a glance so somber and foreboding that I was startled. Just then the car wheels struck a washed-out hole in the road and I bounced almost to the ceiling. Philip said with sharpness, "Don't talk to me when I am driving. That jolt——"

"It didn't hurt me," I said. I wanted to tell him that he must not worry about me, for I saw he was fearful of what the doctor might have to say. But I held my tongue and looked out the window.

The air that would be warm and muggy by noon was fresh and

35

sweet. Along the roadside bank spiders had spread their silver scarves to dry amid the little wild roses. In low places a gray mist stirred lazily, as if earth and cloud had lain together in the night and day had caught them lag-abed. We turned from the gravel road into the main highway now, a little pond flashing like a mirror with a green embroidered frame.

Philip drove faster on the paved road; cars whizzed by. For a fleeting moment as we met I looked into a driver's face and thought how our lives and this stranger's, at twice fifty miles an hour, hung on the turn of a wheel. I did not like this part of the drive. It was all speed, without meaning or pleasure. Yet it brought us quickly into the edge of town. The gray country cabins were left behind and now the houses were painted, set close together on green open lawns edged with purple iris or splashed with the pink and red of rambler roses. No smoke came from the chimneys, for there was natural gas here, brought in cheaply from the Jackson field. It was a great convenience, no doubt, yet without the gray drift of smoke from the chimney top, a house has a forlorn, dead look, as if its heart were burned out and only cold ashes lay on the hearth.

We left Main Street as soon as we came into the edge of the business district, took a small side lane and came in to the back of the courthouse where there was parking space for the county employees in the shade of water oaks. When Philip had driven in at just the right angle with the car's nose to the wall of the jail, he took out the key and turned to me. "Are you feeling up to it?"

"Of course, Philip. I feel up to anything." I did wish he would not keep asking me how I felt. Miss Kate was just as bad, always saying, "Really, dear, in your condition, should you be doing this?" I wanted to ignore my condition and then just be surprised when something came of it.

I waited while Philip got out of the car and came around to my side. That was one of the many little things I had had to learn, for I felt quite capable of lifting the handle and jumping out by myself and did not see any real reason for waiting helplessly for him. Still, it made me feel taken care of and most properly lady-like.

36

"I want you to promise me one thing before I let you go," Philip said with earnestness.

"Why, yes, of course, Philip. What is it?" I searched his dark, lined face.

"Promise me you will put yourself completely in the doctor's hands and do exactly as he tells you."

"But—" I laughed—"that's what one goes to a doctor for, isn't it? I mean, if you knew yourself——"

Philip frowned. "One never knows. But if you should feel ... poorly ... or anything, have him call me and I will come at once and take you home."

"Oh, Philip, what a worrier you are! But I will call you if I need anything and I'll do just what he tells me, starting the very minute he says it."

At that he seemed satisfied. Yet he did not ask me what I meant to do with the rest of the day. Usually he wanted to know exactly where I would be and sometimes he would even call the library where I often waited for him, to remind me, he said, to meet him at the car at five o'clock. As if I did not know! Once when I was shopping for a hat, he called the millinery shop to make sure I had enough money. Philip was like that and I was used to it, took it as a sign of his concern for me. So I did not mind when he said, "Now, what time was your appointment?" as if he did not trust me to know and had to check on it.

"Miss Kate said she made it for twelve o'clock."

He patted my arm, bent and quickly kissed my cheek. Then he hurried away toward the courthouse steps. I was startled. I stood staring after him. For Philip thought any public exhibition of affection was in the worst possible taste. What had got into him? I wondered, as I set out by the little dirt path that cut through between two buildings and brought me out on Main Street. The shops were just beginning to open, the sidewalks still empty of shoppers. When I came to the little hole-in-the-wall place with a pink and blue sign, GIFTE SHOPPE, I saw that Miss Ida was just putting up the shade of her tiny show window. I knocked and went in without waiting for an answer because Miss Ida was quite deaf.

She was still at the window, bending to rearrange some white handbags so they would show better. She had a curved, busy look, like a little gray bird arranging her nest, and she gave me a fierce birdlike glance over her glasses as she turned. "Why, it's little Bentley Carr—I mean Churston. Can't get used to your being grown-up and married. Just a minute——" She spoke in a flat toneless voice. "I must put out these figurines."

I stood looking over the crowded little shop. Gadgets and doo-dads cluttered the counters. There was a hit-or-miss arrangement of baby caps, nylons, pottery and hand-painted trays. Suddenly, down in one corner of a shelf behind the cash register, I saw a little red pincushion. It was one my mother had made. It had a glass standard, like a goblet's, and it was shaped like a strawberry. My mother had made these pincushions in spare moments all one winter, long ago. For a moment I was back in the shabby small room we shared, seeing the bright red scraps spread on the counterpane, seeing my mother's slender shape, stooped from bending over her needle, her lips grave, her eyes intent on her task until I spoke. Then she would look up with her quick, bright smile.

"I . . . I want that," I said, my voice breaking as I spoke.

Miss Ida could not have heard me, but she was quick to catch the direction of my gaze. "Oh, yes, one of your mother's. The last I have." She darted back of the counter and pounced on it.

I took it from her quickly, not wanting anyone else to touch it. My fingers went over it, feeling the tiny French knots, the smooth silk. It was cruel, the way things lasted, while their maker—— I fumbled at the clasp of my purse.

"Take it and welcome, dear," Miss Ida said. "People have got out of the way of pincushions. Such tiny stitches—your mother was an artist with a needle. The stuff I get nowadays——"

I thanked her, then I said, "Could you sell some smocked dresses for me, the way you did for her?"

A shrewd look came into her gray eyes. "What's that?" She bent an ear in my direction. I knew she had heard me and just wanted a minute to consider, perhaps to wonder why Philip Churston's wife was wanting to do such a thing. For most people thought Philip and Miss Kate had money. They had the air of it, that was all. "Maybe." She scratched the tip of her pointed nose, her eyes going over me, probing, exploring. "You want to make some?"

I nodded. "I love to make them ... and I don't have enough to do." I had to shout it over again before she heard.

"You can still get servants in the country and I suppose Miss Kate runs the house. Going to make your own baby clothes?"

I shot her a startled glance. In my blue linen suit I thought no one could possibly tell. But Miss Ida's eyes made up for her poor hearing. She always knew everything that was going on in town and people came in to gossip as much as to buy. I said, "Yes," and turned away, pretending an interest in the row of horrid little china dogs that sat on the counter. "Will you take the dresses?"

Miss Ida shrugged. "You might bring in two or three to start with and I'll see what I can do with them."

Out on the street again, the pincushion tucked in my handbag, I hurried along, though I had all the day before me. In the town's one department store I found some lovely chambray and chose thread for smocking. I was going to make these dresses so beautiful they would be bound to sell. Then I would make some money in spite of the storm and my poor little chicks.

The sidewalks were no longer empty, but among all those I met there was none I knew except the Johnsons who lived on the place just across the gravel road from us. I said good morning to them, thinking the daughter Ovelia would be quite pretty if she did not friz her hair so and wear such a lot of paint.

The whole aspect of the town had changed in the few years since I had lived there. The store fronts had lost their small-town look and now sported chromium and plate glass. There was an air of hustle and hurry too that was unfamiliar to me. The very crowds on the street looked different, for the burlap bag factory and the overall place on the outskirts of town had brought in new people, and the boys and girls I had gone to school with were grown-up now and scattered. This morning more than usual I had a lost, strange feeling, like a ghost come back to haunt—and haunting was a dull business, I thought.

I had been moving aimlessly, yet my feet had taken their own way and now, seeing I had come to the railroad tracks, I went on with purpose in my steps. At the old corner the barbershop was just the same, only there was a new name across the front. The little bakery, that used to smell so wonderful, was changed to a dirty-looking laundry and through the window I saw a Negro man ironing a shirt. After that—— I stopped short and stared. Where the shabby gray picket fence should have been and the shallow yard with a scraggly Cape jessamine on each side of the plank walk, there was a new filling station.

A car tooted at me and I moved out of its way. Then I saw that the house had been moved back, the fine old hackberry tree I used to climb cut down to make way for it. The house was shabbier than ever and had lost what little respectability it had once had. Bricks had fallen from the chimney and lay untended on the roof. A pane was gone from the front bedroom window and the hole was stopped up with a piece of dirty quilt. As I looked a woman peered out, her face untidy with sleep and framed in frowsy hair.

I walked slowly on, wishing I had not come. Yet somehow, seeing the place as it was now sharpened my memories of the way it used to be, as an old woman looking in the glass might see her young self beneath the sagging mask of age. I remembered how I used to fling open the gate. I could hear the clatter of the plank walk as I ran to the steps, pigtails flying, books under my arm, shabby brown coat flying open. I would shout to my mother first thing, dash to the kitchen for a cold biscuit, dig a hole in it with one finger and fill it with molasses. Then I would go and tell her about school, licking my fingers as I chattered. All over the world, no doubt, countless children ran home from school, but I was this one, just this one, to be remembered now with poignancy. I thought too of the morning when my mother did not wake, when I ran screaming to the hall, and old Miss Teasdale, who roomed with us and cooked on a gas plate because she did not want to go to the old ladies' home, came tottering out to see and to call the doctor. There was nothing he could do except try to comfort me. How kind old Dr. Felting had been!

If he were alive now I would be going to him instead of to Miss Kate's doctor. I had planned to go to his son, young Dr.

Will, when I needed to go to anyone. But Miss Kate had got ahead of me. I would have felt more at home with him. Suddenly I wanted terribly to go to him, to have him look after me. And why not? I was the one who was going to have a baby—not Miss Kate. This was my business and nobody else's. Why shouldn't I do as I pleased about such a very personal thing? I quickened my step as the resolution took shape.

The clock on the Presbyterian Church chimed ten as I turned in at the doctor's gate. His office was a small building set off to one side of the house and reached by a path that led between rows of tall crepe myrtles. The very look of it cheered me because I remembered coming here with my mother. The old doctor's name was gone but everything else was just the same. I opened the screen door and went into the waiting room. I would have half an hour to wait till office hours began, but I would be the first in line.

The room filled slowly and the doctor was late, but he was worth waiting for. He knew who I was—not just that I was Philip Churston's wife. He had a look of his father, his hands were sure and skilled. And when I was out on the street again I felt like dancing and skipping. Everything was going to be perfect. I was a healthy young woman, it seemed, and all I needed to do was eat and exercise as usual and come once a month for a checkup.

I was so relieved and happy—for Philip's anxiety and Miss Kate's "if anything is wrong" had been weighing on me in spite of myself—that I was in the drugstore having my lunch before I remembered the other appointment. It was 'way past the hour. How could I have forgotten! I gulped the rest of my soda and hurried to the telephone booth. It would be awkward explaining but surely any reasonable person would understand.

"Dr. Whitlow?" I began. "This is Bentley Churston, Mrs. Phil——"

"Where are you, Mrs. Churston?"

His question took me aback and the little speech I had planned went out of my mind completely. "I'm in Layton's Drugstore. I forgot to call you and I'm sorry. I——"

41

"Just a minute—" And vaguely in the background I heard a woman's voice saying, "No, he left quite a while ago." Then the doctor's deep voice demanded, "Are you all right?"

"What? Oh, yes, but why——"

"It's your husband, Mrs. Churston. He is very anxious about you. He's been trying to reach you."

"Oh—but is anything wrong? Is he ill? What——"

"N-no. But naturally he was quite concerned when you did not keep your appointment here and——"

"Oh, dear, I should have . . . I should have told him, and you, too, of course. You see I just decided all of a sudden to go to Dr. Felting. His father used to be our doctor and——" I was making a mess of everything and Philip was going to be furious with me.

Dr. Whitlow's heavy voice was rumbling in my ear and for a moment I could not think of what he was saying. I was filling up with dread. ". . . just a slight misunderstanding of your plans, no doubt——"

I broke in on him. "No, he thought I was going to you, and I was, only I just decided all at once—I mean, after I got to town, after I left him."

"I see. Well, it's quite all right as far as I am concerned, Mrs. Churston. It may well be for the best. Anything such as your former association with Dr. Felting's father, anything that gives you confidence at this trying time is extremely helpful. And you are in good hands with the young man. In your condition you need——"

My condition! This trying time! Thank heaven, I had not gone to him, the old windbag! I interrupted him, "But my husband—where is he now?"

"Oh, yes. That chap worries too much, Mrs. Churston. Not at all the thing with his heart and I told him so. I said, 'Now quit your fretting. The little woman's off buying a hat or something.'" His laughter struck my ear like a blow. And if there was anything I hated heartily it was being called the little woman. He went on talking while I took the receiver from my ear and wiped the sweat from my face. It was close in the phone booth and I felt sick all over.

"But where is he now?"

Again the doctor laughed. "Said he was going straight to the police. He was sure you had met with an accident. But I persuaded him to try walking up and down Main Street a few times first. You will probably——"

"Oh, thank you." I slammed down the receiver and tore out of the drugstore, looking left and right, searching the noon crowds. I kept telling myself there was no reason to be upset, or for Philip to be, but he was beyond reason when he took one of these notions about me. He would think I was in love with young Dr. Felting—no, no, he did not know yet I had been to see him. But that was what he would think when he found out. Oh, it wasn't worth it, nothing was worth having Philip down on me.

I had been the length of the street once and was coming back when a wave of nausea swept over me. I stopped in front of a little dress shop and waited for it to pass, leaning my forehead against the cool surface of the plate-glass window, pretending to be looking in. After a little I saw myself reflected in the glass, hair disheveled, hat on one ear. I lifted one hand to straighten it and stood transfixed in that stupid pose. Philip was behind me, his face drawn and tense. In an instant there came swooping down upon me the memory of other times when he had been angry with me, so that I suffered not only for the present but for the past, all the in-between good times wiped out as if they had never been.

My arm came down slowly, like something hung on rusty hinges. I turned, speechless, and no doubt the picture of guilt. Always at these times I seemed to say and do the wrong thing. No matter how innocent, I could not present an air of innocence. There was something about being under suspicion that drove me to behave unnaturally. I knew I looked guilty and that didn't help any either.

"Bentley," he said through tight lips, "where have you been?"

"J-just around town. To the doctor——"

"This time I know. You did not go to the doctor. You——" He glanced around as if suddenly aware that we were in a public place. "Come to the car."

43

I had to take little running steps to keep up with his long strides. Where is your care of me now? I thought with bitterness, holding my package tight against me, my breath noisy between parted lips. We crossed the street and had two blocks to go before we could turn in between buildings by the dirt path that cut through to the back yard of the courthouse. Once I tried to speak but he silenced me with a gesture.

At the car, under the cool shade of the oaks, he faced me, not meeting my eyes. It was as if in his heart he knew better and was ashamed. "Now," he said in a cold tone that shattered the beginnings of pity within me, "now let me hear what you have to say."

I moistened my lips, tried to speak naturally. "Oh, Philip dear. It isn't anything. I'm sorry you were worried. I should have let you know, only I did not know you would phone the doctor, or go there or anything. I meant to phone and break the appointment——"

"Break the appointment?"

"Yes, yes, that's all it was. You see, I just got to thinking—I didn't really know your doctor and I did know Dr. Felting because he took care of my mother and——"

"Dr. Felting is dead."

"But his son——"

"You went . . . to . . . young . . . Dr. . . . . Felting?" He spaced the words so each struck my ears like a blow.

"Yes, Philip, I did, and please don't mind. He says I'm fine and all I have to do is eat and exercise and come every month for a checkup, and Dr. Whitlow himself says that he is a good doctor and I couldn't be in better hands. That's all there is to it. I explained to Dr. Whitlow how it was I just suddenly got the idea I'd rather go to somebody I sort of knew and——" My breath gave out.

Philip took off his hat and wiped his forehead with his handkerchief. He opened the door of the car. "If you will get in I will drive you home."

Suddenly I could not bear it. "No, no, Philip. Don't you understand? Won't you understand?"

"I am waiting, Bentley," he said, not looking at me.

44

"Listen," I cried, "you must listen. I haven't done anything to deserve to be treated like this and I won't have it. I know I should have told you but I didn't even think of it till this morning—that I would rather go to Dr. Felting. You haven't any right to treat me like this just because I didn't phone Dr. Whitlow, because I didn't go to him. You——" I was silent. There was no use. It was like beating myself against a wall. I made one more attempt, I tried to shock him into reason. "It's ridiculous, your acting like this. You'd make me laugh if you didn't make me so sick. Go on back to your office. I'll go to the library and read till time to go home and maybe you'll get some sense in your head before then. Or I can take the bus." I turned away as if to go.

"Get in, please." His face was gray with white lines around his mouth, and his hand held my wrist so tight I almost cried out.

I looked at him for a long moment, then the fight went out of me. There was no use. I sat silent all the way home, my eyes on the floor. When we came in by the plantation road to the cedars at the side of the house, he stopped the car, though not until he had turned it round, heading away again. Then he got out, came and opened the door for me, not speaking, not looking at me.

That was more than I could take. "I won't have it this way," I cried. "I won't . . . you can't—— Wait, Philip!"

But he was already in the car, sliding across the seat to his place under the wheel, and the sound of the engine drowned out my words as he shot the car forward.

Blinking back angry tears, I stumbled up the steps, across the gallery and almost ran into Miss Kate. "What on earth——" she began, her voice even more exclamatory than usual. "And Philippe, why didn't he help you in? Come lie down at once, dear. Was it very bad?"

I looked at her stupidly. "It wasn't bad at all. The doctor says I'm fine."

Miss Kate's pale eyes widened till they showed a circle of yellowish white all the way around the dark pupils. "Then why did Philippe have to bring you home?"

"He just did." I was turning away, eager to escape from her, when I saw the blanket and hot-water bottle she held in her arms.

45

She must have thought I'd be half dead when I got here. She must have thought—I did not know what. But she was trying to help me, surely, so I gave her the truth. "He brought me home because he was mad at me for not going to Dr. Whitlow. I went to Dr. Felting."

Miss Kate's mouth was a little round O. Then she stiffened. "What a very odd thing to do! I don't wonder he——"

I went away from her while she was speaking, across the hall, up the stairs, my feet so heavy I scarcely could lift one after the other.

46

· 5 ·

PHILIP's displeasure endured. It lay like a blight on me. I kept myself busy during the day, sewing on the little dresses I hoped to sell, working over the chicks that had survived the storm and throve now in the bright warm weather. I hemmed and dyed the curtains for the room that was to be the nursery. But all the time it was as if a weight were pressing down on me. I moved languidly and often went to lie on my bed even in the morning. Miss Kate ignored me most of the time though when she spoke it was in her usual sweet manner. I would rather she had blazed out at me, for I knew that under her sweetness she was unforgiving, and would be until Philip changed.

That first night, after the day in town, I had said at the end of the miserable silent supper that I was tired and would like to be excused. Philip rose as I spoke. He even went to open the dining-room door for me, saying, "I have to work late tonight over accounts, Bentley. I will sleep in my office so as not to disturb you."

"Yes, of course, Philip," I said. I was glad to be alone that night, being too weary to endure even a reconciliation. I thought perhaps he would come the next night and I would be able then to talk with him quietly, some of the hurt being eased by then. But the days went by, and the nights, and he did not come. I was in despair of ever arriving at any change, for how could we be reconciled if we were never alone together?

Then one night when I was drifting off to a troubled sleep, he came. I heard the door creak and through half-closed eyes saw the yellow light of a candle waver across the room. He entered softly, holding one hand cupped around the flame so it left my bed in darkness. He went to the wardrobe and got out a suit, closed the door carefully and began to move with equal caution across the room toward the door. His hand was on the doorknob

47

when I spoke. "Philip?" I whispered, my voice breaking on his name.

He stood motionless for a little and I thought he was going on as if he had not heard. Then he laid his suit across a chair and moved slowly toward me, the candlelight showing his face, bleak and tortured. He placed the candle on the small table and sat down on the edge of the bed, his dark eyes fixed on me with reproach and dumb suffering.

For he had suffered too. I saw it now and my heart melted so there was no more pride and anger to hold me back. "I . . . I'm sorry, Philip." The words burst from me with a sob. "I can't bear it any longer, I love you so."

Philip looked at me a moment more, then he bent and hid his face against me. His arms came round me, holding me fiercely so that I almost cried out because I could not breathe. I could scarcely hear his muffled words. "You . . . you do really love me, Bentley? I thought—I don't know what I thought—that I should never have married you, so young and lovely . . . when I have nothing to give you. I thought——" He drew a long shuddering breath.

Little by little I felt him relax against me while I stroked his head and held him close and told him over and over that everything was all right, that he was my dear Philip and nothing should ever come between us again. For so it seemed to me in that blessed moment of relief.

Yet when he had risen and set about undressing for the night and I heard him whistling softly under his breath the way he did sometimes when he was happy, I lay there against the pillows and wondered at him. Incredibly he seemed to have forgotten both my hurt and his own. For him it was all over and past, as if it had never been. He was in fine shape, restored completely. I . . . I was exhausted in body and spirit and still sharply aware not only of these days just past but of other such periods that had come and gone, all in the same pattern. Would the time ever come when I could not recover even under the charm of Philip's gentleness? I was like a rubber ball that was thrown down again

48

and again, each time losing some of its elasticity. Someday—but I would not think of that now.

Philip had put on his bathrobe and, knotting the belt around his trim waist, he smiled down at me. "How about a glass of hot milk, dear? I'll put a bit of spirits in it and we'll both have a nightcap."

"That will be wonderful," I sighed. But the truly wonderful thing was being loved and taken care of and having Philip himself once more. I looked after him as he went from me across the room, and as I saw the neat compactness of his body, the curl of his dark hair at the back of his head where it was rumpled and sweetly boyish, it seemed to me that I loved him more than ever before, and I thought it must be that one loves best what costs most—in hurt and heartache.

Those were golden days that came now, and if there were clouds low on the horizon I turned my eyes from them and basked in the sunlight as if it must endure forever. No one could have been more kind and thoughtful than Philip, and generous, too. One evening we sat, the three of us, on the gallery where the night wind blew in soft and cool from the river, fragrant with the spicy scent of the cedars. A high moon poured its light down in pools of silver.

Philip stirred restlessly in his chair. All evening I had sensed excitement in him, some anticipation he had not shared with me. "Aunt Kate," he said at last, "have you got your program ready for the Clef Club?"

"Almost, Philippe. I was just thinking I really should run over one song again—if it won't disturb you."

"Of course not, Miss Kate," I answered for both of us, thinking she knew how to take a hint when Philip gave it. "It will be nice to hear you. This is such a lovely night." Indeed I felt so at peace that I would not have been upset by a caterwauling on a back fence.

She rose at once and went in, her step light and silent as always, her bulky figure casting a mighty black shadow across the gallery as she passed through the lighted hall. A moment later we heard

49

her from the music room to the tinkling accompaniment of the old piano. "Sweet summer breeze," she sang, "whispering trees..."

Philip took my hand and led me into the square of light that lay like a transparent carpet on the floor of the gallery. "What in the world, Philip?" I laughed, teased by his air of mystery.

He put one hand in his pocket and I remembered then that he had been feeling in that pocket all during supper as if to make sure something was there. "Just a little present for my wife," he said with pride. "I had to wait to get it engraved." He took out a small velvet box and laid it in my hand.

I stared at it, reading the name across the top. Borden's Fine Jewelry, it said. I touched the spring and the lid flew up as if eager to reveal the gold wrist watch that shone against the purple lining. For a moment I could not speak, not just because it was so beautiful and I had never owned a watch, but because I could not help thinking how much it must have cost. More than I could earn with my needle, more than my chickens would sell for. Oh, my poor dear Philip! I thought, my eyes blurring. If he had money to spend how he would love to give me things. And having so little he had yet managed this apology for those miserable days, the only apology he could make. For he was not a man to whom humble words came. All this went through my mind while his eyes rested on me, full of pleasure in what he took to be my pure delight. I struggled for words but I could not speak.

He put his arm around me saying, "There, there, dear. It's just a small thing. Nothing to what I would like to give you." And when he had fastened it on my wrist, he took pleasure in turning it this way and that to catch the light, explaining how it must be wound. He had even counted the number of turns the tiny stem must be given, so that I would know when to stop winding.

Yes, those were good days and they lasted all that bright warm summer, with the crops growing well and the river running clear and shallow as it always did at that season, the woods heavy with foliage, the lands across the river and the swamp to the south of us spread out to the sun, lush and steaming. I bore lightly the heaviness of my body, for it seemed a part of the fertility of the land. If now and then I found Philip watching me uneasily, with apprehension in his eyes, I thought that he was dreading the ordeal ahead of me, and I put it down as evidence of his love.

I took my daily walk along the river or by the plantation road to the letter box. Occasionally I had a glimpse of Jeff Wheeling in his dugout, fishing or paddling alongshore. Once he saw me and waved and perhaps would have turned in to talk with me had I not walked on as if bound for somewhere. I did not want to break the happy spell that lay upon me. Without the least possibility of Philip's knowing, I would do nothing that might threaten my tranquillity. For even then I knew that it was brittle and impermanent.

I stayed away from town. I sent by Philip for samples of cotton prints and percales and, though he did not relish carrying bundles, asked him to take the finished dresses to Miss Ida. We went always to church on Sundays. That was my only outing. I had made myself a two-piece black rayon that covered me neatly and, walking down the church aisle behind Miss Kate in her sober Sunday clothes, with Philip following me, tall, dark and distinguished-looking, I had an innocent pride that I was so evidently one of them, a Churston, bearing a Churston child. When Mrs. Mall and Mrs. McCall came in, late as always, only more shriveled and shrunken than ever, their black veils streaming, then I would remember the days when I sat with my mother in the side pew watching them, watching Miss Kate and Philip and the other, Hollis with hair in golden curls, fair as an angel.

Perhaps I grew careless, feeling so full of pride and ease, secure in Philip's pleasure in me. One Sunday as the ushers went by, taking up the collection, my eyes followed the tall young man who passed the plate to us. He was new to me, a stranger, and what caught my attention was the way his coat collar was turned up on one side. I wondered that one of his fellow ushers had not straightened it for him. Perhaps I smiled a little, seeing him so proper and dignified, marching to the altar with a turned-up collar. It might even be that he caught my eye as he came back and looked longer than need be, puzzled at my amusement.

About that I do not remember. It was such a small thing, without meaning.

When one loves, one is alive with feelers, sensitive to the least change. So that Sunday morning, settling back to listen to the sermon, I was all at once aware of a bleakness and a chill around me. I felt it as one feels a prickling of the scalp in time of danger. I turned slowly and looked at Philip. His face was set, his lips were pressed together in a thin colorless line. But what had I done?

We came down the church steps to the sidewalk and stopped to wait for Miss Kate who was delayed by some ladies in the doorway. I said something about the nice warm sunshine but Philip made no answer. His grave dark face was turned toward a group of men waiting on the corner for the traffic to clear. "There he is," he said, scarcely moving his lips with the words.

"Who?"

"The usher who interested you so much in church."

"Oh, Philip, no!" I cried.

But he ignored me, left me standing alone while he went back up the steps to help Miss Kate down.

The miserable days passed, and when our reconciliation came at last, I could not rally as I had before. My spirits lagged behind Philip's; I could not adjust myself quickly. Sometimes I thought that I could support any state if it would only remain constant. It was the changes that wore me down. And they came more often now, for Philip was worried about many things and easily upset. For one thing the potato crop was doing poorly. The county agent came and walked over the field and gave his advice, but Philip did not like being told what he had done wrong, and he resented suggestions.

"Stupid, stupid," he said that evening, telling us about it, walking up and down the library as he spoke. "I know more about the cause of the trouble than he does. All he could say was 'Come down the road and see a crop that's really good.' "

"Where was that, Philippe?" Miss Kate asked.

"The old Wheeling place."

I looked up from my sewing. "Did you go?"

"Yes, I let him run me down there. What good did that do? Jeff Wheeling tends his crop himself; he does not have to leave it to a bunch of trifling Negroes. That makes the difference."

"But he is teaching school a good part of the time," I said, "and besides he's out on the river almost every day." I just did not care. If Philip wanted to get suspicious and go off in another of his gloomy spells, let him.

"Why, Bentley, how do you know?" Miss Kate asked.

"I see him on the river quite often. In fact he pulled me out of a crosscurrent one time when I got mixed up with a lot of driftwood."

"Yes, he told me. Said you were good with the skiff, handled it well."

I stared at Philip. How unpredictable he was! There was no understanding him. "What did you say to that?"

"Why, I said I had taught you myself and I knew you were good."

Miss Kate said, "I have heard some very odd rumors about that young man. At the last club meeting——" She paused to catch a thread she had dropped in her crocheting.

"What did they say about him?" I was interested and almost brazenly I showed my interest, dangled it before Philip.

"Why, they say he is a Communist—or something like that. At the P.T.A. meeting he said terrible things about the government. Then he had the nerve to claim they were quotations from Thomas Jefferson."

"Did anybody check on it?" I asked.

"Why, Bentley dear, who's going to read everything Jefferson wrote, to find out?"

"Just rumors," Philip said with scorn. "I think it's much more likely that he is tied up somehow with some of these organizers who have been through here. One of those men was picked up in front of his place. Jeff Wheeling lived in the North too long." Philip came back to his chair by the table and took up the *Picayune,* adding, "But I wish I had a field of potatoes like his. My crop is going to be an almost total loss."

He said it in a matter-of-fact way, but I knew how deeply he was disappointed. For the county agent who had persuaded him to put in such a large acreage had given him high hopes of getting a good price from the new potato-drying plant that had just been started in the little town below us. I slipped from the room and hurried upstairs. This seemed to be the moment I had been waiting for. All these weeks I had been putting away my earnings, not counting up how much I had made with my sewing and with the sale of my fryers which Old Sam had taken to town for me last week. I got the shoe box from my bureau drawer and brought it down. I laid it on the table beside Philip with a triumphant air. "Don't feel poor. Look what I've got for you!"

Philip was amazed—and so was I—the way it added up. "It will be a great help, Bentley dear."

Miss Kate exclaimed, "How very clever of you!"

I sat smiling, looking from one to the other, all aglow with pleasure at their praise. I thought I could maybe set up a shop of my own and sell dresses and other things, or I might start a chicken farm on a grand scale. Oh, I was full of large ideas just because of a little success. But I only bent over my sewing, saying, "Well, this may not be enough to cover my hospital bills but at least it will pay the doctor."

How could I have been so stupid? Or were Philip's moods an illness that came on him without true relation to outside happenings? At any rate my innocent satisfaction at being able to pay the doctor precipitated us into another unhappy period. This time I could make no effort toward bringing Philip back to himself. Perhaps my lassitude was due to my physical condition, perhaps to the untimely hot weather which came again in early October after we had had a taste of cooler temperatures. I let the days drift by and the lonely nights. I was caught in a nightmare from which I could not escape.

When the time came round for my monthly visit to the doctor, Philip took me without protest. But the ride into town was a dreary one with Philip silent and cold beside me. Even the sight of the countryside could give me no pleasure. The land had a dry and weary look, with the leaves beginning to brown and shrivel, and the dust lying thick on the roadside and rising in a white cloud behind the car and, with any slackening of speed, enveloping it.

When we parted at the parking place back of the courthouse I said I would lunch at the drugstore and then wait at the library for him to pick me up. Philip bowed in the terrible, formal manner he wore always now and I went on to walk stupidly up and down Main Street till time for my appointment with the doctor. I was tired and downhearted and my mind was a parliament, one part debating against the other.

"Oh, it is too much, to keep on like this," one part said. "Philip, forgive me . . . and . . ."

"Forgive you? Forgive you for what? What have you done?"

"But I must have some peace. I am tired, I need it so. Now of all times. I will do anything to get it."

"You should never humble yourself again or ask pardon, not if this should go on forever. It is unjust and horrible, and he should be asking your pardon."

"Pardon, pardon? In true love there can be neither pride nor humbling."

"True love? Where then is your love gone? Can something that was all your thought and life be gone—like this—just . . . gone?"

"But I must love him still or he could not hurt me so."

That was how I talked with myself as I walked through the town, lost and bewildered. But in spite of my unhappy state of mind it seemed that my body kept on about its appointed task. The doctor said I was doing well, and he did his best to cheer me. But I was past cheering. In the library with the long day ahead of me I sat near the window in the periodical room, a magazine in my hands, while my thoughts went round and round in their little trapped circle.

At last out of sheer weariness I looked down at the page I held open before me. This was a literary review I had picked up by chance and my attention was caught by the sheer incongruity of the advertisements on the back pages. There were requests for correspondents, for jobs, for rides to the West Coast; there were sure cures for snoring and places to stay where there was food and quiet.

Quite suddenly the idea came to me. We had rooms aplenty, there was always food in abundance, fresh out of the garden, and there were the swamp and the river. Wouldn't Cedar Bluff seem romantic and glamorous to people who had read historical romances of the South, and who wished to escape from a Northern winter? I searched the column for some indication of the prices charged, and I could scarcely believe it when I found that people were expected to pay as much as forty dollars a week for room and board in a place which actually boasted of having no radio. Forty a week—it would be our salvation. Not just in the cash alone but in the ease of mind. Philip had been so difficult lately because he was worried about money. Clear that up and everything would improve. Things would be as they used to be with us. Oh, money would make all the difference in the world!

Eagerly I searched my handbag for pencil and paper and began to compose my ad. I offered escape from Northern cold, a refuge in mild Mississippi, one wing of a colonial mansion—though I hesitated to call it by so pretentious a name—Southern cooking and freedom from the confusions of the modern world. I laughed to myself; that would be worth forty a week, if one had the forty to spend. I begged a sheet of paper from the librarian and copied the lines neatly, signing it "B. Churston, Cedar Bluff Plantation, R.F.D. Sherrysburg, Mississippi." It looked good to me, the way I had written it and everything. My spirits rose.

There was just time for a trip to the post office and a hasty sandwich, for my appetite had come back all of a sudden. Then I had to hurry lest I keep Philip waiting at the library. It was still ten minutes before five when I rounded the corner, but Philip was ahead of time. He was standing beside the car looking anxiously up and down the street.

I hurried toward him, puffing a little with my excitement and with my quick walk. "I'm sorry, Philip. But you're really a bit early." It was the first time I had spoken to him with complete naturalness in a long time. But he did not respond to the change in me.

He closed the door after me, went round to the other side. As he started the car, he gave me a quick sharp glance. "Your visit to the doctor seems to have cheered you." His tone was hard and bitter.

Now it was my turn to say nothing. It was as if the wall that had been growing up between us had become, with those words, too high and too wide to reach across. I could not tell him what I had done, nor could I share with him the hope that it had given me.

57

· 6 ·

THE days were cooler now, the sky a bright October blue. At night it seemed heavenly to need a blanket again. I began to revive after the heat of the long summer, and in this period of physical well-being I was better able to support the alienation from Philip. The protective shell which I had put on against his displeasure thickened in these days and within it I moved with something that was almost indifference. I had given up smocking dresses for Miss Ida's Shoppe and spent all my time making baby clothes, taking pleasure in the tiny stitches and delicate materials.

On coming in one evening from dinner to the library where we sat by the fire now, I saw a package on the brown-covered center table. Miss Kate, opening a new murder story which Philip had brought from the library, said, "What's that, Bentley?"

"I don't know," I answered without interest, taking my place in the little low rocker and opening my sewing basket which I had left on the floor beside it.

"Aren't you going to look and see?" Philip stood with his back to the fire, one elbow on the mantelpiece.

I gave him a quick glance and dropped my eyes, for I had seen his pathetic eagerness and it hurt me. "Is it for me?"

"Of course."

He was smiling. I knew without looking directly at him. I put aside my sewing and took the bundle in my lap, my hands trembling at the string that fastened it. Time, just time and nothing I had said or done, had brought Philip out of his suspicion and coldness. Time had taken the place of the apology I had withheld. Relief mixed with wonder spread through me, yet the tiny core of bitterness within me remained undissolved. I was a pitcher gone too often to the well, a sapling blown upon too long by stormy winds, a ball that had lost its elasticity.

The paper fell aside and Miss Kate exclaimed, "Why, how very lovely! You have always had perfect taste, Philippe."

"Yes," I murmured, bending over the material—a dark-brown wool with tiny woven rust and gold stripes. He had remembered that I liked stripes. Even then I felt no warmth stirring in me. I spoke only because he was waiting for me to speak. "Thank you, Philip. It is beautiful."

He crossed the room, saying something about bringing some papers up from his office downstairs. He paused at my side to look down at the cloth, laying one hand on my shoulder. "It will be very becoming." Then he went on out of the room.

I sat moving my fingers over the fabric. Philip had not noticed my lack of response. Everything seemed right to him once more and he took it for granted that I felt the same way. "It must have been expensive," I said.

"Yes, indeed," Miss Kate agreed, taking up her book again. "There is no one more generous than Philippe when he has the money."

"He . . . he has money?"

"Oh, dear, yes. The potato crop brought much more than he expected. The price is 'way up."

He had not told me, though he had told Miss Kate. I laid the cloth on the table under the lamp and picked up my sewing. Yes, it was beautiful material; it was kind of Philip to bring it to me. Yet I could take no great pleasure in it, or in my return to his favor. I was beginning to be insulated against good and ill alike, shut away from him.

Living thus, independent of him on whom I had been so dependent, I began to seek other sources of happiness, less variable, less external to myself. I began to realize one should never let one's life lie wholly exposed to another's whims and moods. There is an inner core that must be kept inviolate. It is that part of oneself which must stand alone, stripped and hard, against the onslaught of physical pain; it is that essential self to which one clings in the face of death—and which alone must persist, if there is anything beyond.

Yet it is not a miserable small thing, this essential part of one's being. There are richness there, tranquillity and understanding, a kinship with all living things; there may even be a kind of inward gaiety, though true gaiety takes two to make it. These were the ideas toward which I was fumbling now. Perhaps it was only the process of growing up, and it may be that when need drives him to it, every human being experiences this tapping of his inner resources. I do not know how these things are. I know only that in this period I turned inward for strength, and I took satisfaction in doing well the small tasks that fell to me, such as the making of baby clothes, the preparation of an old clothesbasket to serve as a crib.

That part of the housework which Miss Kate allowed me I did with meticulous care. I even opened the unused parlor on the other side of the hall, and the downstairs bedroom behind it, dusting and putting all in order. For I still hoped to get some response to the advertisement I had sent away. Only one answer had come—from a couple, writing people, though I was not familiar with their names. They had asked about private baths and hot water and heat and such conveniences, so I had been obliged to write that we had none of those things. That was a disappointment, yet I accepted it without dismay and went on hoping.

The change that was taking place within me extended to my feeling for Miss Kate. I was no longer so intolerant of the little ways that had been an irritation to me. I saw the essential bleakness of her life in spite of her trips to town to meetings of various kinds. She had no real friend who troubled to come to see her, and the murder mysteries she read were like an anesthetic to dull her to what she lacked. Sometimes I even questioned her about a club election, or inquired into the history of the family. Of Philip I demanded nothing, accepting his attention as I had borne his neglect.

And while I had always loved the countryside, being townborn and new to it, I now took a deeper pleasure in woods and river, sun and rain. I looked forward, too, to the coming of my child. But this I kept to myself, seeing that neither Philip nor Miss Kate wished to speak of it. Sometimes I thought that was because of a

60

quaint Victorian attitude which they had; again it seemed to me that they shared some inner dread which I could not understand. I felt physically better than I had in a long time. I felt a gathering of all my resources, a building-up of vigor against the day when I should need it.

I walked daily along the riverbank and I made it my habit to go each morning by the plantation road to the letter box. I took my time, stopping by the cow lot to watch old Peggy eating grass or just chewing her cud, her soft eyes looking into mine with dumb patience and tranquillity. I went by the barn sometimes and took a sugar lump to Ergo, once Philip's saddle horse and now humbled to the plow.

This morning, passing the pecan grove, I saw the bare gray branches and the clusters of nuts, the outer shells opening like dark petals to autumn buds. Then, following the plantation road, I came to the part that was worn deep into the earth by the long passing of wheels. It was a tunnel roofed with branches, partly bare and laced with gray moss. The fallen leaves whispered under my feet and I stopped now and then to pick up a crisp red one or a bright yellow from a scalybark tree. One great bare root projected from the wall of honeysuckle and woodbine and I sat down on it to rest. A pool of sunshine lay around me and in its brightness I examined the leaves and a bit of moss I had picked up. The sunlight magnified the veins in each leaf, made the wisp of moss alive in my hand.

In the stillness I heard someone singing, and steps rustling in the leaves beyond the turn of the road. It was a young voice singing a juke-box song, one that was an imitation, almost a caricature, of a Negro river song. What should have been pure and primitive was raw, graceless, false. I wondered who could be singing like that, punctuating the words with little rhythmic grunts.

Then I saw Callie coming round the curve of the road, a tin pail balanced on her head, her arms akimbo. She moved in the raw rhythm of the song, swinging her hips, unconscious of my eyes. Seeing the enviable slenderness of her body, her easy motion, I thought that out of them the song was reborn and made pure

61

again. Lost in wonder at this strange alteration, I did not move nor speak until she was almost upon me. At my good morning she shied away like a young colt. The song snapped into silence, the pail toppled over, spilling corn pone and side meat in the road. She bent quickly and with her face averted began to gather everything up, her pale-brown hands moving jerkily.

"Too bad," I said with a little awkward laugh, for there was always something in her manner that made me ill at ease. "I must have startled you, sitting here so still." I had caught her off guard, too, carrying a pail on her head—something the young Negroes never did.

"Reckon it won't hurt none to eat a little dirt." She moved on while she was still speaking.

I watched the ants gather quickly round the crumbs that remained among the leaves and I wondered why this slim brown girl could make me so uncomfortable. I looked after her and just at that moment she shot a swift backward glance at me. Its impact was like a blow. But why should she hate me—if it was hate I had seen on her face? I had no dealings with her, never spoke to her save in casual meetings such as this. I knew nothing about her really, only that she was Old Sam's granddaughter who kept house for him and took his dinner to the field. I knew nothing about any of the Negroes on the place. Even Minerva whom I saw every day was a mystery to me. I got to my feet and went on slowly down the road.

When the banks opened out and I could see across the field, I made out three seated figures against the far hedgerow. Callie was eating lunch with the field hands. She must have run, to get there so quickly. I quickened my own step now, eager as always to see what mail there was. I unfastened the chain that held the big gate shut, pushed it just wide enough to squeeze through and hurried to the letter box.

Nothing—nothing important. Only a farm journal for Philip, a bill or two, some business letters. But as I fastened the gate behind me, another letter fell from inside the folded market bulletin. I snatched it up, seeing even before my fingers touched it that the bold large handwriting spelled out "B. Churston,

62

Cedar Bluff." I leaned against the gatepost and tore it open, my eyes skimming through it. ". . . Several weeks ago . . . your ad in the . . would like to come January fifteenth . . . do not require luxuries, only privacy and cleanliness . . . through the spring . . . gathering material . . . sociological study . . . research in the field . . . reply at once . . . check inclosed . . ."

I looked in the envelope again and found the check, on a Boston bank, properly signed, Eliza M. Stockbridge, the sum of forty and no hundredths dollars I pressed it to my cheek I was so happy. She would come, and there would be another such check every week after the middle of January. Eliza Stockbridge—it had a stout New England sound. She must have money, and Miss Kate would be impressed by that and the quality of the stationery. Best of all Philip would be eased of his worry.

In the hall I met Miss Kate. "You've been a long time going after the mail, dear. I was about to send Minerva to see if you were all right."

"Oh, I'm sorry. I sat down to rest on the way." I was still breathless from my quick walk home, the letter clutched tight in my hand. I was in a hurry to get upstairs and read it all over again. I didn't want Miss Kate to know about it till I had told Philip.

"Was the mail all for you, dear?"

"Oh, of course not." I leaned down over the banister and handed it to her. Then I went on up the stairs, my step light in spite of the heaviness of my body. It might be that now everything was going to be better. Although something was gone from our relationship, Philip's and mine, yet it might be—oh surely it was possible!—that something even richer and better could grow up between us.

· 7 ·

AFTER dinner, in the library, I waited with impatience for Miss Kate to leave us. She often said good night early, going upstairs to take off her corsets and lie abed reading till she got sleepy. But tonight she seemed rooted in the big rocker with the swanneck arms, fixed in the tent of light falling from the student lamp on the table. Philip, opposite her, read the *Picayune* carefully and slowly, turning a page at long intervals. I had shifted my chair so the table with its brown-fringed cover like a long skirt kept the heat of the fire from me. I was warm-blooded and did not like to be too near.

My needle flashed in the light as I featherstitched a tiny blue jacket, and whenever I shifted my position the letter from Miss Stockbridge crackled. Of course I could have taken it out right then and told them both about it, but somehow I wanted to let Philip know first. So in my mind I kept saying to Miss Kate, Bed, bed. Go to bed. Your corset's too tight. Bed—you could lie on the pillows and be comfortable abed. Bed, bed—— It amused me to try to communicate the idea to her and when she stirred restlessly, I smiled to myself, thinking I was really having some effect on her.

After a while I saw her stifle a yawn, glance at the little clock on the mantel, and mentally I clapped my hands. But she did not go. She said. "Bentley dear, you did such a lot of cleaning today and had that long walk to the letter box—aren't you sleepy?"

"Me?" I said stupidly. "Oh, no, that is, I think I will finish this jacket before I go to bed."

Miss Kate sighed and went on with her reading. But now, watching her with sudden suspicion, I saw that she was not turning the pages with her usual rapidity. She had a little habit of licking one small finger to turn the page and I was always conscious of it because I disliked it so heartily. She was just sitting there staring at the same page all the time, a waiting look on her

64

white face. I wanted to laugh. Both of us waiting like this! Well, I would just sit her out, if it took all night.

But I was the first to lose patience. Miss Kate seemed so solid, so fixed, that I despaired of outsitting her. Besides, the room was filling up with waiting, with a tension I could not fathom. There was no air left for breathing and the fire had sprung up afresh as a log burned through and fell into the red-hot embers. I laid down my work. "I'm going out for some fresh air. It seems too hot in here."

Philip said, "Don't go out of call."

"Oh, nothing will get me."

"Bentley, you must not go out of the yard." Philip spoke with sharpness. "You grew up in town. You don't understand. No white woman goes out in the dark in the country."

"All right," I said from the doorway. "Don't worry. I'll stay close."

Miss Kate called me back. "Put my shawl around your shoulders, dear. Here——" She pulled the crocheted blue shawl from the back of her chair and held it out to me. "It will do you good to walk in the fresh air. You'll sleep better."

I went through the hall door, out across the gallery and down the steps. I did not want the scarf—it smelled too strongly of Miss Kate's face powder—so I hung it on the railing and went on, picking my way carefully in the darkness. The air was cool and damp. I breathed deep, filling my lungs with the clean, dew-wet pungence of the cedars.

At the brink of the bluff I stopped, looking out over the river. It was blacker than the earth, it was night itself, melted and stretched out in a lazy curve. The sky hung low, a spangled velvet shawl flung round the earth to keep it from the high winds of heaven. I felt my way to the old cedar stump and sat down. A boat was coming round the far bend of the river, its lights reflected in the water, elongated and broken, like bright crooked claws. I leaned over, elbows on knees, chin in hand. I would stay till the boat had passed and surely by that time Miss Kate would have finished whatever she had to say to Philip.

I tried not to think of anything at all. For in this period of turning in on myself I had found that when I was alone, blank-minded, with earth and sky, my own small secret self could feel its relationship to both. As the least molecules in their motion and behavior are akin to the stars in the vast reaches of space, so it was with this small me and the great universe about me. I felt a blending with the earth, so that I was conscious of the curve of its surface, of its motion through space, of the forces that held it on its course; and looking far up into the night sky, I felt freed from the laws of gravity, as if I could drop up as easily as down. Were these leftover feelings from some lost freedom, or were they intimations of a release to come? Or both, perhaps?

The sound of the tugboat, pushing its barges upstream, came over the water with a steady rhythmic beat. Below me the current nibbled at the shore. Around me were small sounds in the bushes—a rabbit moving haltingly, a bird stirring on its branch. Suddenly through these sounds there broke the slow dip of a paddle. I could even hear the light fall of the drops that followed its motion toward another stroke, and the whisper of the boat's passing, like a snake weaving through grass. Then close under the bluff I made out the shape of man and boat. For a moment I considered calling, "Hi, Jeff," just to startle him. But I gave up the notion and sat silent as the stump, a part of the bluff, unknown to him as he passed downstream with the current. I was like a small wild animal watching a human, wondering at his ways.

He was a strange man, I thought, spending his life in this lonely fashion, teaching a tiny country school, finding his pleasure in swamp and river. What restlessness had brought him out in the dark where only night creatures stirred? He was a long way from home. He would have to go several miles down the river to a break in the wall of the bluff where the black bayou led inland. After following its winding way, he would turn off by a small branch that ran behind his fields. In my mind I followed him homeward, thinking how he would tie up the dugout, his hands slow and sure at the knot, how he would move with limping step along a narrow path and come at last into his own yard, past the big woodpile, under the blacker darkness by the single water oak and into yellow light that shone out through bare vines to welcome him. It would be midnight perhaps before he got there.

The barges and their laboring tugboat were out of hearing now, the stern lights limming in the distance. Then they were lost around the far curve of the river. I rose, feeling refreshed and renewed. Now I must go in and tell Philip about our boarder. In the hall I stopped to listen. They were still talking. But they had talked enough. It was my turn now. I made my step noisy and went on to the library.

Philip was saying, "Yes, of course, she must be told."

I blinked in the light, and was at once aware of tension in the air. I went to the low needle-point stool in the chimney corner and sat down, looking from one to the other.

"You have been out too long," Philip said. "Aren't you chilled?"

I shook my head, but to pacify him held my hands out to the fire, waiting, puzzled, vaguely uneasy. I saw now that Miss Kate had an open letter in her hand and I quickly felt the front of my dress to make sure mine was still there.

"There is something you will have to be told, Bentley," Philip said, frowning. He looked to Miss Kate.

She gave the letter a shake, as if she would shake away the news it contained. "It's just this, dear. Philippe's mother——" She began again: "As you know, for many years Philippe's mother has been in the state hospital at Jackson. After her complete nervous break-down we could not give her the proper care at home." She spoke it like a piece she had memorized and spoken many times. "Now we have a letter from the superintendent, a new man. He writes that the place is seriously crowded, that it is necessary to ask the families of all patients who are not . . . whose conditions permit . . . to take them."

"Oh!" I breathed and my eyes turned to Philip.

"There is nothing else we can do," he said.

"Of course it can be managed if it has to be," Miss Kate went on. "She can be kept in her old room."

"You mean downstairs—the bedroom across there?" I pointed toward the hall, the closed door opposite. That was the room I had advertised.

"But no, no," Philip was saying. "That was her room and my father's. After his death she moved——"

Miss Kate interrupted. "The room just beyond the one you have been working on, dear, upstairs in the ell. That will be much better. I mean she will be less disturbed there."

I nodded. "Perhaps I could take care of her."

"No," Philip said quickly. "Someone else——"

"But I could," I broke in with eagerness. "I know I could, and I won't have too much to do even after the baby——"

"That would not do at all," Miss Kate said hurriedly. "I feel that Minerva——"

"I thought we had settled that, Aunt Kate," Philip said with annoyance in his tone. "Minerva has enough to do, with the cooking, cleaning, the cow to milk, now that she is going to freshen soon. Besides, she would probably refuse. Callie can have a cot bed right in the same room. After all, she has had a year's training as a nurse."

Miss Kate gave him a sharp look. "I didn't know that."

"I believe it was under the WPA, one of their classes."

"But Callie——" I began and turned my head to stare at the fire. I would not like to have Callie looking after me, or anyone I loved.

Philip's fingers were rapping a muffled tattoo on the table. "She is young and strong, capable, and will no doubt be glad of the extra money—and that brings me to something else." Again he looked to Miss Kate.

"I suggested, and I'm sure you will take it in the right spirit, dear, that you stay here instead of going to the hospital. Many of the girls are doing that now, Mrs. Bellows Woodworth tells me, because the hospital is so crowded! And the expense——"

"But expense doesn't matter. Look!" I snatched the letter from my dress. "See—the first check, and there will be more, right along every week." I ran to Philip, holding out the letter, breathlessly explaining how I had put an ad in the magazine and now here——

Philip read the letter through in silence while I stood watching. Then he passed it over to Miss Kate. I sat down again on the stool by the fire. This was not how I had planned to tell

Philip, but surely—— My eyes went from him to Miss Kate. Had I been too bold? Had I made too free with their house? It belonged to Miss Kate but eventually it would be Philip's and . . . and mine. "If it makes extra work, having her, I can do it. I just thought——"

Miss Kate's fingers had been moving over the single sheet of paper, testing its quality. "Evidently a person of means, of some taste," she said, lifting her large pale eyes to meet mine. "My first thought was that you had been a bit—— But no matter. After all——" She looked now at the check which Philip held out to her. She examined it with the same slow care. "It comes most conveniently."

Philip took the check from her. "The money will be a great help with this unexpected expense. And she need not be a part of the family. It is a purely business arrangement." He took a pen from his coat pocket, unscrewed the top as he rose. "If you will just sit here and endorse it, Bentley, I can settle that little bill at the fertilizer plant right away. They have been quite annoying about it."

I drew a sigh of relief as I signed my name. They were really glad I had done this. Miss Kate, still studying the letter, said, "I don't understand this—about field work, research. What can she mean?"

"It was a literary magazine. Maybe she is a writer, getting up background material or something," I said. For the first time I began to think about her. Was she young or old? Anyway, it would be interesting to have somebody new in the house. Soon there would be several new people in the house, I thought with wonder.

· 8 ·

MISS KATE and Philip were going to Jackson to get his mother. They were to drive up one day, spend the night and come back the next and they had a fine cool October morning for the trip. I walked to the end of the gallery to see them off. Philip, uneasy, depressed, said little, but Miss Kate seemed cheerful at the prospect of a journey, for no matter what reason.

"It's a fine day, and I am hoping we will get to Jackson in time to drive about a bit before dark. There have been so many changes there since my last visit." She straightened her hat and went quickly down the steps behind Philip who was carrying her old-fashioned alligator satchel.

He put it in the back of the car and then walked around examining the tires with more than usual care. There was something so harassed and worn in his look as he bent to study the right rear tire, which was the weakest of them all, that I ran down the steps, laid my hand on his arm and said, "I do hope it will be all right, Philip—everything, I mean."

"It's a bad business." He touched my hair with his lips. "I don't like leaving you alone even with Minerva sleeping on the lower floor. Be sure you lock up. Maybe you had better have Minerva bring a cot to the hall just outside your door."

"Nonsense, I'm not the least nervous." But it warmed me that in the midst of this new worry he should be thinking of me. "I'll just rest and be quiet and you will be back in no time."

"Come, Philippe," Miss Kate called. "It's a long drive and we may have car trouble."

"Coming, Aunt Kate." He patted my shoulder, went round the car and got in.

When they had jolted out of sight down the plantation road, I looked around the empty yard and was glad of old Humble sunning himself in a splash of sunshine beside the althea bush. It seemed emptier than other days when Miss Kate went off to town with Philip. I went through the house and heard Minerva rattling the breakfast dishes and the homely sound was reassuring. Then I went upstairs to get my knitting. I had been saving it to do after the weather got cooler so the yarn would not stick to my fingers as it did on hot days. First, though, I thought I would have a look at the end bedroom on the upper ell porch, make sure everything there was ready for Philip's mother.

The morning sun shone in brightly through the eastern window, lightening the gloomy mahogany furniture. The ruffled curtains were starched and clean but they could not hide the wooden strips which Old Sam had nailed across the windows. The sight of them now gave me a queer feeling. There was a wooden bar across the door, too, that could be let down on the outside—as if the lock might not be strong enough. I shivered. What a homecoming for that poor soul! Would she recognize the octagonal mirror of the bureau, the carved morning-glories on the tall headboard of the bed, the little washstand with its blue flowered bowl and pitcher? Might not the change have a good effect, perhaps restore her to some degree? I resolved to come and sit with her often, to talk with her and try to bring her back to herself. At any rate I would see to it that Callie gave her every attention. I did not trust that girl.

I had much more confidence in Minerva, gruff though her manner was, and slipshod her cleaning. Could she have dusted here at all? And Old Sam had left his stepladder in one corner. It was a good thing I had come to look the place over. I got a dustcloth and set to work. After all these years in an institution, Philip's mother deserved to have things nice.

In the quiet as I worked, I heard mice scampering about overhead. They were always in the attic but I had grown used to hearing them there and in the walls. Now I wondered if they would disturb Philip's mother, and I thought I would speak to Philip about setting some traps. When I had finished my dusting I looked around with satisfaction. I would just drag the step-

71

ladder out and then there would be nothing more to do. Then it was that I noticed how the dust danced in long bright shafts where the sunlight came through the barred window. I had stirred up no dust with my oiled cloth—where could it be coming from? I looked to the ceiling and saw the crack through which it was sifting down. Worst of all, the small trap door was not completely closed. That would never do. Every time a mouse ran across the floor, more dust could come down.

I found a broom, got some old papers from my room, thinking I could cover over the crack. I dragged the ladder into position and mounted to the trap door, pushing it aside with the broom handle and tossing broom and papers up ahead of me. Then I climbed carefully up. Sunlight shone in by a window at the eastern end, revealing the dust of generations thick on floor and cobwebbed rafters and the boxes and trunks that stood under the eaves. Through the shrunken floor boards I could see light coming from the room beneath me. I swept as well as I could, spread the papers and weighted them down with some schoolbooks that were heaped untidily on the floor. Mice had made a nest of papers beside one of the trunks and I swept it up, though I thought as I did it that this was really a job for Minerva. The dust was making me sneeze.

I was just turning away when, in the heap of shredded papers at my feet, I saw some stamps, unusual ones that might be valuable and worth saving. These were old letters that the mice had been at. Farther in the corner was another bunch of letters. They seemed to be spilling from a hole gnawed in one side of an old leather trunk. I lifted the lid and looked in. But there were no papers there of any sort, only a rotted blue silk dress, some scraps of lace and several carved fans.

That was curious, I thought. Letters were falling out the side of the trunk and yet there was none in it. I got down on my knees and explored the opening in the side, a big round hole neatly nibbled out. There must be a false bottom—what fun! I swept a small clean spot and sat down on the floor, reached in to pull out one handful of letters after another and laid them in the small square of sunlight on the floor. Mice would destroy them completely unless I put them away, and some of them looked very old. Miss Kate might like to look them over, I thought.

The ink was faded, the handwriting fine and slanting after the fashion of long ago. Most of them seemed to have been written in the 1840's. One was headed "Cedar Bluff Plantation" and began:

"My dear wife:
It is now three weeks since I left you with your sister at her commodious abode on the Amite River. I trust these lines find you in good health."

How quaint and formal it was! The signature was Henry Churston—Philip's great-grandfather, the one Miss Kate talked about so much, the old judge. I took up a pack of yellow letters held together by a faded ribbon that fell to shreds as I touched it. They were all in a round young hand. I opened one and saw that it was headed "Avery College, Louisiana," and began "My dear parents." A schoolboy, writing home. He had acquitted himself creditably in the public examination in Mental and Moral Philosophy; he thanked his father for paying his debts of honor and promised that henceforth he would shun the gaming companions responsible for these deplorable losses. The letter was signed "Respectfully your son, Carrol Churston."

Carrol? He was the one in the portrait over the hall sofa. Philip's grandfather, Miss Kate's father. Even the stiffness of the pose, the dark, flat style of the painting could not obscure the fire in his eyes, the determined set of his jaw and the idealistic sweep of his brow. He was self-willed, no doubt, and probably got into many a scrape at college.

As I laid the letters in the main body of the trunk, I had a new sense of the reality of those lives that had come and gone long ago. The family that Miss Kate talked about so continually had come alive to me, and I resolved that instead of letting my attention wander as I usually did, I would listen more carefully to her stories about them. As for the letters, stored safely away in the trunk, they might be found again by another generation after mine and read with pleasure. The thought pleased me and I

73

salvaged all that were not too torn to be legible. I even reached for back into the secret compartment to get them all out, though I shivered a bit as I did so, lest I put my hand into a nest of baby mice.

The last lot I found was wrapped in a scrap of linen, yellow with age and splitting on the creases. I opened it and recognized the handwriting—it was Carrol's again, though more mature now. The dates were in the late sixties, and I saw at once that they were love letters. Surely after so many years, the writer and his sweetheart both so long dead, it would do no harm to read them.

Little by little as I turned the pages, careful not to break them where they were folded, the story grew in my mind. On his way back to college, in his last year—and I thought it must be that the Civil War had interrupted his schooling—he had lost his way. He must have been on horseback, for he wrote, "Oh, blessed chance that led me astray at the end of that long day's ride and brought me, a wayworn traveler and a stranger seeking lodging at your father's door!"

I sighed, with pity for them that they were dead, with wonder that these yellow faded pages could make their passion live again. "My angelic Thérèse," he wrote. "Thérèse, my dearest." Now and then he broke into verse, as though mere prose could not do justice to the charms of "one whose lips were redder than the red moss rose, whose eyes were dark and bright, a mingling of the day and night." He wrote from college, impatient for the next vacation when he could fly to her side. Then after the visit he wrote in great happiness because his suit had found favor in her sight, and her father had not withheld his consent. His only regret was that her mother's health had been such that he was unable to pay his respects to her in person, but he wished his dear Thérèse to convey to her his deepest respect, nay his affection, for was she not the mother of the fairest flower of Southern womanhood?

I took up the next letter and moved nearer to the window to keep in the warmth of the sunlight. This was from Carrol's father, Henry Churston, and it read:

"I have perused with interest your communication of February eleventh. I have no doubt that the young lady in question is all that my impetuous son declares. The Du Quarl name is not wholly unknown to me, a proud name and one held in high regard."

In the stilted roundabout language of the age, he went on to hope that his son would not be too hasty. They had known each other but a short time, and while Carrol alone, since the death of his two brothers in the war, would be sole heir to Cedar Bluff plantation, it might be well in view of the unsettled conditions of the time . . . On and on he wrote in such vein. Caution, elderly caution, I thought, and hoped that Carrol paid no attention to it.

Eagerly I took up the next letter dated some months later and addressed to Carrol Churston, Esq. Sub Rosa Plantation, East Feliciana Parish. It bore no stamp, only a line in one corner of the envelope: "Kindness of Gilbert Blakely, Esq." I hoped it would tell me what happened next, for this was worse than reading a continued story. It read:

"My dear son:

"Your letter telling me of your approaching marriage to Miss Thérèse du Quarl arrived by the same post with a communication of so grave and pressing import that I send this by your cousin who is en route to New Orleans and will pass out of his way to deliver it direct to your hand and no other.

"As soon as it became apparent to me that your intentions with regard to the young woman were serious, I at once set into motion a series of inquiries regarding her family and antecedents. The results of my investigation, which was wholly confidential and of unimpeachable accuracy, have revealed certain facts which it is my duty to communicate to you, and acting upon which you will at once break off your engagement and withdraw from the untenable position in which you find yourself."

Heavens, I thought, turning the yellow page and bending closer to decipher the flowing ornate hand, why couldn't the old gentleman say what he had to say without all this circumlocution? The old judge went on:

"That this will be a blow, especially to one of your warm and impetuous nature, is well known to me, but in revealing these unpleasant facts to you, you must know that I am but acting in the best interests of not only yourself but future generations."

Future generations—that's me. I chuckled and read on:

"I shall be brief, and again I assure you that brutal though the truth may seem, it has been carefully substantiated and I have in my hands certified copies of all the records involved.

"On the eighth day of May in the year of our Lord 1841, André le Moison de la Cour du Quarl, late of Montevideo but presently residing at Sub Rosa Plantation, East Feliciana, was married to Antoinette Gresham, a woman of color, and so registered in the Black Book in the city of New Orleans. To these two, by official record were born four mulatto children whose names it is not necessary to give save that of the youngest, Antoinette Thérèse, whom you have proposed to make your wife."

Whew! I drew a long breath. The Black Book? I had never heard of such a thing. Poor Carrol, what a blow this must have been to him! I sat a few moments thinking how he must have felt when he read the lines I had just finished. And how did he escape from such a dreadful situation? But there was more of his father's letter and I read on:

"May I add that without doubt the mother pleads invalidism in order to avoid making an appearance which would at once reveal her color. I have every confidence, my son, in your ability to extricate yourself with honor from this unfortunate affair. May I suggest that, much as we would like to have you at home during the approaching months, especially in view of your mother's failing health, it may be well for you to spend some time in foreign travel? With this in view I am depositing to your order at Willoughby, Wheaton and Gill's, Commission Merchants of New Orleans, sufficient funds to cover your expenses. Your mother, who suffers with you in this blow to your hopes and plans, joins me in affectionate salutations.

"Your father, Henry Churston."

I let the letter fall to my lap and pressed my fingers to my eyes which ached from the strain of reading the faded fine script. I could imagine Carrol on shipboard, gloomily watching the horizon. I could see him wandering through Europe trying to forget, crushed and disconsolate, but thankful surely to have found out in time. Yet he must have recovered his spirits eventually and married, for he was Philip's grandfather, Miss Kate's father. No heartbreak was beyond repair—or had he married only out of duty to his family? Had he perhaps cherished always the image of this beautiful and charming girl with lips as red as the red moss rose—and the tragic taint in her blood? In the long summer evenings here at Cedar Bluff did he remember and mourn for his lost love? Or was his love in an instant turned to revulsion, or even to hate?

I shifted my position on the cold floor. It had all happened so long ago. Now for many years Carrol had been lying beside his father and mother in the little burying ground in the shade of the great magnolia trees at the edge of the bluff, the river moving now as then below the wooded slope. The woman he married was beside him—second choice. I felt sorry for her, for she might have sensed what no one would ever have told her: that she was not his first love. Her stone was the one that had fallen on its side, the inscription lichen-covered, indecipherable. I had seen it there and wondered at its being so neglected—Miss Kate's own mother's stone.

I rested my head on my hands, overcome with a sense of the transience of life. Yet there was a certain continuity. Life had come down through this ardent tragic Carrol, and his grave father the judge, to Philip and through him to the child I was to bear. I straightened up at last. The sun was going from the window and the attic air was growing cold. I was eager to go downstairs and look at the portraits in the hall. I would see them now as real people, not as mere emblems of Miss Kate's pride. I would not look at them and say I would like to throw them all out and start over. One could never do that. These people were a part of the present, living on as long as a Churston walked the earth.

There were but two more letters and I almost laid them away without reading—they would be but a sad anticlimax after the events of which I had read. But something quavery and feeble

in the old judge's handwriting made me draw out the yellow
sheet. He wrote:

"My dear son:
"I cannot believe that you will persist in taking this disastrous,
this suicidal step. May I ask if you have considered the conse-
quences, not only in the blasting of your hopes and ambitions
but those of your children to come? Can you so lightly and selfishly proceed in full knowledge on a course which will blight the
lives of others? Can you so easily destroy the happiness, the honor,
of your father and mother? Do you not realize that such a marriage will brand you as an outcast in all decent society? For these
things are known; there is no concealing them. In those rare
tragic cases where such a taint is in the blood, there is no hiding
of it. Never delude yourself in this fashion. Oh, my son, ask yourself, is such an infatuation, such a momentary madness, worth
the terrible cost? Have you no more regard than this for the
Churston name? For God's sake, stop before it is forever too late!
"Pray let me hear by return post that you have come to your
senses. Only your mother's serious prostration and my grave fears
for her life prevent me from coming at once to your rescue. You
must know that her condition is largely due to the suffering and
anxiety which your conduct is bringing her. As for me, I make no
plea, but for the sake of her who bore you, for the sake of your
children to the third and fourth generation, I beg you to recon-
sider while there is yet time.
"Your father."

Poor old man! I sighed, my sympathies all with him now. It
was cruel of Carrol to worry him so, knowing in his heart no
doubt that he could not really go through with such a marriage.
He must have known that, even in his madness. And what about
his mother? Did this anxiety really cause her death? There was
but one more letter and I saw with relief that the father's hand
was again firm and steady. He wrote:

"My dear son:
"This is the last time I shall thus address you. You are that no
longer. Should you ever return to Cedar Bluff during my lifetime,
the door will be closed against you. This communication is
merely to advise you of this fact, and of the fact that my will re-

mains unchanged. At your mother's death which is now immi-
nent, and mine, Cedar Bluff will be yours to do with as you will.
May God have mercy on you is the prayer of one who for the last
time signs himself

"Your father."

The letter fell from my cold fingers. Carroll had really married
her then! He must have. I got stiffly to my feet, threw the letter
in the trunk with the others and closed the lid. I was dizzy. The
air in the attic was unbearably close. I dropped the broom
through the trap door and let myself down. I even replaced the
wooden square that closed the opening. With my feet safely on
the floor I leaned against the ladder until the room stopped
turning round and round. The girl Thérèse must have died.
Wives died off fast in the old days. They got t.b. or they died in
childbirth. She must have died, and so Carrol could marry again.
It could not be any other way.

Yet I must find out. I had to be sure, now that the question
had entered my mind, ridiculous though it was. What was the
name of Philip's grandmother? That would settle it. But I could
not wait to ask Miss Kate for her mother's name. I had to know
right now. How could I? The gravestone! Of course. I could tell
by that—dates, name, everything.

I went quite slowly down the stairs, seeing nothing, my mind
like a top that had been started spinning and could not stop. I
brushed past Minerva in the hall, scarcely hearing and not at all
heeding her "Lawd, Miss Bent, what happen?" Out the front
door and down the steps I went, talking aloud to myself now,
saying it could not be, saying I was just a silly fool, a plain damn
idiot to get such a notion. It was just because it was near time
for the baby—women got foolish fancies then. I would sit back
and laugh at myself when I got to the graveyard and found
Elizabeth or Ann or Susan on the fallen stone. But why had it
been neglected? Why? I stepped over a fallen log, walked straight
through bushes, feeling nothing but this gathering dread that
gripped me tighter and tighter. I had not been running, yet I
had no breath left when I jerked open the rusty iron gate, stum-

bled through the crisp magnolia leaves and dropped to my knees beside the sunken grave.

Wind and weather had worn down the lettering; gray-green lichens obscured it. I snatched up a small stick and scraped at the words. "Beloved wife of Carrol——" But I knew that. The name must be higher up on the stone. The stick broke, my fingernails broke, but I went on digging at the lichens. I could hear my own breath coming harshly, I felt the blood pounding in my ears, so that there seemed nothing else in the world but my frantic self and this crumbling stone with its secret.

The first letter was *T*. But it could be Tabitha, Tildy, anything. It must be. *H*—but it still could be Theodora or Thomasina or—no. The whole name stood forth plainly—Thérèse. But the date? Perhaps she had died early with no children. I scraped again at the stone, all feeling gone from my fingers, until I could read the whole:

DIED ON THE 20TH DAY OF JUNE
IN THE YEAR OF OUR LORD 1895
MAY THE LORD HAVE MERCY

Have mercy, have mercy . . . I kept reading the line over and over, clinging to the words the way a drowning person snatches at anything to keep himself from the watery depths. I thought of odds and ends of things . . . her lips were red as the red moss rose; the crackling in the dead magnolia leaves . . . Philip's grandfather walking. And now at last I knew why he must keep on walking forever. Your children and your children's children. The Black Book—I saw the Black Book, magnified and horrible, the Doomsday Book, the Judgment Book, and on its pages the Churston names—and the name of my unborn child.

Oh—now I was to come to the crux of the whole matter. My child —part Negro! I looked down at my body and revulsion seized me like nausea. This—this excrescence, this alien thing. I struck at myself with my open palm. I gasped with pain and struck again.

A hand caught me by the wrist, and whirling I faced Minerva. She had both my wrists now, she held me fast. That infuriated me. "Let me go! Take your black hands off me! Get away from here! Let me go, I say!"

But she held me all the tighter. "You done found out," she said, her lip curling.

I stared at her, my arms going limp, the fight going out of me. "You . . . you know?" The words were only a whisper. There was the thing itself in all its horror, and here now its magnification, reflected in a mirror, in countless mirrors. "You know?" I repeated hoarsely.

"I knows."

"D-does everybody?"

Slowly Minerva shook her head. "Ain't many."

"White people?"

"Some white, some black."

I moistened my lips. "They . . . they talk about it?"

Again she shook her head.

"Why? Why don't they?"

Minerva shrugged. "They got a respect for the family, I reckon. Churstons, they hold their heads high."

Yes, they had to, I thought with bitterness. I leaned toward her. "You mean those that know don't . . . don't talk?"

"Could be awhisperin'. Ain't sayin' they ain't. When somethin' happen—like when Mr. Hollis kill hisself."

I caught my breath. I knew why Hollis had killed himself. "When something happens," I repeated. Something had happened. I was going to have a Churston child. Suddenly I remembered Mrs. Mall and Mrs. McCall in church, as we were leaving, how they had noticed me, how they had whispered. They knew I would have a child that would be part Negro. "But I won't," I cried, "I won't have such a child." A kind of darkness came over my mind. All feeling was wiped out so it no longer mattered what happened to me. My eyes turned to the bright river.

"You ain't goin' do nothin' like that."

"Why not? Why can't I?"

" 'Cause it's a sin befo' the Lawd."

"A sin! What do I care for a sin? What did they care?" I stamped on the grave at my feet. "What did they care?"

Minerva's laughter stopped me. She let go my hands and threw back her head, she bent double, holding her sides. It was terrible laughter.

"Stop!" I cried. "What's the matter with you? What do you mean?" I caught her by the shoulders and shook her. But still she laughed. I covered my ears with my hands but I could not shut out the sound.

At last she leaned against the trunk of a magnolia tree and wiped her streaming eyes with the back of her hand. "I could die alaughin'."

I was furious then. "There's nothing to laugh at, you fool!"

"Ain't they? Oh, ain't they?" She shook again with laughter and her words came brokenly through it. "I could plumb kill myself alaughin', seein' a body take on so account a little drap of nigger blood."

I stood with my mouth open, blinking at her stupidly.

She drew herself up with dignity. "A drap of nigger blood. Supposin' you hadn't nothin' but. Look at me. All black. I'se human, ain't I? I got feelin's one way and another like to the lily-whitest they is. I done been born, I been livin', breathin', eatin', drinkin', lyin' abed with a man. Ain't I? Ain't I?" She thrust her dark face close to mine, spitting the words out at me. "Cut me and my blood run red as yourn. Split me wide open and look at my guts—ain't no different from yourn." She snorted. "You . . . you, takin' on like crazy—you, makin' such a to-do. Carryin' on like a plumb fool. Fixin' to end up like Mr. Philip's ma."

I gasped. I saw it all now. "She turned against us," Philip had said.

"God!" I whispered.

"Yeah. That's how come. You's gettin' your eyes open. You's seein' things now. But you ain't see it all yet." She leaned closer, her black eyes blazing. "You listen to me, what I'm sayin'. Didn't you never stop to think colored folks is human, too? Didn't you never take it into your head to git a notion how it might be, knowin' you's human and seein' yourself set down lower 'n a dawg? Lower 'n old Humble that come and go like he please in

82

and out every door they be. Reckon you'd rather have old Humble's blood runnin' in your chile. Reckon you'd say, Oh, that don't matter, long's it ain't nigger blood. Yeah, that's what you'd say." She drew herself up, tall with scorn. "Then you ax me, what for you laughin', Minerva, and how come you laugh so loud and long? I swear to Gawd I could die alaughin'."

I turned away. I hid my face in my hands trying to shut it out. Wasn't it enough that I had looked into the Churston hell? Must I look now into another? "I never thought," I whispered. "I . . . never . . . thought."

Minerva wiped the sweat from her face. "Time you's thinkin'. Time everybody in the world was athinkin'." Her voice died down now into its customary grumble. "Reckon you better git on back up to the house. Likely wore yourself out with all this here plumb foolishment."

Foolishment, I thought, and abruptly the strength went out of me. I knew nothing but my own weariness. I stumbled blindly across the graves, out the iron gate and along the path, Minerva shooing me along the way she drove the cow into the barn, saying, "Git on now, keep agoin'. Git on."

· 9 ·

ALL that afternoon I lay on the four-poster bed in my room, my room and Philip's, and I looked at the ceiling. There was an irregular spot where the roof had leaked and stained the paper. As I stared at it, the brown lines and blurred patches took on strange aspects as if my mind were a projector throwing pictures on a screen. There were faces, grotesque and grinning, bent inhuman figures that faded into turbaned, faceless heads. Then animals came—great shadowy rabbits leaping and fleeing from unseen danger, raccoons wearing dark-rimmed glasses on their evil faces, monkeys with lips drawn back like snarling dogs. As long as I could keep my mind on them, I needed not think. It might even be that I could rest forever in this unreality.

Minerva came and went, bringing me food which I could not touch, putting a hot-water bottle to my feet and covering me with blankets which I could not feel. With darkness I slid imperceptibly into sleep. When I awoke late the next morning, reluctantly opening my eyes, the same strange numbness held my mind. I was covered over with scar tissue, quick-grown, impervious. Minerva made me take my coffee, though I did not want it.

"Got a pain ary place?" she asked.

I shook my head. Then, as she turned to leave, I asked, "Why are you so kind to me, Minerva?" For no armor is complete against kindness.

She gave me a dark look. "Told you I'se human, didn't I?" Then she added, "I ain't forgit how it is to be young and come on trouble the first time."

"But I've had trouble. My mother died; I was all alone."

"Anybody's mother bound to die, if you live long enough. That's in nature. Trouble hurts the worstest is the kind that ain't in nature. This here ain't." She went on to the door, her step solid and flat. There she stopped, not looking back. "Another

84

thing I ain't forgit—how it come on me the first time what color I was."

I stared at the empty doorway where she had stood, wishing I had not spoken to her. Why did I have to know these things? Why did I have to understand? And why did she have to be so good to me? The slow tears blinded my eyes, and I turned my face, to hide it in the pillow for shame. Old black Minerva—not hating me or anyone. And all the time deep down under my numbness I was hating everybody, hating Philip, hating this . . . this child I had to bear. But no, no. Why should I be ashamed? I sat up suddenly, wiping my blubbery face with my hands, pushing back my hair. I had not done anything wrong, to have all this come on me. It was not fair, and I was not going to be caught like this and made to think, to know. Why should I, Bentley Carr, be mixed up in such things? I looked down at the alien mound on my body. When that was gone wouldn't I be free as ever? Free to go far away somewhere, anywhere, and live out my life. There was no . . . no Negro blood in me. I was young. I could go alone—as I had been before I married Philip—and I could forget, as the years went by. I must start forgetting at once. I got out of bed and began to dress. I saw it clearly now. All I had to do was to live through the next few weeks, live as if nothing were real, live untouched, waiting to flee. One could stand anything for a little while, knowing that escape was near.

In an old wool skirt and sweater, a loose smock buttoned around around me, I sat on the rocker at the far end of the gallery, my needle flashing in the bright October sunshine that came in warmly between the cedars. When I heard the car coming I did not move. The springs squeaked, the engine wheezed as if the long drive had left it breathless. In the silence after it came to a stop, I heard a shutter turn at one of the windows in the music room and thought that Minerva must be looking out. Or was it Callie? I dropped my sewing and walked quickly to the front hall. I pushed the sliding doors wide open, and their creaking protest matched my tone in sharpness. "What are you doing here?"

Callie whirled about. Her lower lip protruded. "Ain't doin' nothin'."

"Well, you can do it upstairs, in Mrs. Churston's room," I said. "Turn down the bed and get it ready for her." I turned away and stood waiting in the front doorway. Then I heard Callie's slow sullen step as she began to mount the stairs. But I could not let her go yet. "Not that way. Go by the ell porch steps."

Callie stopped. She did not look around or speak; she just stood there, one brown hand on the railing.

"You heard me," I said. Only then did she turn and come slowly down and go out by the back hall door to the ell.

When she had gone out of my sight I covered my mouth with my hand. Was it I who had spoken like that? How could I? That was the way Philip spoke. O God, no! I must not.

The car door slammed. Now I would have to meet them, face them, knowing what I knew. I stood there waiting while I got hold of myself, while I froze over, hardening myself, numbing all my feelings. Then I went to the head of the steps.

Miss Kate was already out of the car, Philip was helping someone else out, a shrunken, frightened old woman. She was hatless, and her hair, once that glorious gold, was faded to dull brown streaked with gray. Uneven wisps, blown across her sunken, sallow cheeks, gave her a bedraggled, unkempt air. But her eyes, as Miss Kate and Philip took her, one at each side, and helped her up the steps—her eyes were the worst of all. They were blank and unknowing, mirrors that reflected nothing.

I watched their slow progress up the steps, Miss Kate saying, "There now, we're almost home. Just a little farther," and Philip silent, his lips compressed. I made myself look at them as if from a great distance. I kept saying to myself, I have nothing to do with them really, and I have only to see them for a little while, a few weeks, maybe. When Philip looked up and saw me, I even smiled a little. I think I did. At any rate, my lips moved while my eyes searched their faces with bitter knowledge.

"Bentley, are you all right?"

"Just fine, thank you," I said and moved aside to let them pass.

"Where's Callie, dear?" Miss Kate asked.

"I sent her upstairs to get the bed ready."

"That's good."

They went on, through the hall door and slowly up the stairs, the little old woman moving meekly between them. I stood clinging to the newel post with both hands, hardening myself against the pity that welled up within me. I made myself look at them as a stranger might, a knowing stranger. Each was different and yet shaped in his own cruel and inevitable pattern. As two and two must make four, as something let go in mid-air must fall, as a seed must grow after its kind, so in the remorseless working of things they had become what they were. For them there was no escape. But me—I would not be caught. I would not let myself be caught.

Philip flung open the arched door to the ell porch and they went through it out of my sight. I wiped the cold sweat from my upper lip with trembling hand. A little longer, just a little longer, I would live on the edge of the trap; then I would escape forever. I would not let myself be sorry for them—for Miss Kate who filled her empty life with club activities and dulled her senses with romances and mysteries, who moved with unimpeachable propriety under her armor of sweetness; for this poor old woman, Philip's mother, too fragile to stand up under the knowledge when it came to her; and for Philip, warped and twisted, not wanting to marry, yet because he saw and loved me—— I caught my breath in a sob, choked it back. No, no, I would not let myself think these things. I was not going to be concerned with them any more. They had nothing to do with me. I would live in the house with these three people for a little longer because my body was trapped, but I would keep my heart and mind free of them. Just a few weeks—one could stand anything for a few weeks. When they were over I could make definite plans.

The time passed slowly, each day dragging behind the other. I found I could sit in my room by the window looking away toward the pecan grove where the nuts hung in little bunches against the sky, or to the far pine trees at the plantation gate. I could look by the hour, my mind empty, my spirit hushed and waiting. I was like someone serving out a sentence, waiting for the day of release.

I kept the door to the nursery closed so I would not be reminded of the high hopes I had had, so I would not be conscious of the old woman in the room beyond. Her presence made little change in the household, for she was always in her room. There was only Callie, going back and forth with trays or a pitcher of water. I met her sometimes in the hall or on the ell gallery, and, if I did not say good morning, she did not speak, but passed lightly on in silence, her eyes averted, her slender shape graceful, her walk saucy and bold as if in coming to work at the house she had achieved something to be proud of, as if she had triumphed over me.

Philip spent some time each evening with his mother in her room, coming out worn and silent. Perhaps being occupied with her was what kept him from noticing any change in me. Only once he said, "You are so quiet, Bentley. Are you all right?"

I said, "I'm all right, Philip," my voice level and apparently untroubled.

Another time, as we left the dining room, Miss Kate walking ahead of us as usual, he laid his arm across my shoulders. I shivered and drew away from him. I could not help it, but I moved ahead of him quickly, making an excuse of passing through the door, for I did not want to hurt him more than I must. He overtook me in the hall, lowering his voice so Miss Kate would not hear. "You do not like me to touch you?" There was bright suspicion in his eyes.

"It's just . . . the way I feel right now," I said, turning my head away, moving on toward the library door.

Another day, walking idly about the place, I passed under the kitchen window and heard Miss Kate speaking to Minerva, asking her if anything had happened while they were away. I stopped and held my breath listening. I could live through this time only if they did not know. But if they knew that I knew, that would be more than I could bear.

"Didn't have no time to be awatchin' every minute," Minerva grumbled, "her walkin' in the woods like she do."

"I suppose it's just that it's getting near the time," Miss Kate said.

"Takes some that-a-way," Minerva said. "Moody-like, that's what."

88

I spent most of the day outdoors now, for the house oppressed me. Only in the open air, along the riverbank with space around me, only then could I breathe easily. I stood among the great trees that stretched their branches out over the bluff and I tried to be like a tree myself. A tree did not feel; it stood rooted in the earth, bent this way and that by the wind, yet steadfast and without pain. The clouds too, I would think, seeing a shadow pass over the bright water, the clouds did not think. They moved untroubled across the sky. The water knew nothing, only to go, forever to go, it mattered not where. That was how I would go too, when the time came.

One day as I stood with my hands pressed against the gray bark of a bare hackberry tree, liking its feel of hardness and impenetrability, I heard a crackle in the underbrush and turning quickly had a glimpse of a dark figure dodging back out of my sight into the thick underbrush. "Minerva?" I called. And when she came forth, ungracious and a bit shamefaced, I said, "You needn't be watching me all the time. I'm not going to . . . to do anything I shouldn't."

Minerva grunted, avoiding my eyes. "That all you fixin' to say?"

"That's all." I looked back at the river, forgetting at once that she was there. The water was hypnotic in its brightness, easing me into a deeper blankness of mind, free from thought and hurt.

"Same old thing," she said with scorn. "All over again."

I drew my mind back from nothingness, annoyed. She was like a mosquito buzzing around me. "What are you talking about?"

"Took her just that-a-way. Same look in the eye. Face like a empty dish, for all the world."

"Who?" I turned now and faced her.

"You and Mr. Philip's ma. Like as two peas."

"What do you mean?" My voice sharpened.

"Don't mean nothin'. Ain't none of my business."

"What are you trying to say?"

Minerva's lip twitched. "Pull the plug and let the brain seep out. That's what she done. And that's what you's doin', Miss Bent." Abruptly she turned and went away.

I stared after her, aghast. Me? Was I like that poor, faded, wispy wreck? Was I going that way? I stumbled across to a log and sat down, bent over, head resting in my hands. She had been once the young girl of the portrait, with hair like sunshine. She had escaped into blankness, an empty dish; her brain seeped out. Oh, why did I have to see, to understand, to ache so for her, knowing how easy it was, because I was doing it myself? But I wouldn't. My hands clenched. I wouldn't be like that.

But what other way was there? None that was easy. Only the hard way, not drawing back from pity and understanding, no matter how they hurt, not avoiding reality but facing it, naked and exposed. Suddenly I was intensely aware of everything around me, of the hard log beneath me, of the sunlight on the bare tree trunks, the sound of the current eating away at the bank below the bluff, of the rustle of a bird in the underbrush behind me, of the smell of brown leaves, of the crisp autumn air. I felt sharply the ache in my back from sitting still so long. The sun was low above the still, flat swamp beyond the river, a bright orange ball dropping visibly behind a strip of gray cloud, red-rimmed. It was time for me to go back to the house. Philip would be coming.

As I came in sight of the cedars and the low, brooding roof that contained the gallery, holding it in, close, secretive, the last rays of the sun were slanting in between the shaggy tree trunks and penetrating to the white wall of the house, to the fanlight over the door, and the small panes of the windows, making them blaze red as fire, as if fire were eating out the heart of the house. I stood under the moss-hung cedar branches and looked, thinking of all the people who had lived in that house, who lived there now, of myself, living among them, being for the moment—for I was still resolved on going—a part of them. And as I stood there, evading no knowledge, no reality, a new strength rose to meet them. As if all the forces which had been busy evading, dulling, numbing, had turned, and in turning gathered power. Like a bird that had fled before the wind, and in wheeling rose against it, mounting to new power. Out of nowhere I remembered a line, from the Bible or maybe from some old hymn: "And as thy days may demand, shall thy strength ever be." This was how people stood things, I thought.

That night I could not sleep. Every hard lump in the mattress seemed to press in upon me with malicious intent. My backache was worse and I thought I must have taken cold, sitting so long on the log by the river. It could have nothing to do with the baby's coming, I thought; for no one had told me where the pain would be.

The moonlight came in bright as day across my bed. I closed the shutters against it but still I could not sleep. In making myself aware of everything I had rather overdone it, I thought, smiling wryly to myself. I was too aware of everything. I heard a rooster crowing off in the chicken yard. I heard a bird's low night call and the stirring of a faint wind in the bare branches. I heard the night creaking of the old house itself. At last, weary of tossing and turning, I got up and put on my bathrobe and sat by the window.

Around me the old house breathed and stirred, its boards and beams shrinking as the night grew colder. All my senses alert and sensitive to every sound, I heard then a faint whispering movement from the ell porch, a slow, stealthy step. Was it Philip's mother, I wondered? Could she have stolen past the sleeping Callie and come out into the night? I went quickly through the nursery and silently swung open the door to the upper porch. There was no one there. I moved to the railing and looked down. The courtyard was a pool of blackness, for the moon had not yet risen above the level of the roof. I stood there a long time, listening, one hand pressed to my back. There was no one there, and yet I knew it was a step I had heard.

I went to the door of Philip's mother's room and bent to listen at the keyhole. There was a faint sound of movement in there, then silence again. I turned the doorknob gently and the door swung open with a faint sigh. Callie's cot bed was empty, so was the big bed. Against the brightness of the moonlit window I saw a small bent shape. Philip's mother was sitting there looking out through the wooden bars.

The old woman turned her head. "Come in," she said, her voice poignantly sweet, like a little bird's in the night. "Don't be afraid. Nurse is gone."

I took a low stool and placed it close by the window in the bright moonlight. I sat down and took her hand in both of mine, stroked it with gentleness, unable to speak.

She peered down at me. "You are so young," she said. "Most of us are old. Old beyond the measure of time."

"You were young once."

"Was I?" Her hand, like a little bundle of bones, lay in mine. It was cold, and my own hands could not warm it. I went to the foot of the bed and found her dressing gown and a blanket. I put them round her and tucked them in, then sat down again, my elbow on the window sill, my head resting on my hand.

"I think," she began, after a long while, "I don't know who you are."

"I'm Bentley," I whispered.

She shook her head. "I don't know. But I think you must be someone I should know and love."

"Yes, yes," I said with eagerness, lifting my head. "I am that. Please believe it." Her worn, sunken face blurred before my eyes. There was no reason, no thought here, and yet something stronger than either had reached out from me to her and touched her. It must be, I thought with wonder, that love and pity are stronger than reason.

We sat silent, looking at each other. Then she shivered and turned her eyes to the window. "Have you seen it?"

"What?"

"The night."

"Yes. It is beautiful."

She nodded slowly. "That stays. You can keep that. It doesn't hurt."

"You mean," I began, fumbling toward the thing she was trying to tell me, "you mean that no matter what else hurts—or goes—there is the beautiful night."

"When the nurse goes you can have it, all to yourself, when they think you are asleep. It's a secret. You won't tell?"

"I won't tell. But the nurse, this one—is she good to you?"

"They are always good to me. I don't make them any trouble. They like that. When you make trouble, that's bad. You won't make trouble, will you?"

"No," I said and choked on the word.

"That's right. That's best."

We said no more, just looked out into the night, into the shadows and the moonlight and the dark shapes of trees, moonfrosted on one side. After a while she said, "Better go now. Nurse will be coming back. We don't want to make trouble."

I stood then. "I'll come again." I bent and put my lips to her cheek. It was soft as a baby's.

"Thank you," she said in her sweet, slow way, not moving, not turning from the window.

I went out softly, closed the door and let the bar fall again across it.

· 10 ·

Two ways, I thought, fumbling toward thought. Two ways of finding respite. I had discovered them in the hours of that night and day. One was hard, one was easy, and both quite ... quite legitimate, not cowardly. The hard way was through pain. Pain was a bright, blinding wall, a shell enclosing, shutting out all else, shutting out thought and sound—Philip's step in the hall, Miss Kate's breathy whispering, Minerva's harsh monosyllables, the doctor's deep voice. I lived within the shell alone for a long time, knowing nothing but the fierce, white purity of its walls.

The other way was by oblivion, soft and dark. It began with a mask fitting over my face and the doctor's voice saying, "Breathe deep now, deep, deep." How sweet it was then, the darkness, the surcease! Letting myself slide into it, I thought. How easy, how easy to go and never come back!

But slowly, after time without measure, in spite of myself, I was coming again into a world of thought and feeling. There was at first only a question in my mind. I could not open my eyes to see or my lips to ask, but I knew a way to tell. Little by little I moved my hand, walking it on fingers, creeping it like a crab across the sheet, up the mountain of one thigh until I could feel the blessed flatness of my body. I was free, free! I drew a deep breath and drifted off again.

Coming out a second time into life, I heard voices, the doctor saying, "I'll go along. Call me if anything—— Oh, yes, you may go in now."

Miss Kate's voice next, exclamatory and yet oddly broken, "Well, Philippe! You escaped—this time."

Philip's voice sounded tight and strange. "There will not be another time."

Darkness came over me again, and when it had passed I woke into a sound of crackling. This time, slowly, I opened my eyes.

It was night again now, and firelight danced on the ceiling, crooked the bedpost shadows across the wall. I watched them and drifted in and out of consciousness. Then above the blazing of the fire I heard a rustling movement, a hard flat step. Minerva's dark face floated over me. She was speaking, and after a long time her words took on meaning. "Ain't you gwine look at your chile?"

I shook my head. All my thoughts—what few I had—were turned inward. I had no interest in any child, only in myself, free now. Free. My lids began to close again, but Minerva's voice kept after me, prodding me. She had brought the lamp and set it on the table by the head of the bed. It made a yellow circle of light around me, around me and . . . another living thing. For now I felt a warmth beside me, beyond my body, independent of me, extraneous, separate.

"Come on now, look," Minerva kept saying. "Just look. Ain't agoin' to hurt you just to look."

There was no escaping her insistence. I turned my head. But all I saw was the blue blanket in a little mound beside me, the blue blanket I had knitted, with scallops round the edge. Minerva lifted my shoulders and thrust a pillow in to hold me up. She pulled back the blanket and held it away with her black, bony fingers. But I had closed my eyes. All at once I was afraid, afraid to look.

"Aw, come on," Minerva said with brusqueness. "What you scairt of?" She laughed, a harsh, astringent sound. "Afeart he's black, ain't you?"

"Oh, damn you!" I cried and jerked myself up on my elbow, eyes wide open now, staring down. When I could hold up no longer I dropped back on the pillow, but I could still see that small, wrinkled face, a pale fuzz of hair, lashes dark against the cheek, familiar even in its strangeness, a snub of a nose, a pointed small chin, delicate, parted lips, the breath coming lightly between. "It's all pink and gold," I whispered.

"Ain't no it. It's a he," Minerva said with indignation.

I raised up again but fell back, too weak. "Is it . . . is he . . . all there? All his parts—all right, I mean?"

95

Minerva, blowing out the lamp, laughed under her breath. "Now you talkin', now you gettin' some sense in your haid. Course he's all there. Seven and a half pounds of him near as I could read it on Miss Kate's preservin' scales, and about as purty a white chile as ever I see."

"You mean . . . you'd think he was prettier if he . . . if he wasn't so white?" I stammered.

"Shore would, for a fact." She sat down in a low rocker beside the fire, stretched out her long, lean legs and kicked off her gray felt slippers. "Got to catch me a nap now. You go on back to sleep."

I lay still, my eyes closed, but I did not sleep. When I heard her breathing deep and even, I got up on my elbow and I sat upright. I drew back the covers and looked at the baby. I felt of his arms and legs and his tiny toes. Sound and perfect he was, as Minerva had said. There was only firelight, but a log flared up brightly as I studied his small face. I saw now why he looked familiar. It was because he looked like me. Yes, like that baby picture of me, the one that used to stand on the mantel between the clock and the knobby blue camphor bottle that had belonged to my grandmother Bentley.

Slowly I eased myself down on the pillow again, and slowly the bitter tears formed and slid down my cheeks, wetting my hair, wetting the pillow. Free? I had thought to be free. But I could never go away and leave this child. He was complete, an independent being, yet he was part of me. No matter what blood ran in his veins, I was too closely bound to him for escape. Where I went he would have to go.

The doorknob turned, the hinge creaked, and I settled my head deeper in the pillow so that my face was in the shadow. Philip's step crossed the room. He came to the side of the bed and bent down. Perhaps he looked at me first. I could not know, for I had closed my eyes, but when I opened them just enough to see through wet lashes, I found him pulling aside the blue blanket, bending closer. Two small fists stirred. He took one in his hand, pressed back the little fingers and studied the palm. Then, with a long sigh, he let the tiny hand close around his finger. He stood there a long time, bent over, motionless, his face softened to tenderness, a tiny smile twitching at one corner of his thin lips.

As he straightened at last, I closed my eyes tight, breathing deep and slow till he had tiptoed from the room. Then I turned my head and hid my face in the pillow and cried myself to sleep, knowing now that this was Philip's child too, and that I could never leave. I was caught now and forever, to the third and fourth generation.

And I thought, as sleep overcame me, I shall call him Henry. Henry Churston, after the old judge, who had looked ahead—to the third and fourth generation.

· 11 ·

THE days' demand was greater now. Yet as physical well-being and activity returned, I felt my strength rise to meet it—a strength born perhaps of a fierce protective feeling for my child. Somehow, I did not know how, but some way or other, I would keep him from hurt and from warping. For his sake I was able to accept everything as it was. Because of him, I became intensely Churston. I was on the Churston side, furiously, defensively, against all the world.

Philip was a help to me in these days, and as if he sensed my new allegiance, unspoken though it was, he seemed eased of suspicion and fear. He was thoughtful and tender. He praised me and said I was more beautiful than ever. Yet there was one difference in him, in our life together. If he forgot and put an arm around me or a hand on my shoulder, he drew back quickly and covered his withdrawal by talk of this or that or by a question about the baby, so I would not see. But of course I saw, and I remembered what I had heard him say: "There will not be another time." So this was how it was going to be, I thought, and took it as I was learning to take other things, for one cannot stay forever at high pitch before any misfortune. One accepts and bears what is inevitable. All my care and attention were centered on Henry now. Bathing him, feeding him, seeing him thrive and grow, I was able to set all else away from my conscious mind.

In mid-December Philip brought home a package. "It's a Christmas present for the baby," he said. But he would not wait for Christmas to open it. He carried it right upstairs to the nursery with me following, smiling at his eagerness. It was an electric train. An electric train for a month-old baby! I watched him set it up with bolts and batteries and wires, his long, slender fingers fumbling at the task, because he was not in the least mechanical

98

and it was hard for him. "I want Henry to understand how these things work," he said with earnestness.

I took the baby up and hushed his crying—he was frightened by the noise and clatter—and as I stood there, holding him in my arms, looking down at Philip while he adjusted this bit of track or tightened a wire, I was filled with pity and sadness, for him and for all parents the world over, longing to see in their children what they had missed, hoping in new lives to find fulfillment for their own lack. All Philip's lost hopes and frustrated ambitions were revived, for this tiny child. Philip, because of his fear and dread, had not dared fulfill himself. He might have been a lawyer, like his great-grandfather, even a judge. But that would have been conspicuous, laying him open to talk and the whispering of the old story. So he had kept to the small position in the county clerk's office, avoiding danger, doing work that must always have been dull and boring to one of his ability and temperament. Only during the war, in a position of responsibility, dealing with all manner of people, only then could he have felt free. That was how he had dared to fall in love, to marry. Oh, now I could understand him as never before, and my heart ached for him as if he too were my child. Not only for his unfulfilled past but for the disappointments that must be ahead.

For I knew—how I cannot tell—I knew that one could not live in another. No man has more than one chance at life, just his own. If that is lived fully, with courage, it is enough. I could see Philip and know this, but I could not see myself as I held the baby closer to me, protectingly, resolved that I would keep him from all hurt and harm, dedicating myself anew to guarding him. I did not know then that one cannot save a child from what comes to him of good or evil, that one can only hope to build him strong enough to meet it.

"Hold him down. Let him see," Philip said.

I knelt, turning the baby in my arms, and indeed for a moment his eyes seemed to focus on the movement, on the light that flashed off and on. That satisfied Philip. He smiled at me, a bit shamefaced, and began to take the thing apart and pack it away.

I rocked the baby in my arms for a little and laid him down in his basket crib. Then Philip took up the candle and we tiptoed out. Looking back, from a distance, seeing our life together as a whole, I think that we were never closer than in this simple moment. For a marriage is not only in words spoken, or even in that great vital force which draws a man and woman together; it is in the simple, daily details of living, and it is there that it is made —or broken.

Christmas came and went almost unnoticed. Philip had taken cold the week before and it developed into influenza. He insisted on going to town as usual in spite of the rain and cold, and that had not helped. He was abed now and I ran up and down stairs, all day and night too, nursing him and tending the baby.

"You should not be down here in this chilly basement room," I said, bringing more blankets and a hot-water bottle for his feet.

Philip shook his head. "I might give this to the baby."

"You wouldn't. I could keep the door closed, go round the other way to his room." I drew the covers up close under his chin, then looked round at the bleak dark room, shivering a little in spite of the good fire Anse had built in the small stove.

"No, no," Philip said fretfully. "The baby's crying would disturb me. And you'd better let Anse take care of me. I don't want you catching this."

He was flushed and feverish now and I did not argue more. I went and called Anse to bring in more pine knots and short wood. But I knew I would never trust Philip to Anse's stupid care. The doctor came, Dr. Whitlow, with his hearty, false laugh. "Oh, we'll have you up and around in no time," he said to Philip. But when I followed him to the gallery after his second visit, he spoke seriously. "Of course, the real trouble is that heart condition of his. He must be kept quiet, not allowed to worry about anything."

"How do you keep anyone from worrying?" I sighed.

"I'd be famous if I knew," he said, and then, returning to his professional exuberance, he gave me a playful glance from his goggle eyes and added, "But I should think a pretty little wife like you could wheedle some of his worries away."

I regarded him gravely, not liking to be called a pretty little wife, or taking much to the notion of wheedling anybody. "I will do what I can," I said.

I did, too. I nursed him faithfully night and day, with only a little help from Anse for the lifting that had to be done. Miss Kate went about looking completely down in the mouth. She was out of anything to read, for Philip had missed his weekly trip to the library. All she could do was crochet, her tiny, boneless fingers working faster and faster as her concern for Philip grew.

I was worried too, for I could see how quick and short his breath came, how painful his cough was. When the doctor had come a second time on the same day, I followed him from the room. "Can't you give him any of these new drugs that are supposed to——"

He shook his head. "This type does not yield to those things," he said, not saying of what it was a type.

But I knew, and Minerva knew too. She came to the door that night. "You better let me set with him. You's plumb wore-out."

I looked at her gratefully, for I was about at the limit of my strength. "For a little while," I agreed. "I'll lie down on the couch in the library. Call me before midnight."

But when I awoke, first dawn had come. I sprang up and ran out by the ell porch, down the steps and through to Philip's basement room. I flung open the door and stopped short, sniffling the air. "What on earth, Minerva?" She roused up from her dozing in the chair by the stove and looked toward the bed. So did I, and ran to the bedside to bend over Philip. His hand was cool to my touch and by the light of the guttering candle I could see the sweat standing on his forehead. His breath came easily and he was sleeping naturally.

Minerva grunted. "Yeah, done took a turn. 'Bout midnight."

I straightened up, drawing a long breath as the long-gathering dread rolled from me. Then I sniffed again. "What in the world do I smell?"

Minerva pulled her old sweater closer round her shoulders. "Made him an onion poultice. That's what done it." She started for the door. "You's out of the woods now, Miss Bent," she said.

But I was not out of the woods. If I had come out for a little,

101

it was only to plunge into another part of them, deeper and darker still. Philip, who had been pitifully grateful for everything I did for him during the height of his illness, was in his convalescence unendurable. Nothing I did pleased him. I even tried to improve my looks, thinking he was probably sick of the sight of me with my hair half brushed and any old sweater and skirt or shabby wool dress thrown on in a hurry. Now I had more time, I tied back my hair with a velvet ribbon and in the afternoons put on a dark-brown dress cut in the new style, full-skirted and fitted in the bodice, showing off my figure that was slender and shapely again. But I could win no word of praise from him. He lay on his pillows watching me through narrowed eyes, apparently just waiting to find fault with me. I could not even draw the covers closer under his chin or measure his medicine or throw more wood into the stove without his blazing at me. I was worn out, worried too, because my getting overtired had made it necessary to put the baby on the bottle.

I did my best to be patient, but one evening when he complained of the broth I had made him, I flared up. "You ought to be thankful to have it. No matter if it does taste like dishwater, it was a lot of work to make."

"It's not fit to eat," he said, and whether he meant to or not, his impatient movement tipped over the bowl and flung the tray and spoon crashing down on the brick floor.

The dish shattered into a million pieces, and I cried out, "You ... you ought to be spanked," and burst into tears, not because of the dish or my new dress skirt, spotted and stained, but for the wasted broth which I had worked over for hours, pressing the juice from the meat, trying to get all the nourishment out of it.

Philip caught me by the wrist. For a moment I thought he was going to strike me, but he did not. He jerked me down to him roughly and held me fast, kissed my eyes, my lips, my throat. And such is the power of passion that though my spirit resisted, I was moved by it.

But now he thrust me from him, turned his face to the wall and would not speak or move. Bewildered, feeling stripped and ashamed, I left him and wandered about the house and would

not go near his room. I sent Minerva with his supper, and Anse
to tend him next day. After that I went in and out as usual, but
I was quiet, avoiding his glance, speaking only when I must
speak. He was cold and formal with me, but gradually the tension, the awkwardness, eased.

Then the day came when he was to sit up for the first time. I
called Anse in and sent him to the library for the big Morris
chair. I stood outside Philip's door and watched him bring it in,
cautioning him not to bang it against the door, to walk carefully
and not trip over old Humble who insisted on coming in now to
sleep on his rug before the stove. I helped Anse spread a blanket
over the stair and stood holding another to go over Philip's knees.

Anse helped him up and steadied him, half carrying him across
to the chair. And when I had tucked the blanket around his
knees, it seemed so good to have him sitting up at last that I
clapped my hands and cried, "That's splendid, Anse! You managed beautifully."

Anse, always voluble and good-natured when Philip was not
berating him about something, nodded and grinned back at me.
"He ain't hard to holp, ma'am. He ain't got much meat to his
height right now."

I laughed right out at his way of putting it—meat to his height.
That was a good one. I looked to Philip, hoping that he was en-
joying it too. But his face was turned from me. "I'll get you some
orange juice, Philip," I said.

Coming out from the dark understory into the dazzling brightness of the courtyard, my eyes were almost blinded by the sudden change. I stopped at the foot of the steps and waited, blinking, till they should adjust to the light. That was how it was that
I heard Philip. I could not understand the words he spoke, but
there was pain as well as anger in his tone. Had he tried to get
up? Or had the rod that held up the back of his chair fallen out
so that he was dropped back? I ran around the steps and along
the dark corridor, colliding with Anse, who jumped aside like a
scared rabbit. I burst into Philip's room. "What in the world . . .
what has happened? What——" I was silent, for Philip sat as I
had left him, in the Morris chair, only now he was leaning for-

103

ward, his hands clasped tight on the chair arms, his eyes fastening on me with bright suspicion. I knew that look too well. I had seen it when we came out of church that day I watched the usher. I had seen it too many times. But how could it be now? There had been no man here except Dr. Whitlow, and with him I had been guarded and careful, scarcely looking at him during his visits.

I stood there in the doorway, no doubt looking like a fool in my bewilderment. I was so utterly unprepared, so defenseless against the words Philip flung at me. I could not even take in their meaning for a little. Even then it was incredible. But Anse was a man, and Philip thought I had smiled on Anse. He thought —— God, how could he! I held to the door frame with one hand, supporting myself. Then as the fantastic unreason of such an idea struck me, I laughed. What a joke, what a riot of a joke! Philip, of all people in the world, Philip thinking I had been familiar and . . . and flirtatious with poor stupid Anse! I laughed the more.

Philip was leaning back in his chair now, his face distorted, the lines from nostril to mouth a greenish white. I was frightened then out of my hysteria. The doctor had said . . . his heart. I turned and fled down the corridor, up the ell steps and through the back hall, calling, "Miss Kate! Oh, Miss Kate!"

Miss Kate appeared in the library door, her crochet trailing after her in crazy white streamers of thread. She was like a startled fat spider in a half-spun web. "Wh-what is it? Bentley! Oh, my——"

"Philip——" I said in a choking whisper. "Go—quick."

I stood alone in the hall, clinging to the back of a chair for support, listening, waiting. There was no sound anywhere about the house. What had happened? Slowly I fumbled my way out again, down to the courtyard. There I sank down on the bottom step, bent over, my head in my hands, afraid to go farther, wondering if I hadn't better call the doctor.

Miss Kate came to me, soundless as always. Slowly, with terrible dread, my eyes traveled upward from her tiny, black shoes, over the firm mountain of her body to her whitely powdered face. She was looking at me with a puzzled expression. "What is the matter with you, Bentley? Don't you feel well?"

"Me?" I said stupidly.

"Yes, you. You came screaming for me, frightening me half out of my wits, and now you sit here——"

"But Philip——"

"Why, did you think there was something wrong with Philippe? He said he was tired sitting in the chair, so I helped him back to bed and stayed till he dozed off. He can't sit up long at one time, you know."

"Oh," I said blankly.

Miss Kate went on past me, up the steps. "He is wonderfully better today. He will get his strength back quickly. The Churstons have wonderful recuperative powers."

"Oh!" I said again and got to my feet. Miss Kate was out of hearing when I spoke. "But me—I am not a Churston. There are some things I do not recuperate from, and never will. Never."

Then after a moment I mounted the steps and went out the runway to the kitchen. I asked Minerva to feed the baby for me and said I was going for a walk. I had been too long in the house.

Minerva only grunted her assent, but I knew she liked being trusted with Henry, and her bony black hands were skillful at tending him. I turned away quickly now from her dark, shrewd glance and went on to the hall closet for my coat. A moth flew out and I slapped at it. The hall needed dusting. One of the portraits was crooked. I heard Callie coming down the ell stairs, dishes rattling on the tray she carried. All these things but danced on the surface of my mind, like little eddies whirling over a tumultuous, tumbling stream.

The sky was gray with lowering clouds. Across the river rain was coming down in slanting, penciled lines. The air was quite still and mild and I wore my coat slung round my shoulders like a cape. There was no use, I thought, my eyes on the ground, on the rotting leaves under my feet. There was no use trying any more.

I followed the river path till I came to the sand bar, long now, stretching out into the shrunken river. There I sat down on the willow log, bent over with my head in my hands. There was no use building, building with slow, heavy labor what would only

105

be cut down and destroyed, taking me down with it. I felt as if I had come to the end of the world. Perhaps I had been close to it before, but this time—— Oh, didn't I have enough without this? I had been hoping that now, with the baby here and that worrisome time past, Philip would never again be suspicious and accusing. And here it was, all over again—and about Anse. Anse of all people! How could he? All I had done was laugh at the poor, stupid thing. I thought back over the other days when Anse had helped me with Philip. I tried to remember if there had been anything, but how could there have been?

The rain walked across the water on a thousand feet, surrounded me and covered me and I lifted my face to it. Perhaps it would wash me clean again, clean from Philip's terrible accusing. Tears ran down my cheeks and the rain washed them away; it ran down my coat that covered me like a tent, and the sand drank it up as fast as it fell. I heard no sound but the whispering water and the fall of the rain. I did not hear the dip of a paddle or the dugout nosing into the sand. Only the voice, an untroubled, easy voice speaking just ordinary words with a faintly humorous note. They came to me as if out of another world.

"Hey there, taking a shower bath?"

I turned and wiped my face with my hands, fumbled for a handkerchief and blew my nose. "Sort of," I said. I even smiled a little, blinking the drops from my lashes, looking at Jeff Wheeling with a kind of wonder. He seemed steady as a tree, large as the sky, untroubled as the earth beneath my feet. "Been fishing?" I asked, when the silence had lengthened.

"Got one, before the rain started."

"Let's see him."

He bent down and lifted up a small catfish, opalescent where the raindrops struck. "I'll cook him for my lunch."

"Nice," I said. Commonplace words they were, but healing. So was the sight of him, sitting there hunched over the narrow seat, the rain streaming from the back of his wide-brimmed, brown felt hat, falling down the slope of khaki raincoat, making a shower within a shower.

106

"I was just heading for cover," he said.

"Cover?" I looked around at the rain-pocked river, the bare willow branches, the drenched underbrush of the bluff.

"It's down the river a bit, back, off the bayou. Ever been there?"

I shook my head.

"Want to come?"

I looked back at him sharply. His deep-set blue eyes held only tranquillity and kindness. If he saw the state I was in, if he felt my stunned distress, he gave no sign. I stood abruptly. "I'd like to."

As he helped me aboard, his hand, wet and cool, swallowed mine, holding it briefly, but long enough for me to feel the warmth coming through. When he had shoved off and got out into the current he reached under his seat, opened a little door and took out a bath towel. "Better wipe your hair dry and then pull up your hood."

"Oh, yes. Thanks." I did as he told me, rubbing my dripping hair till my head was in a glow. I must look a sight, I thought, but I did not care. All that I wanted was to keep hold of this quiet, this peace that emanated from him. I folded the towel and gave it back to him. "You seem to carry everything you need," I said, seeing the skillet, the cup and the plate in the small compartment.

He nodded, swinging his paddle. "The Compleat Angler, that's me. And the title of my favorite book. Ever read it?"

I shook my head.

"I'll quote you a line about fishing: 'An employment for his idle time, which was then not idly spent . . . a rest to his mind, a cheerer of his spirits, a diverter of sadness, a calmer of unquiet thoughts, a moderator of passions, a procurer of contentedness.'"

God! I thought. I'd better take up fishing.

He paddled in silence now, his eyes passing over my face, moving on to sky and water. There was only the fall of the rain and the rhythmic dip of his oar, soothing as a song in minor key, only that and the echo in my mind of the words he had quoted. We dodged a floating log, making an easy curving passage round it;

107

we skirted a projecting point where driftwood had been piled high and left by the receding current. The bare roots and branches of a sycamore were white as bleaching bones.

"Haven't seen you in a coon's age. What have you been doing?" he said at last.

"Me?" I did not want to think of myself, but the question waited to be answered. "I've just been busy—having a baby, and things."

"So I heard. Boy, isn't it?"

"Yes."

"Fine."

I turned the talk from myself. "Why aren't you at school?" He laughed. "At Christmas and New Year's there are holidays. Remember?" Behind his laughter his blue eyes studied me shrewdly.

"Oh, yes. Of course." My glance fell. He must wonder at my not thinking of that. For all I knew, today was New Year's. "I've been . . . occupied. I mean, one gets involved."

"Yes." He let the word fall gently and said no more. The dugout moved swiftly now in a shallow channel between shore and a long, low island, thick with green cane from which oak and ash and bay trees lifted bare, rain-blackened branches into the gray sky. He turned the nose of the boat and shot it shoreward through a gap in the wall of the bluff. This was the bayou where but a faint current moved. The banks rose high for a little way, root-tangled and dark, with here and there a spray of green rattan and a clump of green cane. Moss-hung branches met overhead as the way narrowed and the banks declined. The rain ceased abruptly, so we moved in stillness with only the soft drip from leaf and twig.

"You know your way about," I said, when he sent the boat sharply around a cypress root and into a still narrower channel.

"Every branch and stream through all the swamp. Duck now, there's not much clearance."

I bent double, my eyes on the still water and the unbroken ripple of our passing. It was like sliding over a gray mirror that wavered and healed as we went.

"Okay now," he said and I straightened up as we came out into an open space. Cypress trees ringed it round. They rose dark and majestic, unbranched to dizzying height. Moss hung down, fragile as foam, patterned like lace, black lace laid on the silver sky. The fluted cypress knees were like turrets rising from underwater castles. Out in the open still water, bare to the sky, black, dead remnants of trees stood, weathered down to grotesque, distorted shapes.

"Like statues," I whispered, as Jeff sent the dugout slowly out among them. I looked in wonder, openmouthed. Here a black branch hung down like a drooping arm; there a trunk had partly rotted, leaving the shape of a bowed head, a twisted body fixed in some arboreal agony. In the still, gray water each form was reflected, complete and three-dimensional so there was no telling where reality ended and image began. There was no surface to the water. It seemed to be all sky, hung with these haunting forms among which we moved as if suspended in mid-air. It was a place to put a spell on one, so that words could not be spoken.

Slowly the boat moved on between the cypress trees, and Jeff said, his voice hushed as if he too were caught in the enchantment, "A kind of druid circle. They take on a thousand forms and meanings with the changing light." Rain began again, and looking back I saw the dark reflections dancing under the fall of drops as if to some music which neither we nor the rigid, tortured shapes could hear.

We passed on in silence, weaving in and out among the great trees, hearing only the silken whisper of falling rain. Then quite abruptly we came on a tangled wall of green. I bent over, thinking we would surely crash into it. But with a turn of the paddle Jeff sent us through it by a narrow opening and then, lifting his paddle, let us drift to stillness.

"Here we are," he said, taking off his hat and shaking the water from the brim. "No rain can reach us here."

I looked up into a green roof of tangled cane and vine. This was a snug green cave, the water still and dark. A red bird, startled by our coming, flashed over our heads. Beside the boat a moccasin swam, his undulations leisurely and graceful. "It's a wonderful place. Out of the world," I said.

Jeff took a knife from his belt and picked up the catfish from the floor of the dugout. Leaning over the side, he cleaned it deftly, cut it up. Then from under the seat, out of his little compartment, he began to take things: a tin tray, a metal stand, a skillet to hold the fish, a box of sterno.

"What in the world——" I began.

"Aren't you hungry? I am."

I watched in amazement while he placed the things on the floor of the boat at his feet, put a strip of bacon on the skillet over the flame, then the fish with salt sprinkled over it. The smell of it rose deliciously, and it cooked with a gay, sputtering sound.

I laughed aloud. "What a wonderful picnic!" I took the cigarette he offered me and we smoked in silence while the fish cooked. The smoke rose slowly in the moist, mild air. It was as if we sat by a campfire, settlers come down the river to make a home, camping by the way, shut in by the rain, snug and safe from all harm.

Jeff turned the fish with his knife. Then he looked at me, smiling a little. "What are you thinking about with that faraway look in your eyes?"

"The early settlers, how they came through the woods and swamp, like this."

Jeff leaned forward, resting elbows on his knees, his face lighting up. "I just got hold of a book the other day, recollections, crudely written, but fascinating reading. It told about one family that came up from New Orleans. It was easy enough coming down the river, you know, but coming up—that was really tough. They had to pole their way alongshore and, where the water was deep, sling a rope round a tree trunk, pull alongside, then throw it round another tree, progressing literally by inches."

"Did they make it?"

Jeff shook his head. "The man got caught in a current. The boat tipped over and he lost everything, family, goods and all."

"Oh! What did he do then?"

"One of the planters gave him a scrap of land, and off his first crop he made enough to buy slaves and plant more acres. And in the end he married the planter's daughter. The land was rich then. But when the land goes down, the people go down too. That's the trouble with us here now. It will be a long time and hard work before we get back what we squandered in those days." As he spoke he got out a corn pone, rolled in waxed paper, split it and laid it in the skillet. Then, when it was hot, he served me the food on a tin plate. He brought out a thermos bottle from his compartment and poured me a tin cup of hot coffee.

"Am I taking your only plate?"

"Oh, I've the skillet, and the thermos top, and fingers were made before forks. You can have the knife—but don't cut yourself. Use the corn pone for a scoop."

As I lifted another delicious morsel to my mouth, saying I'd never in all my life tasted anything so good, quite suddenly I thought of Philip, and my hand stayed poised motionless, halfway to my parted lips. If Philip—so jealous of a glance in church, so uneasy about the doctor who attended me, so . . . so degradingly suspicious of a yellow stupid Negro like Anse—if he could see me now, deep in the swamp, alone here with this man, this stranger, the rain shutting us in like a curtain, the food shared between us, the silence all around—— "God!" I whispered.

"What is it?" Jeff asked and leaned toward me.

I shook my head. "N-nothing. Just tell me some more—about the settlers, the Indians—" my eyes fell—"about anything." Then I went on eating, forgetting everything as I listened to his stories. He told of the Indian days and how Bienville was offered the hand of Cadillac's daughter and when he refused was sent by Cadillac against the whole Natchez nation with only a few pirogues of soldiers. "But Bienville had a way with the Indians and he made out all right. High water came while he was camped below Natchez, and they had to lash logs together to have a dry place to sleep."

I looked down at the water, up at the green overhead, and I imagined how it must have been. I thought of the night sounds they would have heard, the frogs croaking, the wildcat's scream, the panther's cry. "The mosquitoes must have eaten them alive."

"They had 'barres'—that's where we get the name mosquito bar." He took my empty plate, washed it over the side, the skillet too, stowed these things away in his small compartment while he talked. We had cigarettes with our coffee, and he went on from one tale to another. I listened gratefully.

The rain had stopped when we came out of the cove again into the open, cypress-circled space. The air was colder now and a mist rose from the still water. It swirled in ghostly scarves among the black, distorted shapes, all struck motionless in the midst of dancing, with only their veils still moving.

Jeff paddled steadily now, out into the bayou and upstream. It was late afternoon and fog lay over bluff and river. The bare, black trees stood out distinct in every branch and twig against its gray blankness. They were cutouts hung in space, unreal and strange. At the sand bar Jeff hesitated, his paddle uplifted. "Shan't I take you on to your landing?"

"N-no. I'd rather walk."

He helped me ashore, standing on the sand, holding the boat with his paddle. "I hope you'll come out again with me," he said.

"It's been wonderful, and thanks a lot," I said in a rush, awkwardness overtaking me. Then something in his pose, the way he turned his head, looking down at me with good will and kindliness, made me say what I knew was true, that I would come again.

"That's good." He nodded.

That should have been all, but suddenly I found myself saying, "You don't know how good it's been." I bowed my head against his gaze. "I wish . . . before I go . . . I wish you would say again those lines—the ones you quoted."

Slowly, gravely, his voice lingering on each word, he repeated them: ". . . a diverter of sadness, a calmer of unquiet thoughts, a moderator of passions, a procurer of contentedness."

I looked at him now, unashamed of the tears in my eyes. "That's what you have been to me. And I—" my voice faltered—"I thank you." Then I turned and left him. He was still standing there motionless when I looked back from the crest of the bluff and waved.

· 12 ·

In some other world it may be that a spirit can circle unceasingly the flames of torment, or that ecstasy can hold forever the high pure note. But there, in that other world, surely, one need not interrupt these eternal preoccupations to earn a living at a dull office job or to sew on a button or tend a baby or eat dinner or sleep and wake to a new morning.

So it was with Philip and me that the fine edge of his suspicion, the sharpness of my hurt, were worn down, dulled by the relentless daily mechanics of living. He recovered quickly from his illness and began going again each day to town. I moved in my familiar routine, watching with a new hardness how his cool, precise formality passed into the dark reproachful stage, knowing that next he would praise me for some small thing that other times might go unnoticed, or that he would bring me a present and think that all was well again. Yes, I was bitter then. It is not easy to be generous and noble while one moves in the midst of things. Only afterward does that come, when one is at a distance, untouched and secure. Then one is driven to godliness willy-nilly and there is small virtue in it. For surely it must be that a god is godly out of necessity, as we are human.

Into this dull and static living the postman came, driving in from the outside by the plantation road, knocking at the door where no one ever knocked, bringing a special-delivery letter from Miss Stockbridge. It plunged me at once into the excited activity of cleaning, planning, all with high expectation. I read the letter aloud to Philip and Miss Kate that evening as we sat in the library after dinner.

"I expect to arrive in Sherrysburg at six twenty-one P.M., Central Standard Time, on Thursday the sixteenth of January. Will you kindly see to it that I am met at the station which, I understand, is located on the corner of River Street and Walker Avenue? I shall have two suitcases and a small overnight bag.

"Sincerely yours, Eliza Stockbridge."

113

"Well!" Miss Kate exclaimed as I folded the letter and looked from one to the other. "She certainly believes in being specific. As if everybody in the county didn't know where the station is!"

Philip gave the *Times-Picayune* a little shake to emphasize his words. "A very proper and businesslike letter. Sam can take the car to meet her. I see no need for any of us to make the trip."

I put the letter back in the envelope with a childish sense of disappointment. Somehow I had been wanting to go myself to meet her. She was my experiment, my idea, and I would have liked to have the first look at her. But it did not seem worth making a point of. I would see her when she came, and meanwhile I had plenty to do.

With Minerva to help me I began the next day to get her two rooms in order for occupancy. They had been so long unused that the air seemed hopelessly musty. Then I discovered that the parlor curtains were mildewed. They had to be taken down and washed and sunned and aired. The brown brocade shattered at a touch, the lining let my fingers through. I tried mending with needle and fine thread, but each stitch made a new tear. All I could do was readjust the fullness and hope that the rents in the brocade would not fall across the torn places in the lining.

Minerva scrubbed the floors and laid fires in parlor and back bedroom. I took hammer and nails and crawled underneath the big mahogany bed to make the sides more secure and stop the slats from falling out at the least provocation. Even so it worried me to think of what might happen if Miss Stockbridge turned out to be fat or given to nocturnal tossing.

With all this activity in addition to my daily round of tasks, I had no time to walk by the river. Only once, late in the afternoon, I quit work and, after telling Minerva to keep an ear open for Henry while she was cooking dinner, I set out along the path. As the river was running shallow now, I went down the bluff by the worn steps cut from its side and followed the lower way. Since that day when I had gone to the little graveyard in fear and left in despair, I had avoided when possible the upper path along the crest of the bluff. While I could I wanted to ignore the knowledge that had come to me then. I could not forget altogether, no more than a man may forget a weight on his back. But I could and did, through constant usage, become accustomed to it, as one does to the heat or cold of the climate where one lives, knowing there is nought that will change it.

When I came to the sand bar, I found it empty as the wide, bright river. I sat on the log and there was only loneliness to keep me company. I had never been lonely here before and I took myself to task for it now. Why should I expect Jeff Wheeling to be here when I came, as if he were a tree or a bush, as if he had no life of his own apart from me and my need? I rose and walked slowly homeward, a bit startled by the keenness of my disappointment.

I went again on Saturday, in the middle of the morning when I had bathed and fed the baby and tucked him in for his long nap. It was a bright sunny day, one of those days we have sometimes in January when it seems as if the calendar has got befuddled, mistaking winter for spring. The birds too had fallen into this seasonal confusion. Cardinals darted across my path, and high on the bluff a mockingbird sang, shaking out his song as if a madness had struck him. Even before I came within sight of the sandy point, I saw rising and dissolving in the bright morning air the smoke from Jeff's cigarette. I hurried my step and came quickly to where he sat on the log, whittling on a willow stick. Always, when I saw him, a kind of peace came over me, and now I rested in the manner of his movement as he rose at my coming and then sat down again beside me. My senses sharpened so that the morning took on new beauty, the air was sweeter to my breathing. For when I was with him, each moment had a value of its own, drawing on neither the past nor the future for its richness, but seeming to hold in itself all that was needful.

"I thought you must have gone away on a visit or something," he said, giving me the slow smile that lighted up his craggy face.

"Off for a visit?" I laughed at such a notion. "No, I've just been busy, getting ready for a . . . a boarder." And then I told him about Miss Stockbridge's coming to live in the two rooms that were never used and how I had been trying to make them presentable. "Of course there are no conveniences such as she is

115

probably used to, but somehow she doesn't seem to mind. She can have a good fire going all the time, and with Minerva and me to wait on her——" Before I knew it I was telling him everything I had done in the two rooms, how I had mended the bed and the leg of the parlor settee, how I had turned the rug so the worn place would be under the armoire. And he listened as if all this were of interest, for he had that way about him, of making one seem important, even to such small details as this.

"It's done you good to have all this to do," he said when I paused for breath. "How did you get hold of her?"

"Oh, that was fun!" I cried, and told him about the magazine and my ad and the other letter that had come, and then finally Miss Stockbridge's, enclosing a check. "I can't wait to see what she will be like, whether she is young or old or what. I feel as if . . . as if I had invented her, but in the dark." I laughed. Then I told him how foolishly I had worried over what I had done, putting in the ad without telling anyone. "I didn't know how they would take it. I mean, after all it is Miss Kate's house, really. But it turned out all right. It seems to me that when I think everybody is going to be upset, they aren't, and then when I least expect it——" I caught myself up short.

"I see." Jeff nodded.

Perhaps he saw more than I had meant him to. I sat silent for a little, my eyes downcast. "I . . . I don't know why I'm telling you all this. You can't possibly be interested. Why should you? It's only that I don't have anybody to talk to, and when I get started——" I was silent again. For he would wonder why I could not talk to Philip or to Miss Kate, or even to Philip's mother. For surely everyone must know, must have heard somehow, that she was at home again, though they might not know in what condition.

But Jeff only said, in so matter-of-fact a way that I could think nothing of it, "I'm interested in everything. After all, I lead a rather solitary life myself."

"You? Solitary?" I stared at him in amazement.

"Oh, I see people every day—the children at school, other

teachers, neighbors up and down the road. But——" He was silent for a moment. Then he said, "By the way, I brought you a little book I thought you might enjoy." He limped across to the dugout and reached under the seat to the compartment there, bringing out a small volume wrapped in brown paper. "I've been carrying it around to give you when I got a chance." He unwrapped it and put it in my hand. "It's an account of the yellow fever epidemic of 1838, how the fever broke out on one of the river packets coming up from New Orleans and how they stopped the boat beside an island and buried the dead and all their belongings, because they thought then that the fever was carried in clothes. I've a notion the island mentioned was the one right here, downstream a bit. I'd like to know what you think about it."

"Oh, yes," I said with eagerness, "I'd like to read it." I turned the volume in my hands, opening to the flyleaf, reading his name written there, seeing for the first time how he wrote it, in a square, firm hand, just the kind of hand I would have expected. "Wait," I said, when he began to crumple the paper. "Let me have it." I took it from him and folded it again around the small volume. "Someone might—I mean, it looks like an old book. It might be valuable." My fingers fumbled, pressing down the paper, and I bowed my head so my hair would hide my shame from him, shame that I could not openly take home a book to read, that I must hide it and slip it in unseen.

But all he said was "Did you know your hair has gold glints that shine where the sun strikes?"

I glanced up quickly and caught a look like wonder on his face, as if he were surprised that he had said such a thing. "I used to be a towhead when I was little."

"It's more than that, more than just your hair that shines," he said, studying me. "There is a brightness all over you. It must be yourself shining through."

I turned from him to hide the quick tears that came to my eyes. It was so good to . . . to be liked. Just to be liked, without involvement or consequence. "Thank you," I faltered.

"For what? That I have eyes in my head?" He laughed.

117

"But no, no. For . . . for seeming to . . . to like me."

"That is not hard," he said with gravity.

"And for being around . . . for me to talk to." I rose, still not meeting his eyes, and said it was late and I must go. I went quickly from him, along the path, not trusting myself to turn and look again.

As I came into the yard and passed under the cedars, the book tucked close under my arm, I saw the car coming. Philip got out and we met at the top of the steps, he mounting on one side and I by the other. "Well, Bentley," he said, smiling, "what have you been doing, having a walk?"

"Y-yes." I held the small book tighter under my arm. But he was not noticing. He had a package of his own.

"Here. I brought you a present."

"Oh, what is it?"

"Open it and see." He smiled down at me, watched eagerly as, with awkwardness because of the book under my arm, I tore open the paper.

"Why, Philip, it is beautiful!" My fingers moved over the dark flowered silk. "A dress for me?"

"Of course. I thought you would like to make yourself something new for the christening?"

"The . . . the christening."

"Yes. In February there is always a Sunday when children are christened. Don't you remember?"

"Oh, yes. I know." We went on into the house together side by side. But a christening! I was thinking with dismay. To march up and stand before all the congregation! Some would be peering with evil eyes, wondering, thinking, whispering—a Churston baby . . . How could they dare? . . . What is he like? . . . Does she know? . . . I shivered.

"You stayed out too long," Philip said. "Come in and I'll build up the fire."

"Yes, in a minute. I'll just take this up to my room." I ran quickly up the stairs.

· 13 ·

RAIN had fallen in the night and frozen white on earth and twig. It was a rare and beautiful sight, but I was not properly appreciative, for this was the day Miss Stockbridge was to arrive. Looking out the window as we sat at breakfast, seeing the cedars, like stiff bundles, ice-wrapped, the plantation road aglare, I said, "What will Miss Stockbridge think? Here she is expecting to find sunshine and balmy air! Oh, why couldn't it be springlike the way it was last week?"

"Surely she won't hold us responsible for the weather," Miss Kate said.

"But I put it in the ad——"

Philip said, "I'll try to get the car out to the road when I come home, leave it at the gate so Sam can be sure of having it to meet her."

"Will you trust Sam to drive at night over icy roads?" Miss Kate asked.

I bit my lip. Why did she have to bring that up? Suppose Philip said the car should not go and there was nobody to meet Miss Stockbridge. She might be upset and go back. She might——

"Well—" Philip shrugged—"someone has to go, and certainly I cannot be expected to. More coffee please, Aunt Kate."

Miss Kate rang the bell for Minerva, and I said, "I could go." I turned to him with eagerness. "I know I could drive all right, Philip, and——"

"What! Alone, at night! What on earth makes you say such a thing? Besides, you might have a flat tire."

I could drive and no doubt change a tire if I had to, I thought resentfully, and night was not much different from day. But I made no answer, knowing it useless. There had been a time when I would have put Philip's words down as evidence of his care and concern for me, and indeed that might once have been true.

Or even now it could be partly so. About that I could not be sure. But I only felt that he was purposely holding me back from doing what he saw I wanted to do. It was as if he sensed that his hold on me was slipping and that he must assert and reassert his authority. I saw this in many other small ways, such as the detailed directions he gave me about a thousand small things.

He began now: "You must keep the baby warm today, Bentley. The wind is from the north. And," he added, laying his napkin beside his plate and preparing to rise, "you had better keep fires going all day in Miss Stockbridge's apartment. See to it that Sam brings in some good dry logs——"

"They'll be too heavy for Old Sam, with his lame back," Miss Kate broke in. "But I'll send word to Anse."

Philip was on his feet now and he turned to her sharply. "No. I don't want Anse about the house."

"Why, Philippe! But of course, if you say so. Only——"

I kept my eyes on my plate, not breathing. Philip did not answer until at the door he said, "If it should be raining at five-thirty, have Sam hitch Ergo to the surrey and come to the gate for me."

The wind shifted to the south before noon and in a few minutes, while I watched from the window, the icebound branches were freed, tossing, crackling, limbering as if they rejoiced in the return of their freedom. But the sky did not clear, and in late afternoon rain began. Sam drove the surrey down to the gate for Philip, for the plantation road was deep in mud and standing water. The last vestige of ice was washed away and melted, so the roads would not be treacherous for Sam's driving to the station, but what a night it was going to be, stormy and wet!

Darkness came on early and the noise of the rain was loud on the roof. There was a leak in the nursery. I set a pail under it, and the drops striking the tin bottom were loud and persistent. Undressing the baby for the night, feeding him and rocking him in the chair by the black, rain-washed window, I worried about Miss Stockbridge. Had Sam got the car to start? Suppose the engine was flooded and would not go.

After dinner when we sat in the library, Philip as usual reading the paper and Miss Kate absorbed in a new historical novel Philip had brought her, it suddenly occurred to me that someone would have to drive the carriage down to the gate to meet them. "Oh, dear!" I cried. "How are they going to get in from the gate?"

Philip lowered his paper. Miss Kate's large pale eyes blinked at me over her book, as if the story of the hyper-bosomed hussy who waved a sword on the book's bright jacket had her all befuddled. Philip said, "It seems to me that you are unduly upset over all this, Bentley. Maybe it is going to be too much for you, having Miss Stockbridge here."

I shook my head, not trusting myself to speak. Maybe I was too much upset over it. There was always a point of truth in Philip's sharpness, so that however my eagerness ballooned, in anxiety or pleasure, he could prick it, leaving me disconcerted, flat.

"I have arranged everything," he said, taking up his paper again. "Sam drove Ergo down and hitched him under the pines at the gate before he took the car."

"Oh . . . I'm sorry," I said, rebuked. Miss Kate returned to her book and I sewed on in silence, now and then stealing a glance at the clock. After a little I slipped quietly from the room and went through the back hall door to the rain-splashed ell porch. I thought I would see to it that Minerva had a clean apron on. I wanted her to come in with hot milk or whatever Miss Stockbridge had need of, perhaps unpack for her. Then she would realize that she was going to have service, even if conveniences were lacking. I had considered asking Minerva to wear a white cap, but I had not dared. And besides, no amount of trappings could transform to a proper lady's maid Minerva's lank, graceless shape, her flat, uncompromising step.

But across the courtyard the kitchen was dark. Miss Kate must have told her to go on home before the storm grew worse. Oh, dear, everything was going wrong! I turned back into the house and went on past the library door to the music room. I pressed my face close to the window but I could see nothing. It was too soon anyway. Coming back, I paused to look around the hall, seeing it with a stranger's eye. Even by lamplight it seemed bleak and bare. I went on into the parlor that was to be Miss Stockbridge's sitting room. In spite of the blazing fire it was not a room where anyone would want to sit. The air was still musty, after all my cleaning; the delicate chairs and sofa with their gold brocade seemed pretentious—and spindly. In the ebony whatnot the collection of tiny figurines which I had so admired as I washed them were only cluttery and confusing now, the whatnot itself a silly thing. I rearranged the chairs and table, but I could not make them informal or inviting. They persisted in looking as if they were waiting for a funeral.

The bedroom was a little better. I laid another stick of wood on the fire and stood with my back to it looking around. The bed was big enough for an elephant, and the pillow sham that covered bolster and pillows was white and starched. The doors of the armoire shone, dustless in the firelight. The washstand was tidy with bowl and pitcher and fringed white linen towels.

The clock on the mantel behind me struck eight. It was a small black clock shaped like a tombstone and it struck the hour with internal wheezings, with a raucous clang, and hurriedly, as if to remind mortals that time was going fast, and an unpleasant judgment day would soon be upon us. Would it keep Miss Stockbridge awake? I considered stopping it, then gave up the idea. There was nothing more depressing than a dead clock with fixed hands and blank unchanging face. I poked the fire, rearranged the logs. Then I lighted the lamp on the bedside table and went out to the gallery.

The rain was lightening a little, I thought. It was not so noisy now, and above its fall on the roof I could hear the trickle of little streams running across the gentle slope of the yard into the worn ruts where the road began. Surely by now the car must have arrived at the gate. The old surrey would be groaning through the mud, Ergo's slow feet sounding *kerflop, kerflop.* Across the field Miss Stockbridge might see the dancing firelight through an open cabin door or—— I ran to the end of the gallery. Yes, at last, surely that was the creak of the carriage. Then I saw the lantern swinging crazily from one side, shining on Ergo's wet flanks, silvering the lines of rain against black tree trunks.

I tore back into the house, snatching my coat from the closet under the stair, calling, "Here they are!" There was no answer from the library, so I ran to the door, flinging my coat round my shoulders as I went. "Here they are!" I cried. "Aren't you coming?"

Philip said, "I see no reason why she should be met by a delegation, Bentley. She will be tired from her trip, and the kindest thing would be to show her to her room with as little formality as possible."

"Oh," I said. He was right, of course. I turned and ran to the gallery.

The carriage was jolting to a stop. "Here we is, ma'am," Sam was saying.

"Whoa! Will he stand unhitched?" Miss Stockbridge's voice was high and clear, her words quick-spoken and each one as finished and complete as an egg. I saw to my amazement as Sam unbuttoned the waterproof curtain that she was driving.

"Stand?" he echoed, climbing out on the far side. "That's what he ain't fixin' to do nothin' but."

Her laughter was a high contagious cackle. Some of my tension eased at once. Anybody who laughed like that——

"Where's the step?"

"You just wait, ma'am." Sam came round to her side of the carriage. "I'll holp you." He stood there holding out one hand to help her, a bent, black gnome, his face a dark blur under the wide brim of his hat.

"Holp? Hope? How do you spell it?" Miss Stockbridge demanded, hanging poised halfway in and out of the carriage, her coat gleaming yellow in the lantern light, her head hidden under a fisherman's yellow hat.

"Ma'am?"

"H-o-p-e? Like I hope you're well?" she asked. "No, it must be——"

"Yassum, I'se right tolerable, exceptin' for the rheumatiz. And now if you'll just——"

"I mean how do you spell it?"

"Well, ma'am," Sam pushed back his hat and scratched his

123

head, "I don't rightly know about all that, but if you'll just set one foot here——"

"No matter . . . later . . ." And with that, disregarding his hand, she took a flying leap and landed in the midst of the althea bush. "All right, it's all right. Just hand me the brief case off the front seat."

"You git on in, ma'am. I'll bring yo' bags."

"No, no. I always carry that one myself."

I stood at the end of the gallery, looking and listening, the rain splashing my ankles. Then, as she scrambled out of the bushes and Sam pointed the way, I hurried around to the steps to meet her. She mounted quickly, swinging the brief case at her side. On the open platform she paused, looked out to the black yard where, by the light from the open hall, the shapes of the cedars loomed, dark and somber. She looked at the square gallery posts, at the high ceiling, the fanlight over the door. Then she advanced to meet me, thrusting out her hand.

"B. Churston, I presume?"

"Yes, I'm Bentley. Come in." Her hand was bony, small and strong, and though she was enveloped in the yellow slicker and hidden under the wide-brimmed hat, I had the feeling that she was wiry and tough, like an old hen. She stopped in the light that came from the lamp in the hall, unbuttoned her slicker and shrugged it off. She took off her hat and shook the water from it.

"I'll . . . I'll t-take them," I said, stuttering in my amazement, for she was old. There was no telling how old. Her hair was perfectly white, clipped short and brushed upward so that it stood up in a kind of ruff or coxcomb on the top of her head. Her features were regular and delicately formed, her eyes wide apart and dark.

"Your rainy season, I presume," she said, straightening the collar of her brown tweed suit.

"Well, we don't exactly——" I waved her ahead of me through the door. Where did she think she was—in the tropics?

She stopped just inside and looked around, her head turning quickly as her dark eyes swept over the portraits, took in the height of the ceiling, the turn of the stair. "Ah!" she said.

I did not know what she meant and I could only indicate the open sliding doors to the right. "In here, this way, please."

In the center of the parlor she stopped again and looked around, her nose crinkling up a little as if she sniffed the musty air. "Yes, indeed," she said. Then her eyes fell on the whatnot and she darted across the room to take up one of the small figurines and turn it about in her hand.

"Somebody brought them from Germany, I think," I said. "A long time ago."

"Of course." She put it back and followed me into the bedroom, crossed at once to the fire where she bent, holding her hands to the blaze.

I was spreading her slicker over a straight chair beside the armoire when I heard Sam's shuffling step. "Bring the bags right on in, Sam," I said. "Put them there, against the wall."

Miss Stockbridge turned. "Ah, yes. Thank you, Mr. Wilkins."

Mr. Wilkins, I thought. Heavens!

Sam dropped the bags as if he had been struck and he was scuttling awkwardly out the door when her clear voice stopped him. "Just a minute." She took a billfold from her coat pocket as she went toward him, extracted two bills and thrust them into his limp hand. "There. Good night. See you tomorrow."

Sam looked down at the money in his hand, his eyes widening. "Yes, ma'am, thanky, ma'am. Shore will, for a fact, ma'am, the Lord willin'." He backed out of the room.

Miss Stockbridge came back to the fire. "Very interesting," she said.

I stood there awkwardly for a moment, then I went to the bed and began taking off the pillow sham. "I'll just open the bed for you. I suppose you'll want to get in it soon."

"At the proper time," she said.

I wondered what the proper time was to be, but I went on taking off the pillows and bolster, folding the marseilles spread. I could see her looking the room over, her bright brown eyes inspecting the wide floor boards, the marble-topped bureau, the high tester, and then coming to rest on the washstand with its yellow flowered bowl and pitcher. Her lips parted and I waited motionless, holding the spread half-folded, holding my breath, too.

"Well, no matter," she said. "After all, I have visited in rural England."

I did not know what she meant. "I . . . I hope you are going to be comfortable here," I said, a question in my voice.

"Comfortable?" She turned on me, repeating the word as if she had never heard it before. "When I leave home I kiss comfort good-by. Much the best way."

"Oh." I laid the spread at the foot of the bed.

"It's big enough," she said. "Big enough for Henry the Eighth and all his wives at the same time. I hope it's hard."

"Hard?" I drew a breath of relief. "That, to quote Sam, that's one thing it ain't nothin' but."

She was looking at me now with the same intent bright gaze she had turned on every detail of the room. "You are really quite lovely," she said. "Young, intelligent, alive—something better than beauty." As I stared at her amazed, she added, "Don't mind me. Always say what I think and no harm meant. I suppose unconsciously I thought you would be a languid, bosomy Southern belle, wafting a fan in on one hand——"

"And a mint julep in the other?"

She nodded. "Exactly. What did you think I would be like?"

"Well, I . . . I thought you would be big and sort of mannish with flat heels."

She bent and drew off her big rubber boots, revealing brown, low-heeled Oxfords, cotton stockings. "That much is right," she said, kicking one foot out for me to see. "Tell me. Is he stupid?"

"Who? You mean Sam, who drove you out?"

"Yes. I couldn't get much out of him."

"No, Sam is a bright Negro. He practically runs the place, the planting and all."

"I couldn't seem to make him understand. Evasive, that's what he seemed to be."

"Maybe your accent being different, the way you talk——"

"Yes, I talk too fast. No time to go slow—not at my age."

"Oh," I said. "I never thought of it just that way."

126

"Not that I'm really old. I just look old." She laughed her high, quick cackle.

Why she's fun, I thought, and laughed with her.

"It's a secret, you know. You don't find out till you get there. Inside you're never really old—just look it. Now tell me, how do you spell it—that word he used."

"Holp, I think it's a corruption of help—h-o-l-p."

"Of course. I must note that down tonight before I go to bed. Now tell me, who composes the household here?"

"I have a baby, but he won't disturb you—he's off in the ell. Besides him there're just my husband, Philip Churston, and his aunt, Miss Kate Churston. And then of course, there is his mother. She . . ." I hesitated.

"Well, out with it. If there's a skeleton in the closet I may as well hear now as later."

I stiffened. "Mrs. Churston is an invalid. You will not see her. She has her nurse and keeps to her room."

"You needn't sound so huffy. Mustn't mind—it's just my blunt way. I'm always putting my foot in it. I'm sorry if she's sick. What's the matter with her?"

"She had a complete nervous breakdown many years ago and has never recovered."

"Needs a good psychiatrist, probably. Have you——"

I did not care to be quizzed further so I said, "Are you hungry, Miss Stockbridge? Would you like a glass of milk or anything?"

"Why yes, come to think of it. I didn't have any supper. The lunch I brought with me gave out this noon."

I hurried out. The lunch she brought with her! Why, you would think anybody with clothes like that—for I could see that her suit was fine material, beautifully tailored—and with those handsome rings on her fingers and all that money she gave Sam as if it were two bits, you'd think she would eat in the dining car. I took a candle from the back hall table and went out to the kitchen. The tray I loaded was heavy with everything I could find. She must be starved.

Miss Stockbridge was sitting in the low rocker close to the fire, dark-rimmed glasses on her nose. The brief case was open at her feet and she was writing busily in a large looseleaf notebook. "First impressions," she said. "Very important to get them down while they are fresh."

I wanted to ask if she was writing a book, but her face looked tired in the dancing firelight, so without speaking I set the tray on a low table and moved it close beside her.

She laid down her writing and examined the food through her glasses before she took them off. "What's that?"

"Beaten biscuit."

"What kind of jelly?"

"Muscadine. It's a wild grape that grows in the swamp."

"H'm. Raise your own chickens?" She took up a drumstick in her fingers and bit into it. "Very nice. What time is breakfast?"

"Well, we eat at seven-thirty, but you may have a tray whenever you like."

"Breakfast abed?" She looked shocked. "Not while I can get out of it. Seven-thirty will suit me very well."

I wished her good night and turned to go. Before I got to the door, she stopped me. "Is it a family name?"

I stared at her blankly, then I jumped to her meaning. "My grandfather's last name was Bentley."

"I see. Had an idea that all the girls down here were Susie Belles and Annie Mays. Just one more thing. Can you tell me why your horse is named Ergo, and do you spell it with an *E* or a *U*?"

"Why, I'm sure I don't know. I . . . I think there has always been a horse named Ergo. I'll ask. Maybe——"

"Thank you, please do. Ergo means therefore. But why call a horse——. On the other hand if it is *Urgo* it might mean that he had to be urged to go. A very apt name. I must know . . . my research, my notes . . ." She waved a hand in the direction of her notebook.

When I had pulled shut the sliding doors to the hall, I stood there a moment laughing to myself. Of all the surprises! Oh, it was going to be fun, having her! What would Philip and Miss Kate make of her? When I went into the library, they both looked up expectantly.

"But what does she mean—her notes, her research?" Miss Kate asked as I finished my account. "Is she a writer?"

"I don't know. She wouldn't let Sam touch her brief case. Said she always carried that herself."

"I hope she is not one of those Northern agitators who come down here, not knowing anything and trying to tell us how to run our business."

"Oh, no, surely not!" I cried. "She's just—well, just a kind of original character, I think."

"I hope she is not too original," Miss Kate said. "These North, ern women are apt to be eccentric. It might be rather awkward having such a person around."

"Luckily," Philip said, "we do not have to meet her in a social way. After all she has merely rented the rooms, and as her meals will be served in her room, we need have little personal contact with her."

"But——" I began and then was silent. Better let that wait and meet it when it came. "She wants to know why Ergo is named Ergo."

Philip who was taking up his paper again, let it fall to his knees. "Now why on earth——"

Miss Kate said, "What a question! We've always had an Ergo. Why, Grandpapa's saddle horse was named Ergo. The carriage horses were Pourquoi and Peutêtre—the Negroes called them Pork and Potatoes."

"That's beside the point, Aunt Kate." Philip frowned as he gave his paper a shake. "The fact is evident that she has begun by asking questions that have no sense to them. It is likely she will pry into everything. We must be on our guard. And, Bentley, you must inquire discreetly into her business when you can reasonably do so."

"All right," I said, but the fine edge of my pleasure was dulled.

· 14 ·

As it happened, there was no need of my inquiring into Miss Stockbridge's business. In her own way she put an end, temporarily at least, to speculations. I was up early and helped Minerva prepare a tray for her, thinking, after what Philip had said, that it might be better to serve breakfast in her room. I waited in the hall for Minerva to come back and report on its reception.

Minerva returned almost at once bearing the tray untouched. "Ain't there. Done lit out. Ain't hair nor hide of her in yonder."

"Oh, no!" I cried and dashed past her through the parlor into the bedroom. It was true. There was not a sign of her or any of her belongings. But to go without a word! The bed was neatly made with bolster and pillows in place. Suitcases were gone. But how could she get away? Had she walked to the road, hitchhiked?

I heard Miss Kate in the hall saying, "Come, Philippe, breakfast is ready. Where is Bentley?" I turned to leave and my last dismayed glance discovered her toothbrush on the washstand. Then I saw the corner of a suitcase under the bed and I ran and jerked it out. Empty! I hurried to the armoire and flung open the doors. There, all neatly arranged on the shelves, were piles of woolen underwear, of cotton stockings and sweaters, and hanging from the rack were suits and blouses. "Just neat," I said aloud. But where was she?

Then I heard her voice in the courtyard. "Yes, of course, the rest of the family, how do you do? I'm just in time, am I? I thought I smelled coffee. Delicious. Only of course, when you smell it, the flavor is already ruined. Never boil coffee. . . ." Her voice died away amid vague murmurs from Miss Kate and Philip as they all went toward the dining room.

By the time I got there, Minerva had laid another place at the table, across from mine, and Philip was pushing in Miss Stockbridge's chair. He gave me an annoyed glance as I said good morning, and moved to his own place opposite Miss Kate.

130

Miss Kate said, "I hope you slept well, Miss Stockbridge."

"Oh, I never sleep—not more than a few hours at most. But I rest. Delightful bed. So firm and unyielding."

Philip looked up quickly, but Miss Stockbridge, the picture of innocence, was inspecting the hot grits Minerva was passing. She held a spoonful doubtfully in mid-air, then dumped its contents on her plate. "Gravy?" she puzzled as she was presented with the other end of the tray. "What do I do with it?"

"Put it on your grits," I said.

"Oh, I thought this was cereal. I see. Very nice." She turned to Miss Kate with her quick pouncing movement. "Have you lived here long?"

Miss Kate stiffened and the coffee cup she was arranging before her rattled in its saucer. "My great-great-grandfather Churston settled here toward the close of the French and Spanish regimes. He was appointed by President Madison a judge of the district to——"

She was off. I drew a sigh of relief and began to eat my breakfast. I could see Philip watching Miss Stockbridge with an uneasy look. But surely he must see that she was all right, just an eccentric, an original.

"Very interesting," she broke in now as Miss Kate paused for breath. "I must make a note of that." She took a small notebook from her coat pocket and, murmuring an "Excuse me, please," jotted down some hasty lines.

Miss Kate gave a pleased nod and said, "If you are interested in such things, Miss Stockbridge, I have some old records in the library gathered by my brother who was quite a scholar—Philippe's father, really quite an authority—and maybe you would like to read what I wrote up for a D.A.R. paper in sort of story form, an account of my ancestors who——"

"Oh, dear, no. Thank you, but frankly I haven't time. Not at my age." She gave her high little cackle and capped her pen. "At my back I always hear, you know."

Philip regarded her as if she might be out of her head and I asked, "What do you hear at your back, Miss Stockbridge?"

"Time's wingéd chariot, remember?"

"B-but," Miss Kate said in a bewildered way, "I thought you were interested, making notes——"

"Only of the similarity. I thought for a moment I was back in Boston listening to Cousin Lizzie Smugensall." She turned on Philip. "Fascinating place you have here."

"We find it rather pleasant," Philip said guardedly.

"Do you give all your time to marketing your produce?"

"There's not much of it," Philip said, a wry smile twitching at the corner of his lips.

Miss Stockbridge accepted a helping of ham and hot biscuit from Minerva. "But I always have understood that these plantations yield a very high return. With sharecropper labor——"

Philip passed his cup for more coffee. "As a matter of fact, Miss Stockbridge, I am obliged to work in town in order to afford the luxury of living on such a place as this."

"Indeed!"

Philip said, "May I ask if you are preparing to write a book?"

"Oh, dear, no, if you mean fiction. Later perhaps when I am no longer physically able to get about, I shall occupy myself with fiction. Now I am gathering material for my thesis."

"Your thesis?" Miss Kate repeated.

"Yes. Ph.D. Radcliffe College." She laid down her knife and fork. "Perhaps I should explain myself. First"—she sat very straight, her dark eyes flashing—"first, I practice what I preach: that a woman, once she has passed the childbearing age, should devote her energies to the general good. Hence my choice of the field of sociology. Second, I wish to prove to the authorities of Radcliffe, who made some objection on the ridiculous score of age, that the human brain atrophies only with disuse. May I——" She passed her coffee cup to Miss Kate for refilling.

Philip said, "Very interesting." He looked at his watch and rose hurriedly. "If you will excuse me."

"Just a minute, please, Mr. Churston. There is a box of books and papers which must be at the express office, as I sent it well in advance. Would you be so kind——"

"I will be glad to bring it when I come this evening," Philip said, moving toward the door.

132

"Evening? You mean you do not come home till late, after dinner?"

"Oh, no, Miss Stockbridge. Here in Mississippi any time after noon is evening."

"Indeed! Very quaint. Though I believe I have run across a similar usage in some of the English novels of the early 1800's."

Philip paused at the door. "Our stock here is largely of English derivation, Miss Stockbridge. We have very few foreigners and those we have are well treated. We have none of the prejudices of your part of the country."

"You save them for your larger minority, I presume," Miss Stockbridge said, and then before Philip could reply, she added, "Another small matter I would like to arrange before you go——"

"Yes?" Philip said coldly.

"I had thought of hiring a car for small excursions over the countryside. But since you have no second car and we seem to be at some distance from town, I wonder if I might engage your horse and carriage and the services of Mr. Wilkins as driver."

"Mr. Wilkins?" Philip frowned.

"Yes. Isn't that the name? Mr. Sam Wilkins, I think he told me."

Miss Kate let out a small sound, and Philip stiffened, his lips closing in a thin tight line. I bent my head over my plate. Everything had gone so well in spite of her remark about minorities, and now——

"Of course," Miss Stockbridge said quickly, reaching into an inside pocket of her brown tweed suit which seemed to be a veritable nest of pockets, "of course, I would expect to pay extra for this. What would you suggest?" She waited, checkbook in hand.

"Well." Philip hesitated. "No one is using the horse, this being a slack time of the year. He's just out at pasture, and there is no reason why you should not——"

"Good enough!" Miss Stockbridge cried and began writing busily. "Shall we say thirty dollars a week, which will include the driver's services for half a day? Or maybe I had better make it thirty-five. There may be some days when I want to take afternoon trips as well." She was bent over her checkbook, and I was glad she did not look up in time to see Miss Kate with her mouth

133

in a little round O and Philip with a look of utter amazement on his face. I had no notion how I was looking. Thirty-five dollars a week! Why, for that she could "milord" Old Sam and "milady" Minerva every minute of the day for all any of us would care.

Philip took the check. "I will tell Sam. You would like the carriage this morning?"

"Yes, please. No time to lose. Not at my age."

When Sam came back from driving Philip to the plantation gate where the car had been left last night, I went to the end of the gallery to see Miss Stockbridge off on her first excursion. She climbed into the carriage briskly and took the reins from Sam. They both clucked at Ergo and reluctantly he got into action. The carriage creaked and groaned as they jolted away down the plantation road. Where was she going? What would she make notes about? I wished I were going with her.

In the music room Miss Kate began practicing her scales. Old Humble, stretched out at the foot of the stairs where he liked to lie, a stumbling block to the unwary, thumped his tail at me as I stepped over him. I ran up the stairs feeling gayer than I had in a long, long time. There was so much to think about, so much to do, all at once. First, there was the baby to be bathed and tended, his washing to be done as usual. Then I thought I would start some Sally Lunn for dinner tonight—for I meant to do some of the cooking myself while Miss Stockbridge was here, not only to relieve Minerva but because I was anxious to have everything especially nice. Maybe a blackberry pie from some of Minerva's canned berries, thick yellow cream on top. And besides all that I wanted to work some on my new dress which must be ready for the christening. Even that ordeal seemed less disturbing now that I had so much else to occupy me. I whistled to myself as I bathed the baby before the little grate fire in the nursery. I took pleasure in his sturdy small body. He was beginning to smile now, and he laughed aloud as I dried his wiggling pink toes.

When I went downstairs again at last, it was noon and Miss Kate was calling Minerva. "Just bring my lunch to the library, as usual." I came out on the ell porch where she was and she said,

"I declare, Bentley, I can't wait all day for that woman. I'm hungry."

"She's probably stopped at some roadside place to eat."

Callie came from the kitchen with a tray, her eyes avoiding mine as usual, her step light, her movement saucy, as she mounted the ell stairs. She was so quiet, so seldom seen, that I sometimes forgot her presence, and the reason for it.

"I hope Ergo has not run away or anything," Miss Kate said, going on toward the library.

"More likely he's gone to sleep." I laughed and went to the kitchen with the baby's empty bottles.

When I had finished my sandwich and had done all I had to do, I threw a sweater around me and set out for the sand bar, Jeff Wheeling's little book under my arm. I had read it evenings in bed, and now I wanted to get it back to him before anyone saw it. Besides, I wanted to see him. I had so much to tell him.

Down at the river in the mild afternoon sunshine I walked back and forth along the hard yellow sand at the water's edge, sitting on the log awhile and then walking again. Where was Jeff Wheeling? But at last his dugout came in sight downstream. I waved and called to him. "I thought you were never coming!"

He nosed the bow of the boat into the sand and sprang out. "Oh, I'm out here somewhere every day it isn't pouring, and sometimes when it is." He came across the sand to sit beside me on the willow log. "I was late getting away from school today. We had a visitor—someone you know."

"Who in the world?" I took the cigarette he held out to me.

He lighted it and his own before he answered. "Miss Stockbridge."

"For heaven's sake! Is that where she went?"

"Yes, she came in before noon, had lunch with us at the school cafeteria and visited several classes. She's quite a gal, isn't she?"

I laughed. "I'll say she is. I've been in a state of amazement ever since she got here last night. What did she visit the school for?"

"Just interested, she said. She came into my room last of all and then afterward we got to talking. That's what delayed me.

She knows a lot of people I know—some of my old Harvard professors."

"Oh." I felt all at once as if I had never been anywhere or learned anything in all my life. "I didn't know you ... you ..."

"I did my graduate work there. And what do you think?" His eyes twinkled. "She is planning to visit the Negro school on the Fayette Road tomorrow. Apparently she isn't going to miss anything. By the way, she asked me to come up to see her some evening."

Come up? To Cedar Bluff? I gave him a startled glance. Nobody ever came to Cedar Bluff. I would not know how to act—with him, of all people. And suppose he said something, innocently enough, as he might, that would let Philip know—— The silence lengthened between us. The longer I waited to speak, the more impossible it became. A kind of trembling came over me and I bent to bury my cigarette in the sand, hoping he would not notice.

Jeff said, "I won't come if you'd rather I didn't." He spoke so naturally, so easily, that my tension lightened somewhat, and I could breathe again.

"It's just that ... not many come ... to the house," I faltered. "I was thinking about that. I don't know why you shouldn't come. I would like to have you, of course." I was silent a moment, and then I said, "I suppose it's just that I've always seen you here, on the river, away from everything, sort of out of the world. I think it must be that quite selfishly I want to ... keep you to myself."

He turned then and faced me, his eyes very bright, as if all his life were concentrated in their blueness. But before he could speak, I hurried on, not wanting him to misunderstand. "You see, one lives along in the midst of one's own affairs, so deeply involved sometimes that it is hard to see clearly. And because you are not concerned in any of that, because we are just ... two human beings who have met here, by chance, apart, it has been something special to me. It takes me out of my life, gives me a kind of perspective, no matter what we talk about. And sometimes one does need perspective. Do you ... do you understand what I'm trying to say?"

"I understand," he said, his head bowed, his voice very gentle and low.

I studied his rugged face, his almost homely face, and I hoped I had not said too much. I hoped he really understood. He looked up and smiled, and it seemed to me I had never seen a more beautiful, understanding smile.

He gave me another cigarette, and while we smoked, at ease now, I told him about Miss Stockbridge's coming. I told him all the small amusing things that had happened. He cut a willow branch and whittled at it while I talked, his knuckly fingers deft and skillful, and his eyes lifted to mine now and then as something I said amused him. When I was silent at last, he gave me what he had made—a willow whistle. "Try it," he said.

I blew and the sound was shrill and clear. Then he took it from me and put it in the crotch of the old tree that spread its bare branches above us. "Now—" he sat beside me again—"if you ever want me and I'm not here, just blow and I'll hear you, even if I am back in the bayou or in the swamp or out on the island." Then we talked about the book I had brought back to him and he said he would take me someday to explore the island and show me the old beech that might have been the tree under which the yellow-fever victims were buried. When I rose at last to go, he said, "Thanks . . . for what you said . . . awhile ago."

At the curve of the bluff I looked back. Our eyes met, and even at that distance, something warm and heartening passed between us so that I was filled with pleasure. I had a friend.

The house was silent when I got home. I went first to make sure the baby was all right, though, as always when I went out, Minerva had been tending him. Then downstairs, going through the hall I passed the library door and saw Miss Kate, book in hand. "Is Miss Stockbridge back?" I asked.

"Who?" She looked at me over her glasses as if she had forgotten there was such a person in the world. "Oh, Miss Stockbridge. Yes. In her room writing up her notes. And listen to this, Bentley. I was coming in from out back and as I passed the kitchen I heard Old Sam telling Minerva." Miss Kate leaned forward and her voice sank to a breathy whisper. "Miss Stockbridge asked him to come and have lunch with her, wherever it was she was eating. She invited him in to sit at the table!"

"He didn't go?"

"Of course not. Sam has good sense. He was shocked at the very notion. You can imagine how Philippe will feel about this." She took off her glasses and wiped them on her skirt.

"But nothing happened. Need you—— She's paying so much."

"I know, but such things as this! I simply cannot take the responsibility."

"Philip will be horribly upset."

"I won't upset him more than is necessary, you may be sure of that." She took up her book, and I went on to the kitchen. My Sally Lunn had risen beautifully and was ready to knead down. I greased an angel-cake pan and was just putting in the dough when Minerva, peeling potatoes at the other end of the kitchen table, began to laugh to herself.

"What's so funny, Minerva?"

"That Sam. I ax him why in tarnation didn't he go in and eat with the lady. Like to scairt him to death, me just axin'. Worst they could do was slam the door in his face."

I set the pan out of the way and covered it with a napkin. Then I just stood there, holding to the back of the kitchen chair. A shiver went through me and I broke out in a cold sweat.

Minerva leaned toward me, her mouth dropping open. "God-sakes, Miss Bent! Look like a white shadow done pass over you. What's got you?"

I stared at her, not seeing her, my hands tightening on the chair. I shook my head dumbly and, turning, fled across the runway and through the hall and up the stairs. In the baby's room I bent over his crib, twisting my hands, looking down in anguish into his untroubled sleeping face. What if he should someday be barred from going where he would? What if doors were closed in his face?

· 15 ·

FAMILIARITY and custom are blinders. It is possible to live in the midst of a thing and never see it, to move untroubled and unaware in the heart of a hurricane, deceived by the stillness roundabout. So it had been with me. I have lived all the years of my life until now with no concern for the thoughts and feelings of a whole group of human beings who, like me, breathed the soft Southern air, sweated through the heat of summer, saw the day's dawning, the season's change, lived, hoped and struggled. For me they had simply been there, as always, and I accepted their presence on the streets, in the fields, in their small, gray cabins, as unthinkingly as I accepted my apartness from them.

Now because of my child, because of his secret kinship to them, and because of this small incident which brought it sharply home to me, I was thrust, stripped and vulnerable, into a terrible awareness. Through him, whether I liked it or not—and I didn't, oh, I didn't!—I was suddenly a part of all I had been blindly indifferent to. At once I had to know more. I had to find out somehow, for his protection explore this dark, tumultuous other world.

As soon as breakfast was over the next morning I went to Minerva in the kitchen. "Why did you laugh?" I demanded.

She gave me a blank look, her bony black hands busy with the dishes. "What you talkin' about, Miss Bent?"

"Yesterday. What you were telling, about Miss Stockbridge and Sam. You know." For somehow, now I had come squarely up to it, I could not speak the thing right out. My tongue stiffened against it and I was suddenly overwhelmed by my own boldness. It was as if I had done something indecent, offensive to my own dignity, to Minerva's dark reserve.

She turned back to the sink and went on with her work, rattling the dishes in the pan, fluffing up the suds.

I stood rebuked by her silence, her implacable back, the limp,

139

straight folds of her familiar faded gray dress. But I waited, unwilling to give in. I made myself wait before her silence, like a suppliant, my hands clasped tight together. Why wouldn't she speak? Was it that she too could not put the thing into words? Was it too . . . too private? For this was not like the rights of voting and work and schooling about which any might speak out boldly. It was delicate and secret—like Miss Kate's not having her club meet here because I was not eligible. Yet, didn't Minerva know why I had asked? Couldn't she understand the terrible necessity? I turned away, baffled and outraged. I was at the door when she spoke, gruff and unwilling.

"Better laugh than cry," she said.

I stopped and waited again, my back to the kitchen, leaning my head against the doorframe, bowed down and humbled. Then in the silence, without turning, knowing Minerva motionless behind me, I felt something that could never be spoken, a dumb sympathy more real than words, more tangible than the floor under my feet. It stirred and came to life and grew between us.

Minerva spoke again, softly this time, as I had never heard her speak. "Ain't no use kickin' agin the pricks, Miss Bent."

I went slowly along the runway, my head bowed, the hot, hopeless tears brimming my eyes. No use—was there really no use? In the hallway Miss Stockbridge had to speak twice before I noticed her.

"I say, could you possibly arrange to have my books unpacked while I am out?"

I saw then that she had on her gray tweed coat, that she was all ready to go on another excursion in the carriage. "Your books?" I said stupidly.

"Yes. The box Mr. Churston brought out for me last night from the express office."

"Oh. Of course. I'll be glad to."

"Good. I like to have them ready for reference." She drew on gray gloves as she spoke. "I'm off now. Never mind lunch. I'll eat wherever I happen to be."

She was turning away when I stopped her. There was something I had to know. "Miss Stockbridge——"

140

"Yes?" She looked back, knotting the red scarf at her throat and tossing one end over her shoulder.

"I . . . would you . . ." Then I blurted it right out: "Why did you invite Old Sam to have lunch with you?"

Her dark eyes danced and she came a step nearer, clapping her hands together. "So you've got wind of it already! Good enough. I was hoping it would get around."

"But why, why, when you knew he couldn't dare—or be allowed?"

The desperation in my voice must have reached her. She unhooked her glasses from the hook on the front of her coat, set them on her straight little nose and peered up at me. "To get reactions, of course."

"Reactions?"

She nodded. "That's the sort of thing I'm after."

"You mean you are studying——"

"The Negro problem, yes. Or the white problem, perhaps I should say. Same thing." Her voice was crisp and matter-of-fact.

I stared at her, openmouthed. There was something shocking in her gray detachment, her daring, her sureness. Yet what did she know? How could she understand all the complications, the intangibles, the dark despair? She was at a distance, scientific, a sociologist, safe. Suddenly an idea struck me. "Miss Stockbridge, the books—are they about all this?"

She nodded. "I have a rather nice small collection with me."

"Would you mind if I read some of them?"

"Help yourself. Do you good." She laughed her high cackling laugh as she went briskly away down the front hall to the door.

In her room, unpacking the books, setting them upright on the mantel and against the wall on the bedside table, for there was no other place to put them, I studied each title hungrily. I selected one and sat down on the rug before the fire and began to read.

Of course I had known in a vague sort of way that there must be such books, but they had not concerned me. Now I read with pressing eagerness, with a fury of concentration. I took several to my room. After that I kept my light burning late at night, so that

141

even Minerva noticed how little oil was left in my lamp each morning. Daytimes I read in all my spare moments. And as I tended the baby, as I washed and cooked—for I was determined that Miss Stockbridge should find no fault with the food—as I sewed on my new dress that must be done in time for the christening, I mulled over what I had read. Some of the books were written in passionate protest; some were concerned only with reporting; some were scientific studies, and others dealt with broad changes in legislation and reform. And yet in all that I read there was nothing that told me what I, one small human being, caught in a dilemma of my own, could do. No one touched adequately on what seemed to me the vital, the fundamental thing—the way people felt and how to make that better. Maybe that was too personal, too intangible.

I did not talk with Miss Stockbridge about my reading. When she asked me what I thought of this book or that, I could only say that I had found it very interesting. A kind of dumbness came over me and held me back from speaking out what I was thinking. Yet she opened my eyes to many small things. When she took out her notebook and wrote down something Philip said, or when she scribbled away, listening to Miss Kate's tales of old plantation days and the splendor of the Churstons, I was alert and watchful, speculating on her reason for noting down this or that. So my vision sharpened.

Philip complained privately of Miss Stockbridge's note taking, and indeed it was disconcerting to have one's words set down without knowing why. "I don't see what she is getting at," he would say with annoyance. "I don't like it. If it wasn't for the money——" But he made no open protest. Her prompt payment each week of board and carriage hire soothed down his irritation before it reached the boiling point. Some of her questions about plantation affairs had given him the notion that she was writing a history of sharecropping in Mississippi and now and then he would worry lest she be connected with some organization which, he said, was stirring up trouble in the county.

I did not enlighten him. In fact during all this period Philip and I lived in a kind of neutral state, strangely welcome to me. I wanted to escape from all emotional involvement. I wanted to be able to see things from a distance as much as possible. Not that the weight was ever lifted. How could it be when I lived in the house with Philip and Miss Kate and Philip's mother, a bleak reminder? Sometimes I sat with her as I sewed, letting Callie off for an hour or two. I even tried to understand Callie. I made an effort to find out what she was like, really, as a human being. But whether I was feeling impatient with her for her saucy ways, or being persistently friendly, I could get nowhere with her.

Then in the midst of my superficial calm a chance remark of Miss Stockbridge's plunged me again into turmoil.

We were finishing breakfast together, for Miss Kate was going to a club meeting and had left early with Philip. Miss Stockbridge turned to me in her quick, pouncing way. "Tell me: why does she wear a wig?"

I held my coffee cup poised, halfway to my lips. "Who?"

"Miss Kate, of course. Don't tell me you never noticed. Of course I have always said that any woman over fifty was invisible, that so long as she was decently covered it made no difference— and it doesn't. But this is so obvious." She set her glasses on her nose and regarded me sharply. "Sorry, none of my business. I just wondered."

I shook my head. But I should have known. Of course it was a wig. That was why her hair never changed, why it was always drawn back in the same smooth caplike way. Her own hair? I hid my face in my hands.

"Heavens! I'm always putting my foot in it," Miss Stockbridge cried. "I . . . really I mentioned it only out of idle curiosity. Though why it should upset you——"

I lowered my hands, wiping my face clean of all expression. "It doesn't matter. Maybe she's bald. I don't know."

Minerva's flat step sounded on the runway and I was thankful for the interruption. "Want more coffee?" she said. And when we had both refused, she gathered up a tray of dishes and went out with them.

Miss Stockbridge took her last bite of biscuit and ham. "Odd character. Not at all the old-family-servant type."

"No. No, she isn't." I spoke mechanically. I could think of nothing but Miss Kate. With her broad nose, her wide, flat features and with no powder to lighten her skin—no wonder she had to hide her own hair. It must be—— I shivered.

Miss Stockbridge was talking on, had been talking for a long time before I was able to bring my attention back to what she was saying. "So I believe I have recorded their attitudes rather well. Mr. Churston is simple enough, the perfect reactionary, and Miss Kate a fair example of the past generation, consistent throughout. But you——"

"Me? About what?"

"The Negro question of course."

I turned my head away so that my hair shielded me from her. "I have read a number of your books."

"Yes, yes, but you never say a word about them."

I dropped my napkin and stooped to pick it up, "I . . . I don't know anything."

"Don't know and don't care? Yet you seemed so eager to read them. Frankly my curiosity is aroused."

I drew back. What could I say? Where could I hide from her bright, prying eyes. "Really I—— If you will excuse me, please. I have so much to do this morning." I laid down my napkin.

"Well, no matter." She rose. "We shall see. We shall see."

Not if I could help it, I thought, panic giving way to anger. Never, never would I let her see—or anyone else. As Philip, as Miss Kate guarded their secret, so would I, fiercely, against all the world.

· 16 ·

As THE day of the christening drew near, my dread of it increased. Yet, when the Sunday came at last, bright and mild and smelling of early spring, when little Henry was dressed in one of my own baby dresses, elaborately embroidered by my mother's needle, the pride and delight I had in him lulled my uneasiness. I brought him downstairs where Miss Kate was ready and waiting, and even she, who so seldom allowed herself to admire, praised him and touched his cheek with one gloved finger. She really loves him, I thought. Only it seemed always as if she held back from show of affection, as if she was afraid to let herself become too much attached to him.

I laid him on the sofa in the hallway and asked her to watch him while I ran back to put on my hat. It was my last year's hat, just a straight brown sailor with a twist of gold maline around the crown, but it went well with my new dress. I had drawn my hair into a knot at the back of my neck. So, when I was all ready, I looked at myself in the glass and I seemed to be hidden behind a new aspect. It gave me a feeling of security, as if I had put on a new armor against the world.

Philip's eyes went over me approvingly as I came down the stairs, but he only said, "We'd better be going now."

In the vestibule of the church other parents were gathering. I looked at the babies and found not one that came up to my Henry. Philip's eyes met mine, and I knew by the smile twitching at the corner of his thin, taut lips, that he was thinking the same thing. I had a brief good moment there, waiting for the service to begin, seeing how much more handsome Philip was than any of the other fathers, feeling myself protected by the Churston prestige. That fine standing Miss Kate and Philip had built up and guarded all their lives was something to uphold one in a time like this.

The first hymn began and from inside the church there was a

145

rustling as the congregation rose. I bent to make sure the baby's blanket did not hide his dress, and when I straightened up I saw Mrs. Mall and Mrs. McCall in the outer doorway, their black veils rusty in the morning sunlight. Panic seized me. If only they would not notice me! If only they would pass me by! I turned my back, hoping the usher would beckon us, call us in to march up the aisle. Then I felt a tap on my arm and there they were, two black crows, pecking, prying, their dry old lips whispering congratulations, their black-gloved claws pulling at the baby's blanket, their heads bobbing with the slight palsy they both had, and seeming to say, "Yes, yes, it's true, it's true."

As they moved away through the church door, I kept watch and saw the glance they exchanged, the lifted brow, the knowing nod. But they could have seen nothing in my baby's face; they could have found no confirmation of their knowledge there. There was none there to find—or was I just so familiar with his small face that I could not see? I began to tremble, my lips were dry, and the blood pounded in my ears. Blindly I moved when Philip took my arm, and we went down the aisle together.

I went stiffly, every muscle tense. Standing with the others in a semicircle at the chancel I heard not a word of the service. How many eyes in that congregation were fixed on me, prying, questioning, remembering? How many minds were humming like angry bees, stirred by an old tale, a whisper. Little Henry cried out and I tried to relax my arms that were crushing him against me. The service went on, the voices. I responded when my turn came. Once I looked up at Philip's grave, guarded face and I sensed in him the same rigidity, the same proud defiance, that was holding me erect and haughty. O God, poor Philip! Poor me, too, fitting into the Churston pattern, solidifying under the same proud, protective shell! I bowed my head, though the time for the prayer had not yet come. God, let it not strike my child, keep it from him, let him go free! I blinked back hot tears.

It was over at last and with the others we marched down the aisle. It was all I could do to hold back my feet from running. I wanted nothing but to get back to Cedar Bluff and never leave

146

home again. Never, never, I kept saying to myself. I would never enter that church again, meet those terrible eyes.

Miss Kate was staying for the regular morning service, but the baby was my excuse for leaving, and Philip drove me home. As he helped me out of the car, he said, "You look pale, Bentley. "Don't you feel well?"

"I'm all right," I told him. "It was just a . . . a strain." Then feeling his sharp eyes on me still, I added, "I was afraid the baby would cry."

"Matter of fact, he behaved very well indeed. Two of them should have been carried out. I could barely hear the service for their screaming."

"Yes," I agreed, moving on toward the steps. But I had not even heard them.

Philip looked at his watch as he followed me. "I won't try to get back for the service. I'll just go in time to pick up Aunt Kate."

"Yes," I said, only half attending.

"Next Sunday you can begin going again. The baby's old enough for you to leave him now."

I stopped short on the steps. "No."

"Why, Bentley! What do you mean?" He caught up with me and stood looking down at me, frowning. "You can't give up going altogether. Why should you? You can't. It's expected——"

"I won't leave him." Then honesty made me add, "Besides, I do not want to go. I won't go."

"I never heard you speak like this, Bentley."

"Well, you've heard me now." I bit my lip to hold back the words that tried to come.

Philip followed me, saying no more. And not long after when it came about that I did leave Henry almost every day for several hours, he did not remind me of my inconsistency.

Spring came early that year and it was soon time for Old Sam to be working in the fields. Philip was in a quandary. He did not want to lose Miss Stockbridge's extra weekly check for the use of the carriage and Sam as driver, and yet there were other things Sam should be doing. So it came about that one evening as we sat in the library—Miss Stockbridge as usual being in her own quarters—he asked me if I would be willing to drive about with her in place of Sam. The idea took me so by surprise that I could only stare at him, wide-eyed.

"Of course," he hurried to add, "there are other reasons why it would be well to have you go with her. We ought to know what she does, where she goes. I can get nothing out of Old Sam except that she talks with people—and sees that radical Jeff Wheeling rather too often."

I bent over my sewing so that he would not see the eagerness in my face. "I would be glad to go," I said, keeping the excitement out of my voice. "But to leave the baby——"

"There is no reason why Callie cannot mind him. She is right there in the next room doing nothing most of the day and——"

"No, no! I won't leave him with her. Minerva can look after him."

Philip gave me a sharp glance. "Callie is quite capable. She is an unusually intelligent girl, and if she can take care of my mother, I see no reason why she cannot take care of my child. In fact he would be much safer with her than with Minerva who has enough to do without any extra work."

"I'm sorry," I said, "but I would not be easy a minute."

Miss Kate, who had lowered her book when Philip first spoke, said, "Why, Bentley!" in her flurried, exclamatory way. But whether she was startled by my objecting to Callie or by my daring to oppose Philip, I could not tell.

Philip said with coldness, "Have you any reason for objecting to Callie?"

Miss Kate's lips parted, she started to speak, then one small hand rose to cover her lips. As I waited, trying to think how I could express my feeling about Callie, I suddenly felt a strangeness in the air. I looked to the window, open to the black night, now that the evenings were mild. It seemed to me that something, alive yet intangible, alien and hostile, had entered the room. I looked from one to the other and then said, "I haven't any real reason, only that I don't like her manner and I don't trust her. I'll let Miss Stockbridge walk before I'll leave the baby in Callie's care." I spoke with decision, my voice so flat and matter-of-fact that the strangeness was dissipated at once.

After a minute Philip said, "Very well. Aunt Kate, you may tell Callie to help Minerva with the cleaning and dishwashing or something." He took up his paper.

I was too astonished to sit quietly sewing. I had to go and walk up and down the long gallery in the darkness where no one could see my face. I had opposed Philip again, as I had about my churchgoing, and had won my point. I simply could not understand it.

Excitement woke me early the next morning. I made myself lie still a little while looking up at the spots on the ceiling, cherishing the thought that today I would be doing something different. I would be actually earning money—and perhaps I was going to see Jeff Wheeling. For I had not gone back to the river. I had not met him there since the day when, looking back, I had felt something warm and vital spring into being between us. But now, if I saw him, it would be because Philip asked it. So I shifted responsibility from myself and felt free to savor the pleasure that lay ahead.

I did my upstairs work before breakfast, and as soon as Philip had left the house, I hurried to the kitchen to prepare the bottles for the day. Minerva was grumbling. "Tell me Callie can holp with cleanin' the house. Reckon I have to go round after, cleanin' up what she dirty up cleanin'."

"I'll help, Minerva. Miss Stockbridge isn't ready to go yet. What shall I do?"

"Got to do Mr. Philip's room this mornin'. What he want to keep that dawg in there all the time for, hairin' up everythin'?" But she was mollified, and when I asked for the broom, she said, "Baby ain't no trouble. I got no complaint about him."

I smiled to myself as I went down the ell steps to the courtyard. Philip's old baby carriage that had been stored so many years in the carriage house, stood there in the sunshine, waiting. Minerva would put Henry there for his morning nap and keep an eye on him. Old Humble wagged his tail at me and lifted his head from the walk as I turned into the high basement under the ell. He followed me to Philip's room and lay down on the old rug in one corner, so I had to sweep around him.

It was a depressing, dreary room. I had not been in it since that day when Anse helped Philip to sit up for the first time after his flu, and I stood, now, broom in hand, chilled by something more than its bleakness. Philip slept here every night; he did his accounts here at the old desk under the one window. Gradually he had moved most of his personal things here. How far apart we were now in every way! With a sigh I went to work. The cleaning had to be got through with.

Old Humble had a sudden spurt of liveliness and made a jump at the broom as I swept under the bed. He pounced on something I had swept out—an old pink satin slipper—began to worry at it with his sparse old teeth. He must have brought it in from the rubbish heap, something Callie had abandoned, no doubt, for nobody else on the place would have worn such a thing. I shooed him out with it and went on with my work.

Minerva called, "Miss Bent! Aw, Miss Bent! Sam done got the carriage out yonder." So I hastily finished dusting and came out. Miss Stockbridge was already at the top of the front steps. I just dashed up to my room and gave my hair a few quick strokes with the brush before I joined her.

"I'm awfully glad to be going with you, Miss Stockbridge," I said. "I'll try to be as helpful as Old Sam."

"Do you good to get out. Besides I've got about all I can from him."

As I watched her take the long step into the carriage and then went round to the other side to get in, I wondered if she was planning to get anything out of me. Not if I knew it, I resolved.

Miss Stockbridge took the reins from Old Sam. Then she reached in her pocket and got out her billfold. "Here, buy yourself some chewing tobacco." She laughed. "That's from my file of native expressions. I shall try it on a taxi driver when I get back to Boston."

Sam was grinning. "Sure thanky, ma'am, and I'd be pleased to keep right on driving you, only Mr. Philip need me bossing the new field hand he done took on this mornin'."

"New? You mean Anse isn't——"

"Naw'm, Mr. Philip done run him off the place for good."

I was silent. I knew Anse never came to the house any more. Miss Stockbridge gave me the reins and reached in her pocket for her perpetual notebook. "My memory—that's the only thing that bothers me. If I don't make note of these things——" She turned to Sam. "Now do tell me just how Mr. Churston ran him off. Did he take a stick and chase him away, or what?"

Sam scratched his head and snickered under his breath. "Naw'm, didn't take no stick. Didn't need to. Jest told him he'd shoot him daid if he ever set foot on this here place again."

"Ah!" Miss Stockbridge breathed and wrote busily. "And what had Anse done to bring this on?"

I studied old Ergo's shaggy back, but I could see Sam bending over, scuffing at a clod of dirt with the toe of his shoe. "I don't rightly know, ma'am."

"I see." Miss Stockbridge put away her notebook. "We'll go into that later." She took the reins now, clucked to Ergo, and we started off. "It's that sort of thing I am after."

"Miss Stockbridge, he may have said that, but . . . but he didn't mean that he would really shoot Anse. It was just a . . . a manner of speaking."

"Indeed? Does a threat to shoot a man come under the head of colloquialisms?"

"I rather think it does."

"Well, even so, I find it quite significant. The leaning toward violence characteristic in this section——" She waved one hand toward the pecan orchard. "Are the trees all dead?"

"No. They just don't begin to put out till much later."

Miss Stockbridge shook the reins and Ergo broke into a trot, less in obedience than in an effort to keep ahead of the carriage as we rolled down the slope into the sunken part of the road. I was getting somewhat accustomed to Miss Stockbridge's way of pouncing on one with a question, but I was quite unprepared for her next. "Don't you ever go anywhere?" she demanded.

"Why . . . I . . . I went to church Sunday."

"Oh, yes, yes." She clucked to Ergo impatiently. "To have your

151

child christened. I mean, have you no young friends? Don't you ever go out and have a good time? Haven't you any interests beyond the plantation gate?"

"Oh, I see what you mean." I was silent, watching the high banks as we rattled on under arching trees that were just beginning to bud. "No," I said at last. There was nothing else I could say.

"Great mistake. You should be cultivating some interest. What will you do when your children are grown and you live on for forty years or so? You young people never think of that. It's just marry and live happily ever after, you think. China," she added with a backward wave of the hand as we emerged from the sunken part of the road and came out between open fields.

"China?" I echoed, glad of any turn of the conversation from myself.

"Yes. The roads are worn down like this in some parts—the only other place in the world with this exact geologic formation."

"You have been to China?"

"Oh, dear, yes, many times. I talked to the children at the school the other day about China. Quite an eye-opener to them."

"At this school down the road?"

"Yes. The young man there got me into it."

"Wh-what young man?"

"Oh, you know. Your great admirer, Jeff Wheeling." She had spoken casually, but her quick, shrewd glance brought the color burning to my cheeks, and I was in such a turmoil of pleasure and indignation that I could not answer. We had come to the plantation gate and I was glad of an excuse to get out and leave her for a moment. As I climbed down from the carriage, she said, "Nature abhors a vacuum."

My fingers fumbled at the chain that held the gate. What did she mean? Had her sharp old eyes seen the emptiness of my life with Philip? Could she know? I swung the gate wide with an angry push. Why did she have to dissect me and my life? I would not allow it. I would close myself against her prying. She could hint all she pleased, but she would find out nothing about me.

As we drove on down the road, the wheels noisy in the loose

152

gravel, Ergo trotting sturdily along, my anger dissolved in pleasure at being out on the road on this beautiful spring morning. We rattled over the bayou bridge and I looked down into the dark still water that was a black mirror to tree and bush. This was where Jeff passed in his skiff, coming in from the branch that curved back of his house. I wondered if he would seem the same when I met him amid new surroundings.

A group of little colored children on their way to school scattered at our approach, stood motionless at the side of the road, staring as we came up to them. Miss Stockbridge brought Ergo to a stop. She leaned out of the carriage. "Good morning, children. What did I tell you about speaking to me?"

They grinned, some shyly, some with boldness. "Mornin', Miss Stockbridge, mornin', ma'am." Their voices were high and sweet on the morning air, and they edged along sideways, looking up at us.

"They know you," I said with surprise. "Have you talked with them?"

"Not with, to. At their school one day. Told them about Africa. Hey, you three! Yes, you," she called to a little group that was lagging behind. "Come get in and I'll give you a ride. Hop in, right on the back seat there."

They climbed in and sat in a row, dark eyes shining, white teeth gleaming as Miss Stockbridge shook the reins and Ergo broke into his graceless trot. "Any time you want me to drive ——" I began.

Miss Stockbridge shook her head. "Always like to hold the reins myself, can't stand having other people running anything for me. That's why I learned to fly."

"You . . . you learned to fly?"

"Yes, yes, anybody can fly."

"But why? Why should you?"

"Oh, why should anybody learn anything? I just wanted to manage the thing, see what it was like."

"Weren't you nervous about it?"

"Nonsense! Why should I be? At my age. After seventy is the time to take chances. Chances are not for the young. They have

153

too much to lose. Get up, Ergo. Extraordinary names—Ergo and Peutêtre and Possible. They just don't make sense."

I laughed. Miss Stockbridge was a continual amazement to me. "You make me feel as if life were stretching ahead of me, long and rich and full."

"Well, isn't it? If not, do something about it."

I sat as silent as the children on the back seat. What could I do? Just enjoy to the fullest this excursion out of my daily habit. Of that alone was I sure. I looked around and saw we were coming into sight of Jeff's house. It stood back from the road, gray and weathered, the small yard inclosed by an unpainted fence and holding the dark rich green of Cape jessamines. From gate to road in the space where the great live oak threw its shade, the grass was getting green. The bayou woods behind the house were bright with redbud, and the neglected open field at one side was growing up in shiny green pines. I looked hungrily, forgetting Miss Stockbridge at my side. It was a warm and homelike place in spite of its shabbiness. Over my shoulder as we passed, I had a glimpse of a peach tree, pink against the gray wall.

Miss Stockbridge said, "We'll stop in someday after school, maybe."

"That will be nice." I spoke as matter-of-factly as she, but a flood of warm excitement went through me. It was suddenly good just to be alive. Alive and young, not old like Miss Stockbridge. We turned off the gravel road now, crossing a drainage ditch by a shaky, unguarded bridge and heading down a narrow dirt road. "I haven't been down this way before," I said. "You know your way around better than I do."

"You should have been here," she said with a severity she always showed when telling people what they ought or ought not to do. "Everyone should be familiar with his environment. Never lived anywhere myself, no matter how briefly, that I didn't explore, investigate, find out."

We turned again and the road opened out between fields and hedgerows white with haw. Ahead was a small, frame, unpainted school, no more than one room with a stovepipe crooking out one side. On the grounds were two chinaberry trees, still bare of leaves and hung with leftover bunches of yellow berries. There were two iron-frame swings, one of which had lost its seat and was only a loop of chain. Miss Stockbridge drew up alongside the raw bank where steps cut deep in the yellow clay led up to the schoolyard. Several children, early comers, left off their play and stood staring at us. The three in the back of the carriage made ready to descend.

"Don't get out yet. You're early. Let's talk a bit first." Miss Stockbridge handed me the reins and turned halfway about, one arm resting on the back of the seat, so she could look at them.

" 'As'm," said the little girl, pulling down her red sweater over her faded cotton dress. The two boys in corduroy knickers that flapped open at the knee wriggled back on the seat, bare toes dangling.

"Now let me get your names straight. You are Marvelline, I know, but you boys—what're your names?"

The older boy looked down, proud and pleased. "Leroy, ma'am. Him Etheber."

"Ah! Ethelbert, no doubt. Leroy what?"

"Leroy Washinon."

"Brothers?"

" 'As'm," they said in unison.

She had out her notebook now and jotted down their names and the answers they gave to her questions about the number in the family, the occupation of their parents and place of residence. "Now," she said briskly, "tell me, why do you go to this school?"

"To git us learned somethin'," Marvelline said.

"Yes, yes, I know. But why don't you go to the big school up the other way? It's a lot nearer."

"This here where us all goes," Leroy said, and Marvelline added, "That up there is the white chillen's school."

"I know it is. But why don't you go there?"

Leroy giggled. Marvelline said, "That where white chillen go. Us all goes here."

"Why don't you all go to the same school?"

Ethelbert sat with his mouth open, Leroy stopped a snicker with his hand, and Marvelline said, "It jest ain't that way."

Miss Stockbridge drew a long breath. "Not 'ain't,' is not." She turned to me. "Unfortunately human beings tend to accept their environment without question. These children don't even realize——" She put away her notebook as a young colored woman appeared in the door of the school. "All right. You may go now, children. I want to talk to the teacher."

They scrambled down and tore up the bank. Their teacher stopped them with a lifted finger. "Did you thank Miss Stockbridge for the ride?" She had a gentle soft voice and in the sunlight her skin was golden-brown.

The children looked back shyly. "Thanky, ma'am," they said all together, opening their mouths like three blackbirds for a worm. The teacher came down the clay steps. "Good morning, Miss Stockbridge."

Miss Stockbridge leaned across me to shake hands. "Miss Gale, Mrs. Churston. I'm staying with Mrs. Churston, you know."

I said, "Good morning," but did not offer my hand. It was strange hearing a Negress called "Miss."

The girl said, "How do you do?" politely, and added, "Won't you all get out and come in?"

"No time this morning, thank you. We were just passing by. I want to see Mrs. Jones and find out how the meeting went."

"That's mighty kind of you. The children will never forget your talk about Africa, and I won't either." She smiled, her teeth white and even, her whole face lighting up.

"Good." Miss Stockbridge took the reins from me. "I'll drop in another day. There are lots of things I still have to talk over with you."

The girl inclined her head in a graceful motion. "Any time, Miss Stockbridge." Then she looked at me and a slight an almost imperceptible change came over her. "I will be glad to have you, too, Mrs. Churston," she said in her low musical voice.

For a second, looking straight into her dark eyes as she stood there against the yellow bank, I saw something in her guarded glance, her stiffness, that made me remember myself, standing, rigid and defenseless, at the chancel rail, the baby held close against me. I swallowed. One hand rose to my throat. But why not say it, why not? She had as much right to it as . . . as Miss Kate. "Thank you . . . Miss Gale," I said.

Ergo responded to Miss Stockbridge's shake of the reins and we moved away. I looked back after a moment, and the girl was still standing there motionless, her two hands pressed against her breast. O God, it was such a little thing I had done. Did it mean so much to her?

For once Miss Stockbridge seemed to have seen nothing or, if she had, made no comment. After a little I began to attend to what she was saying ". . . graduating with honor. It must be a most unusual school. I shall make a point of visiting it in Jackson on my way north, if I have time. She has the true missionary spirit. Her salary is pitifully small of course. Now here's the house where I want to stop. You won't mind waiting?"

"What? No, no, of course not. I'll be glad just to sit in the sun." I watched her walk briskly along the dirt path to the door of a cabin set back from the road in the middle of a field of ragged, brown cornstalks. She knocked at the closed door. It opened and she went in. A meeting—she wanted to hear about a meeting. Could Philip's suspicions be right? I looked at the cabin uneasily. Yet she had spoken out before me without any hesitation. Oh, no, I decided, she could not be up to any harm.

I let the reins lie loose in my lap, and Ergo nibbled at the green young grass on the edge of the road, pulling the carriage along as he ate one spot bare. Ahead the road curved gently into woods that were delicately mauve, as if a rosy breeze had blown over the gray branches opening the buds to spring. A redheaded woodpecker tapped on the trunk of a sycamore, the sound busy and persistent as a quick ticking clock. A bluebird, the first I had seen this year, lighted on a fence post across the road, his breast rosy in the sun. I leaned back in the old carriage, breathing in the mild warm scent of earth and growing things, letting spring seep into my very bones.

"Sorry to keep you waiting so long," Miss Stockbridge said,

hopping into the carriage in her brisk way. She took the reins from me, slapped Ergo over to the middle of the road. I glanced back at the cabin as we left. That was Anse at the door, an old Negro woman beside him. Now why—— "Got to talking and the time slipped up on me," Miss Stockbridge went on, "but this road is a short cut. It will take us right through to the gravel."

It was only a trail, grass-grown, leaf-strewn. Away from the river here there was little moss on the trees, so they had a clear, sunny look. Redbud flashed between the gray tree trunks and here and there the underbrush along the trail was overlaid with yellow jessamine. I leaned out and snatched off a spray of it as we passed and its musty sweetness filled the carriage. I closed my eyes, breathing it deep, and we seemed to float on a cloud of golden fragrance.

"Delightful!" Miss Stockbridge cried. "Takes me back . . . that winter. Nothing like a smell to bring back a memory. I can shut my eyes and see the blue Mediterranean, the terraced gardens dropping down to it."

I looked at her with a faint stirring of envy. How many places she had known! "You've been about everywhere, haven't you?"

"Almost. Ah, here we are! Hang on." She slapped Ergo with the reins, clucked him into a trot, and we clattered over the loose planks that bridged the drainage ditch, rattled up the steep roadside, gravel flying and the carriage swaying. "Made it!" she cried with triumph. She glanced at her wrist watch and added, "I'll just get there. That class meets at eleven-thirty, right after recess."

"Are you going to a class?" I wanted to ask if it was Jeff's, but I didn't.

"Yes, I promised to talk to them. They're studying Greek History and——" She gave her attention to the driving as a truck came around the curve ahead.

After a minute we turned down a side road and came almost at once within sight of the school grounds. The children were just marching in from recess, a long line, shepherded in by a young teacher with bright gold hair and a dress the color of the small pines that dotted the schoolyard like young Christmas trees. She was so pretty, I thought, with an envious pang.

Miss Stockbridge drove up the steep, washed road that led to the grounds. "Whoa!" she cried and thrust the reins into my hands. "I've got to run. Mustn't be late. Come on in if you're interested. I guess he'll stand—or hitch him or something." She tossed the words back over her shoulder as she hurried to join the end of the line.

I sat holding the reins, unaccountably depressed. I had thought Jeff would come out to meet us. I had thought—I didn't know what I'd thought. I certainly wasn't going poking in by myself. So I just waited, letting Ergo roam about nibbling the sparse grass that grew in patches where the children had not trampled it out.

After a little, as Ergo drew nearer the building, I heard through an open window the sound of clapping and then Miss Stockbridge's crisp voice. I strained my ears to catch what she was saying. Now and then I got a sentence or two: "See this little blue strip of water on the map? We were right there. They didn't want me to try it—said I was too old. Now don't ever let anybody tell you you're too old——" I lost the next, but I could hear the laughter. Then: "Well, I said, Leander did it. I hope you know that story. How many do? . . . Good! I said Leander did it and so shall I. . . . So there I was, smack in the middle of the Hellespont. Deep blue sky, with a few white clouds, bright blue water all around me. I lay on my back drinking it all in—well, not literally, but——" Laughter drowned her out for the moment and I missed the next part, till she raised her voice. "No, no, I'm not drowning. I told them. So I made them leave me. Then I swam on. . . ."

Goodness, I thought, what a woman! I wished I could hear all she was saying. At last there was a great clapping, a sound of scuffling feet and children's voice, and then Jeff came running down the steps.

"Why didn't you come in?" he cried. "I didn't know you were here until just now. But do come and have lunch. I'll hitch your horse." He hurried me in, up the steps, down the hall and out to a cafeteria crowded with children. "Never mind a tray. Teachers get served." He led me toward a table where Miss Stockbridge

159

was already seated with the young teacher I had noticed earlier. Jeff was different, I thought, as he pulled out a chair for me and made the introduction. Different in manner and in looks. I had never seen him in coat and collar and tie. He was a stranger to me here.

The children made such a clatter that I could scarcely hear what was being said at our table. Jeff plied Miss Stockbridge with questions about her year in Greece, drawing me into the talk now and then. But for the most part I sat silent and unaccountably depressed. Amalee, the young teacher, was so pretty, so gay and . . . and uncomplicated. I felt old and serious and weighed down beside her, so I was glad when the meal was over and Jeff escorted us out.

He helped Miss Stockbridge into the carriage. "Wait, I'll do that," he said, coming to take the hitching line from me. Then he added, "Where have you been? I've missed you."

I stroked Ergo's velvety nose. "Just busy." My eyes fell under his keen glance.

"But you will come—soon? I have a lot to tell you." He nodded in Miss Stockbridge's direction, his eyes twinkling.

Suddenly I felt happy and at ease again. "Me too." I laughed. "I'll blow the whistle for you."

IN THE evenings when Miss Stockbridge had gone to her room to write an account of her day's activities, we sat in the library as usual and yet there was a difference. Her presence in the house was not a thing one could ignore. She was a burr, pricking; a mosquito, buzzing; and to me especially, she was a bit of yeast, stirring, working. Philip often questioned me about what we had done that morning. But there was little I could tell him that would ease his concern.

"We go on the back roads mostly," I told him one evening when he began his questioning. "We stop sometimes at the school, the white school. Other days we got to the Negro school, the one off the main road."

"What does she do there?"

"I don't go in with her always. When I have gone, she only examines the textbooks or talks about her travels or asks the children questions—about how many are in the family and what work the parents do. Things like that."

"There's nothing wrong there, surely," Miss Kate said.

"Not on the face of it." Philip laid his paper across his knee and stared into the bright fire, frowning. "But I have heard some disturbing things in town lately. There is someone in this county going around trying to organize the Negroes, the sharecroppers and those who work at the new overall plant, too. It's rumored they have had several secret meetings."

My busy fingers stopped their knitting. Meetings? Miss Stockbridge had spoken of a meeting.

Philip went on: "Pamphlets, definitely Communistic in tone, have been handed out. If they could just catch a man in the act——"

"What would they do to him?" I asked.

"Oh, run him out of the county, I suppose. But first they would

161

find out from him who is back of the thing, for he would be only a tool, someone too stupid to know the risk he was taking."

"It's just wicked," Miss Kate said, "the way unscrupulous people do, taking advantage of a poor ignorant Negro. One like Anse, for instance, and——"

"Anse?" Philip gave her a sharp look. "Have you any reason——"

"No, no, Philippe. I used him only as an example," Miss Kate said. "Now he's quit working here——"

"Quit? I fired him, and a good thing too."

I bent over my knitting. Could Anse be involved? After all, Miss Stockbridge had stayed a long time talking with him and whoever else had been in that house the first morning I went with her.

"Why Philippe, you never told me," Miss Kate was saying. "What had he done?"

"That's just it. He did nothing unless I was overseeing him."

I felt Philip's eyes on me, but when I looked up he was folding the paper.

"I suspected him of stealing something," Philip went on. "I was mistaken, as it happened, but it was a good idea to be rid of him just the same. He'd been an annoyance to me for a long time."

I began knitting again, my needles clicking loud in the silence. This was Philip's apology given at last. This was his way of telling me that he had been wrong in accusing me, that day in his room when he was first sitting up after the flu. I sighed. It would take more than this to make me forget.

Miss Kate, who had lifted her book again, looked across at Philip over her glasses. "I really can't believe, Philippe, that Miss Stockbridge is involved. Why, she was telling me the other day that her maternal great-grandfather was Increase Smugensall, the one who was a colonial governor of Massachusetts or Connecticut or one of those places. And her grandfather was Surplus Smugensall who——"

Philip made a small gesture of impatience and interrupted. "That does not mean a thing, Aunt Kate. I understand that some of the best of the old families up there have been affected by this radicalism. They are more dangerous than the riffraff because they have money to support these crackpot causes."

"Oh, dear!" Miss Kate cried. "I asked her to be my guest at the D.A.R. luncheon next week."

"I certainly would not introduce her socially, Aunt Kate. You must——"

"But she refused, Philippe. She said she was too busy with the present to waste time on the past."

"Just as well. There's nothing definite against her, but it is a good idea to be on the safe side." He rose and began walking back and forth before the fire. "I just don't trust her, any more than I trust young Jeff Wheeling."

"But, Philippe, the Wheelings are one of our oldest families."

"The family has run to seed lately, Aunt Kate, and he was educated in the North. Probably picked up radical ideas."

"Oh, I don't think so," I began, and then bent quickly over my knitting. I resented Miss Stockbridge's prying and the way she told everybody exactly what ought to be done, yet all the time Philip had been talking my sympathies had been with her, with Anse, and now with Jeff. Did I put them before my husband? Cleave only unto him—those were the words I had promised. But if he was wrong——

Philip was saying, "I would not be surprised if he were being subsidized by some organization. No country school could pay enough to attract a man of his education."

I could keep silent no longer. "Maybe he thinks it's the best way to do something for the good of the country. Maybe——"

"I never heard such nonsense, Bentley. You don't know anything about it."

"Oh, dear!" Miss Kate sighed. "If we can't trust the young men of our best families—well, it just puts us in the same class with all those decadent places up North, like Boston where Miss Stockbridge comes from." She lifted her book, Philip returned to his paper, and no more was said.

But next morning Miss Stockbridge gave cause for further indignation, if not suspicion. In the midst of breakfast she announced that as the weather was rather threatening—not that she ever really gave up anything on account of weather—she would stay at home this morning and work on her notes. "But I would like the carriage at three-ten this afternoon, if you please."

"Certainly, Miss Stockbridge, I shall order it for you." The more he disliked anyone the more courteous and formal Philip became. So I was not surprised to hear him ask now, "May I inquire how your thesis material is progressing?"

"I have gathered a wealth of it," she said with her usual lively enthusiasm. "I have so much that the great difficulty will be in knowing what to leave out. And there are so many fascinating facets to each phase of the investigation." Her sharp eyes followed Minerva who was passing the hot biscuits. She took one and buttered it while it was hot, something she had learned to do since coming to Cedar Bluff. Minerva had been indignant at the way she broke off a small bit and buttered it when she first came. "Like they wa'n't hot," she said with scorn; "Like they was cold light bread and wouldn't melt the butter."

Miss Stockbridge waited now till Minerva was out of hearing. Then she said, "Take the whole matter of mixed blood, for instance. I have scarcely touched on that."

"Oh, dear!" Miss Kate exclaimed. "Surely I must have misunderstood. No lady would want to—— Dear me!"

Miss Stockbridge looked as shocked as Miss Kate herself. "Your attitude—— Really! But most interesting. I must make a note of it. I mean—" she glanced at Philip who sat stiffly, his dark gaze fastened on her with distaste—"I mean, one reads of these things in the literature, but to come right on it! How can you evade such a fascinating aspect of the whole matter? Take Minerva, for instance. Is she a full-blooded Negress?"

I kept my eyes on my plate but I heard Philip's slow intake of breath, whether in relief or in an effort at self-control, I could not tell. But he only said, "I should think her pure African, Miss Stockbridge, judging by feature, skin color, wide-flaring nostrils and high cheekbones."

"I see." Miss Stockbridge nodded. "And this girl Callie whom I see around the place, though I've never got close enough to

164

engage her in conversation—just what proportion of white blood would such a person have?" She took a quick glance around the table as no one answered. "Don't tell me you never asked her."

"One couldn't ask a Negro a question like that!" Miss Kate cried. "You don't realize——"

Philip set down his coffee cup with a small rattle of annoyance. "We do not make it a habit to speculate on the ancestry of our colored population, Miss Stockbridge."

"But how very odd, when one can tell to look at her that one of her parents must have been white and——"

"Oh, please," Miss Kate broke in, "you must not put it that way, as if it might have been her mother who was white. Really, Miss Stockbridge, in the South at least, no white woman——"

"I see." Miss Stockbridge nodded with a satisfied air. "Just the point of view I was eager to confirm. Then, let us say, for the sake of argument, that her father was white and her mother— did you know her mother, Miss Churston?"

"Why . . . why, yes." Miss Kate looked at Philip as if for help, but his eyes were on his plate. "Yes, I know who she was—that Ella who used to work for the Walker family in town."

"Was she light or dark?"

"Well, I would say . . . I would call her *café au lait.*"

"Probably half and half, then," Miss Stockbridge said. "Do you have any idea who her father was?"

Miss Kate seemed to be out of breath. "Well, really, Miss Stockbridge, these are not things that one talks about."

"Oh, I am sorry. You see, as a complete outsider, I—— Do forgive me." Miss Stockbridge sounded so contrite that Philip leaned back in his chair and passed his cup to Miss Kate for coffee. He glanced at the window where the first drops of rain were striking. "I hope this will keep up all day. We've been needing rain."

Miss Kate said, "I'm glad this isn't club day."

I was studying Miss Stockbridge. With an air of absorption she was helping herself to more of Minerva's peach leather, but I thought by the gleam in her eye that she had probably known just what she was doing all the time. She was just seeing how

165

upset she could get everyone. A moment later I was sure of it.

"Of course," she said, "there is the obverse side of the picture. I am sure we can talk about that."

"What do you mean?" Miss Kate fell right into her trap.

"I mean the Southern white families that have some Negro blood."

Her words hung on the air, doomlike, inescapable. I who had been a faintly amused listener was knocked out of my detachment. I held my breath. Miss Kate made a small distressed sound, and Philip, when I dared glance at him, was white around the mouth.

He folded his napkin with meticulous care. He laid it beside his plate. "Miss Stockbridge," he said, and his voice was so cold and quiet it sent a shiver down my spine, "many a man has been shot for saying less than that. There is no possible response that one can make to—" his lips twisted—"to a lady." He rose and with a formal bow left the room.

My heart began to pound again in long slow beats. Miss Kate said in a choked voice, "Well, really, I must ask to be excused." She went out mumbling something about telling Minerva what to have for dinner. I drew a long breath and tried to get hold of myself. I could not leave. Someone had to stay and face this woman down.

"Fancy that!" Miss Stockbridge cried with a kind of unholy glee. "I certainly put my foot in it. I hope you realize I never would have said such a thing if I had not been sure that there was no Negro blood in the Churston family."

"Oh," I said. I did not know whether to believe her or not. She was a devil, that woman, the way she saw into things.

She put on a plaintive air. "How could I know they would not like my innocent little remark? After all, what's the difference?"

"The difference?" I leaned forward, startled.

"Certainly, what's the difference?" She poured herself more coffee and put in a liberal dash of cream. "What earthly difference does it make—a strain of Negro blood? At least in the sight of God or any reasoning human. Who cares? Now see here—"

she turned on me with the quick pouncing movement that always made me jump—"you are young, you belong to the new generation of Southerners. Surely you can see that it makes not the slightest real difference."

"Why ... I ..." I could not go on. Oh, if it were true, if it were only true! I swallowed. "I never thought of it like that. I——"

"But surely you must have a more open mind on the subject." She leaned back in her chair and took a pack of cigarettes from her pocket. "What I can't understand," she said, striking a match and puffing as she spoke, "what I simply cannot understand is all this emotion about it. Your husband—don't think I did not see that he was white with rage. If I'd been a man he'd have knocked my teeth out. In fact for a moment I was quite nervous about my lower plate. And your poor aunt—really I felt quite contrite. But why get so hot and bothered about such a small thing?"

"A small thing," I said, aghast. "But it's not a small thing, the way people feel about it." My eyes fell under her shrewd glance.

"The whole trouble is the way people feel, of course," she cried with impatience. "No real foundation for it. Just a purely emotional point of view—has nothing to do with the facts. Biologically the combination is perfectly sound. In fact each race might well enrich the other, and amalgamation is of course the only sensible solution of the problem. Honestly, I get so cross, people are so damn stupid." She rose. "Now if you will excuse me, I really must go and get all this down while it's still fresh in my mind."

I sat there, rigid, for a moment, then I covered my face with my hands. O God, if it were only true that it did not matter! If it could only be true—in time for my Henry!

· 18 ·

THE rain continued all morning but by midafternoon there was only a light mist falling. At three-ten precisely Miss Stockbridge came out of her room wearing her yellow sou'wester and the yellow hat with the wide brim in back. I tied a red scarf over my head and went to the hall closet for my old tweed coat. Miss Kate called from the library where she was reading, "Mind you don't catch cold, going out on a day like this. I never heard of such a thing." But I would have risked pneumonia rather than give up this excursion. I had a notion of where we were going. Jeff had said he would look for us on the first rainy afternoon.

In the carriage with the black rain guard pulled up over us and buttoned at each side, the reins going out through a slit, Miss Stockbridge said, "Some people are afraid they'll melt in the rain. Personally I never let the weather interfere with my plans, and I certainly don't mean to begin at this late day."

"I love being out in the rain." My spirits rose at the prospect of getting away from the house. It was a kind of escape from all the problems that beset me. All day I had been pondering on what Miss Stockbridge had said at breakfast, and although I did not really believe that people would ever feel differently about such things, I was stirred by the thought, my mind torn between fact and dream. I was like one of those mythical creatures, half eagle, dreaming of flying and a cliff-hung nest, and half beast that is doomed to walk the heavy ground. All the while, too, I vacillated between fierce loyalty to the Churston's ideas, to those I had thoughtlessly accepted all my life, and a yet fiercer loyalty to my child and whatever was a part of him. For this is the price that one pays for a child—that his hurt and shame come to one not singly like one's own troubles, but multiplied a thousandfold.

As the carriage began to creak through the mud of the plantation road, Miss Stockbridge said with a nod of her head in the direction of the ell, "I'd like to see her sometime."

"Who?" For I could never get used to her quick changes of subject.

"Your mother-in-law. I worked in a mental hospital during the war and I might be able to suggest something. Has she had a good psychiatrist?"

"Why, I don't know. I suppose so, if they had them when she—— It was a long time ago."

"I doubt if she got much attention in a crowded state institution. Certainly something should be done for her. Have you suggested anything?"

I gave her a startled glance. The idea of my doing anything, or even of making a suggestion, had never occurred to me. "I don't think Miss Kate would like it. I mean——"

"You mean you have never felt the slightest responsibility about it, I presume," Miss Stockbridge said sharply. "Well, I tell you we've all got to be responsible for everything. That's the trouble with these times and all our problems. Everybody leaves it to the other fellow and nothing is done. Everybody is so afraid of making trouble. Of course there's got to be trouble before anything good is ever accomplished. Really, I get so provoked." She slapped Ergo with the lines and he switched his tail in response but did not alter his gait.

I sat silent. One of Philip's favorite objections to any change was always "That will just stir up trouble." But if trouble was something one had to go through with before accomplishing anything, then why not meet it and be done with it? Miss Stockbridge was provoking, the way she was always so sure she was right, yet it might be that she was right about some things. She just made it hard to take, with her righteous cocksureness.

She said no more now, however, and as we came out from the sunken part of the road, I asked—for it had been in the back of my mind all the time—"Are we heading for Jeff Wheeling's this afternoon?"

"Certainly we are. Why else would you have been whistling about the house all morning?"

I was glad her eyes were on Ergo's steaming back as he went *clop-clopping* through the mud. For I could feel the color mount my cheeks. It was true: I had whistled a bit and sung around the house this morning. Yet it was not out of the wicked and unfaithful gladness of which she accused me by tone as much as word. Even now, my heart quickening as we creaked along the plantation road, the gladness I felt was once removed, as they say of cousin kin. It was far off from me, like a ray of late sunlight that strikes the treetop and leaves one but witness to it from the shadow below. It was like a bird song deep in the swamp, remotely heard. So I would not let myself be put out with Miss Stockbridge for her way of thinking, or put off from speaking of Jeff. "Tell me, Miss Stockbridge, is he a radical?" I asked.

Her laugh rang out. "You needn't say it as if it were poison. I hope so. He is about some things. Then again there is a curious conservatism and caution in his way of thinking."

"Are you one?"

"That depends. What is a radical?"

"Why . . . I . . . I suppose it's somebody who wants to upset everything, change things." I was silent. There were some things even I would change, if I could.

"*Radix, radicis*—root. That's what it comes from. Fundamental, reaching to the center or ultimate source, affecting the vital principle, getting to the bottom of things and straightening them out. That's what I'm for. No slowpoky, halfhearted business—like this old nag of yours. Get up, Ergo!" She reached one hand out from under the lap cover to get the whip. Ergo plodded on with no change of pace, only switching his tail and flinging a spray of raindrops in our faces.

I got out and opened the plantation gate, closed it after the carriage had passed through. As soon as I was in again and we were heading down the gravel road, Miss Stockbridge said, "Remember this, Bentley. Nothing is sacred and unalterable just because we're used to it, just because that's the way it's always been. I've been fighting that notion all my life. Last thing I want is to get set in any way of thinking. Especially at my age. Get set then and you're ossified for time and eternity. I don't ever want to stand still—get up, Ergo!—I'll be still enough when I'm dead."

I laughed with her and we jogged along in silence. Now and

then a car passed us, flinging the noisy gravel, splashing the carriage with water from the ruts. We crossed the bayou bridge and I gave up thinking of anything except that soon I would see Jeff and his house. For a house is a revealing thing when one has had the making of it oneself. Of course at Cedar Bluff there was nothing of me, and I might quit it this day and leave no sign, save perhaps the yellow-dyed cheesecloth curtains in the nursery. But Jeff's house had been all his own. It would reveal him to me, like something he had written. For between the lines, unseen among the written words, there is something delicate and intangible which is the man himself.

We turned in from the road across the outer grassy yard, and Miss Stockbridge with a loud "Whoa, Ergo!" brought him to a stop under the widespread live oak, his nose to the picket fence.

Jeff came out at once, bareheaded to the mist, hurrying his long limping step to fling open the gate and welcome us. He tied Ergo to the fence post and led us up the single step, across the vine-covered porch and in. "I've been looking forward to this for a long time." He helped me out of my coat, took my scarf.

"How very cozy and welcoming!" Miss Stockbridge cried, shaking herself free of her big sou'wester and flinging a shower of drops from her yellow hat across the bare pine floor.

While she was exclaiming, her sharp glance busy as her tongue, I stood silent yet looking too. We had entered directly into the main room of the house which ran all the way across the front. A warm room, I thought, warm in spirit. At the far end a wood fire burned in a wide fireplace, the bricks of the hearth rosy in its light, old small bricks, plantation-made. All the colors of the room were mellow and restful—the yellow brown of pine board, the darker beams, the subdued gold and red and blue of books that lined the walls. There was a rough homemade table under the window with a typewriter and papers strewed comfortably about; the chairs were country chairs of hickory with cowhide seats; the sofa was covered over with an old red tablecloth. Everything was plain as any farmer might have, but it was a rich room. There were no curtains at the small-paned windows. All was open, for there was nothing of which one could be ashamed.

171

I was filled with satisfaction that everything fitted in with what I knew of Jeff; yet with sadness that all this, like my anticipation of coming, was once removed from me.

Miss Stockbridge was pointing up to the rafters. "Chestnut, aren't they? This must be an old building."

"One of the slave cabins. There used to be a row of them, but they're all burned down except this."

"A slave cabin! Amazing. I had no idea they were so comfortable. Is there more than one room? Where does that door lead to?"

"Just shed rooms, very small. One is my bedroom, the other the kitchen. Want to see them?"

"Of course. I want to see everything. Don't you know me yet? Ah!" she breathed as he flung the door wide and waved her through. "This is the way a kitchen should like. I'm sick of kitchens that look like the inside of a sterilizer. Wood stove, I presume, a table, a chair, an old couch to rest on while the pot boils, and a good lived-in look."

I had followed her into the kitchen and now, still silent, went into the bedroom with her while Jeff began to make the tea. This room was tiny and austere, with only a narrow cot bed, a chest of drawers and a washstand with tin basin and brassbound wooden water bucket. It was not cold, only spare and strong. Now I knew, I knew Jeff. I had seen into him, like a spy who has looked into all the secret places.

"Neat and Spartan," Miss Stockbridge approved as we came back to the kitchen. "Why will people fill their houses with junk? Personally I am through with things. No time to worry with them any more. Called in my nieces and nephews and let them clean me out. Now I must go see what books you have on your shelves." She placed her glasses on her nose as she headed back for the living room.

Jeff gave me a twinkling glance. "Quite a gal, isn't she?"

I nodded, standing awkward and tongue-tied, conscious suddenly of the four walls about us, enclosing us. Till now we had not been alone in a room. It brought us into an intimacy new and a little frightening. But as I saw him pour the steaming water from kettle to teapot, watched how quietly his hands moved setting three cups on a tray with a clumsiness that pierced me through with the wish to do it for him, some of that quiet spread through me and I rested in the peace of this moment. "May I carry something in for you?" I asked when he had everything assembled.

"Just the cooky plate."

I took it up and would have moved toward the door but that he blocked my way, standing before me with the tray in his hands. "Well, how's my house?" he asked.

"Just like you. I love it." The words, or perhaps the way I spoke them, for they had burst from me without thought, opened his face to me, as drawing back a curtain or a guard from before the fire lets out all the warmth that has been held in. My eyes fell then, and I was abashed as if I had looked into a secret place. "The tea——"

"The tea?" he said, as if it were a new word to him and he must learn it. Then he stepped aside and I went ahead of him into the front room.

Miss Stockbridge, with her glasses on her nose and her head tipped back so they would stay on, was examining the books on the shelves. "A very good collection, though why you want to cumber your shelves with Strickland's *Lives of the Queens of England,* I can't see. Who wants to read about Matilda of Flanders these days? No sugar, please."

I sat down on the long pine bench in the chimney corner and Jeff put the tray beside me. "Will you?" he said.

"Of course." I liked the odd shape of the teapot and the color of it—green and yellow. Pottery of some sort, I thought, the cups irregular in form with each handle differently made as if by an individualist with no wish to ape a set mold. Miss Stockbridge took her cup and continued on her round of the bookshelves, commenting on one title and another. I sipped my tea and let them talk. I was content to sit silent in the warmth of the fire and Jeff's nearness. I wanted to soak up the peace and quiet of the room, so that I might bear it away with me and treasure it and keep it as a refuge in my mind.

173

Miss Stockbridge rapped a disapproving finger on one of the books Jeff had taken down to show her. "Throw that out. Yes, I've read it—merely a plea for the *status quo.*"

"Not at all," Jeff said. "It is a sympathetic story and it has a message we should not overlook: the Negroes must do something themselves, not expect to have everything done for them. They must do their part, improve themselves."

"How can they, ground down and oppressed, deprived of every right? I get so indignant!" She walked about the room, sipping her tea.

"Indignation does no good." Jeff smiled down at her. "You know it's only human nature to resent being told we are wrong. We harden our hearts against it. Especially when it concerns something we have grown up with and taken for granted. We feel we are being attacked in a vital spot and we fight the attack instead of the wrong."

"How are you ever going to improve anything then?"

Jeff came and stood with his back to the fire, resting one elbow on the mantelpiece. "Change, social improvement, comes not through one great upheaval but through many small pushes— pushes made by individuals or very small groups who feel the pressure of the injustice with peculiar sharpness and are directly concerned."

"Young man—" Miss Stockbridge set her cup down on the table with an emphatic clatter—"I come of fighting New England stock. I believe in violence and bloodshed when the cause warrants. The Civil War freed the slaves, didn't it?"

"Yes, but without it they would have been peaceably freed long before this and we would have been spared the Reconstruction bitterness and the fear which hangs over us to this day. Don't misunderstand me. I'm right with you on the matter of equal opportunity for all. The poll tax is already going. The vote is bound to come. But not by national edict or by violence."

"Shilly-shallying nonsense!" Miss Stockbridge snapped. "Clean the whole business up and be done with it, I say. I've no patience with this slowpoky notion of letting things work out of themselves. You admit conditions are bad. Well, change them and have done with it. Very good tea. May I have another cup?"

Jeff brought me her cup, and as I refilled it I said, "It may be irritating to be blamed and denounced for something we have just grown up in the midst of, Jeff. But you know what I've been thinking?" I looked up at him, teapot in hand.

"What Bentley?" He smiled down at me.

"That maybe it is good for us to have somebody—like Miss Stockbridge—opening our eyes, turning on a light for us, a clear frosty unemotional light." I turned to Miss Stockbridge. "You know very well you make us all furious sometimes, but I am grateful to you for some things you have said. Will you have a cooky?" I added quickly, fearful lest I had said too much.

Miss Stockbridge laughed. "Oh, I really do have fun with people. No, no cooky. Never eat between meals. Ruinous to the digestion. Well, just put one on my saucer, or two. They do look good." She sat down on the red-covered sofa in front of the fire and added, "It all seems so simple and clear-cut to me, I am utterly baffled by the amount of feeling which seems tied up with the whole question. Why do people get so upset? Why can't they sit down and reason?"

"You can't fight emotion with reason. You must fight it with another emotion." Jeff stood with his back to the fire. "Only love can conquer fear and——"

"But you hate the Negroes down here. I've always known that."

"On the contrary. We get along very well together. We have done a lot for them and we will do more, if we're let alone. You can't solve such a problem offhand, you know. In the course of time amalgamation will probably settle the matter for good and all."

I looked up at him then. Did he mean . . . did he mean that the time would come when there would be no stigma, when——

Miss Stockbridge cried, "There! The first sensible thing I ever heard you advocate. But why not go a step farther and do something about it right now? Why sit back and wait? Social equality, intermarriage——"

175

"No, Miss Stockbridge. Those are too personal things to be forced. They must come slowly, through natural development if they are to come at all. And I am not saying I advocate anything of the sort. I don't know how it will be. I only say it will come. In a thousand years perhaps. Not in my time, certainly. And if I am honest I will have to add that I am glad it won't come in my time."

I turned away, bending to the fire so that my hair curtained my face from them. A thousand years. What good would that do my child? What good was all this talk, talk, talk about large generalities? All I was really concerned with was Henry and what life would do to him. I sat bowed over, my hands held out to the fire. Jeff, who a moment ago had seemed so close to me, so warm and comforting, was distant now, forever removed from me, from what was my greatest concern.

Jeff put on another log, and Miss Stockbridge said his horseshoe andirons reminded her of certain curious goodluck symbols she had run across in Egypt. Then she was off, talking of her travels. I paid little heed, my thoughts traveling round and round in a dark country of their own. It was not until Jeff put a spill to the fire and lighted the lamp on the table that I saw night had come.

I sprang up. "It's terribly late. Miss Stockbridge, please, we must go." Oh, how could I have stayed so long? Philip would be home. He might set out to look for us, thinking Ergo had tipped us over or run away or something. He would drive down the road, see the carriage here, in Jeff's yard and—— Oh, I was in a fever to get away! I flung my coat around me and fairly snatched the scarf from Jeff's hand.

But Miss Stockbridge dawdled, trying to decide which of two books she would borrow. "Take them both," Jeff said. "Here's one you might like to look over, Bentley."

I took it, scarcely looking at it, my eyes on the window where darkness was deepening. "Really," I said, "I'm sorry but we must——"

"Oh, what difference does it make—half an hour one way or the other?" Miss Stockbridge said with impatience. "Why shouldn't you stay out as late as you like? No one has any business looking so frightened over being a little late. I'll take this book, I guess. Though, let me see . . ." She went to the bookshelf again.

I turned away. I had not meant to let them see how anxious I was, and yet—— "You forget Bentley has a small baby at home," Jeff said.

I was so grateful to him that I had to blink back the tears. "Yes," I said. "Minerva must be busy with dinner at this hour and I——"

"Oh, well, come along then." Miss Stockbridge clapped on her yellow hat. "I don't believe in dawdling once you make up your mind."

I was already through the door and running down the steps, my scarf flying loose and the rain striking me full in the face. Jeff overtook me at the gate. His hand came down over mine as I fumbled at the latch.

"Don't," he said, "don't be afraid. What could harm you?"

"Nothing, of course." Then I saw car lights coming down the road. I stood rigid till the car had passed without slackening speed. Then I let my breath out in a sigh of relief and was suddenly conscious of his hand, warm over mine, of his face bent close, grave and concerned. "It's all right," I said. "I just stayed too late . . . because I . . . I needed to be away. I needed a . . . a respite. You gave it to me. That's why I forgot and stayed. That's all."

"God!" he said under his breath.

Then Miss Stockbridge came bustling out, and a moment later we were on the road, headed homeward. I looked back and saw Jeff standing bareheaded in the rain, outlined by the yellow light from the open front door. He wanted to help me, but no one could do that.

As we drove under the dark wet cedars, I saw that Philip's car was in the carriage house, the rear bumper reflecting light from the kitchen window. He was not out looking for me—I was spared that. When I had run up to make sure the baby was all right, I came with slower step to hang my coat in the hall closet. Miss

Kate called, "Well, you certainly made a day of it! Such weather."

"Yes." I came into the library. "The rain was a bit wet." I stood before the fire drying my ankles, my eyes trying to read Philip's face.

"You mustn't catch cold on these expeditions," Philip said, "and I see no reason for staying out after dark, even with Miss Stockbridge along. It's not safe. Is dinner about ready?"

"I'll see." I hurried out, weak with relief. Oh, I could never tell about Philip. The things I worried most about, he overlooked. Then when I had no notion of having done anything wrong, he would burst out at me without warning.

From the ell porch I called to Minerva, "We're ready for dinner now."

" 'Bout time," she answered. "Got protracted meetin' all this week and I been late every night yet."

· 19 ·

EACH Sunday since the christening I had made some excuse to Miss Kate for not going with her and Philip to church. She had accepted these excuses without question and Philip too had said nothing. But this sunny mild Sunday he sought me out. I was in the nursery when he came in and stood watching. I had the baby on my lap, a towel across my knees, the bowl of warm water for his bath on a chair in front of me. I finished soaping his plump little body and set him in the water, holding him with one hand and sponging him off with the other. He kicked and gurgled and laughed aloud, loving it. I said as I lifted him out and rolled him in the towel, "Pretty nice, isn't he?"

Philip nodded, his face dark and inscrutable. "His eyes are more brown than they were. I was hoping they would be like yours. Will you get ready for church when you are through feeding him?"

I turned Henry on his stomach across my lap and began to powder his back. "I won't go today, Philip," I said, as if we had never discussed the matter. "I like to be with this little rascal some, and I've been out so many days with Miss Stockbridge."

"I don't think you should miss church, Bentley. You have not been in a long time. It doesn't look well."

I slid a shirt over the baby's head. "Look? Does one go to church for looks?" I bent over to pick up a safety pin that had fallen on the floor. Philip and Miss Kate might go for looks. They had to be seen doing the right thing. It was part of their everlasting front before the world. But must I too?

"For Henry's sake, Bentley, I think you should make the effort."

I looked down at the baby, wriggling happily in my lap. "He doesn't know the difference."

"What difference?" Philip asked with sharpness.

179

"Whether I go to church or not, of course."

Philip crossed to the window and stood there looking out while I finished dressing the baby. "Well," he said at last, "I suppose, while he's so small——" Then he went out.

Looking after him, I thought that his shoulders drooped, that his step was discouraged. Poor Philip! I thought with a quick stirring of sympathy; he has to consider always how things look. He has to keep up in every small detail the front of impeccable conduct before the world. No wonder he is short-tempered and difficult, living under this continual strain. Holding the baby tight against me I whispered, "I'll have to do better, darling. I'll have to make it up to him somehow, and to you, too, little one. I must work out some sort of life for you both, for us all."

The resolution comforted me. I went to the kitchen and made sweet-potato pies for dinner, Philip's favorite dessert. Then I sat with his mother for a while, though that always depressed me. For she had never again spoken to me as she did that first night. She just sat looking out the barred window.

When Philip and Miss Kate came back from church I was on the gallery to welcome them. At dinner I kept Miss Stockbridge talking of her travels, and Philip for once relaxed his disapproval and seemed to become interested. I felt cheered. If I worked hard enough at it, I might be able to make Philip happy in spite of everything. When he went out in the sunny bright afternoon to look over the fields and plan the next week's work, I went with him as I had not done in a long time. I questioned him about the crop in this field, admired the cover crop in that one, and asked how the new hand was doing, the one he had hired in place of Anse.

That night I went to my room right after dinner. As I moved the lamp to the marble-top table at the head of my bed, I thought it had been a good day and now I would take my reward. Now I would get into bed and read Jeff's book. I brushed my hair forty strokes and put on my best nightgown, the yellow silky one, remembering that Jeff had once said he liked me in yellow and that there was a brightness in my hair, and in me. I put a match to the fire that was ready laid, for the evenings were still cool.

Then I plumped up the pillows and settled down with the book. Jeff's name was on the inside. My fingers moved across the bold strokes of his pen and I noted the date—a new book, one he must have just bought.

My eyes went over the first page, but I was still thinking about Jeff. I had to put him out of my mind with conscious effort. I must not be thinking of him, remembering that brief moment at his gate in the rain. I had my life here, apart from him, and I must make out with it somehow. Just how, I did not know, but today had given me a clue. I began again at the top of the page and gave my attention to my reading.

I was just beginning to get interested in it when Philip came. He often did, to get another suit from the wardrobe or a shirt from his drawer in the bureau, for he still kept most of his clothes here, there being no proper closet in his room on the basement floor. I laid my book down open on the bed beside me and watched him as he stood before the wardrobe, his brown dressing gown belted neatly around his trim waist. How well built he was, I thought, as I so often had. Yet now I saw him with detachment. I looked at his firm shoulders and had no wish to slide my hands across them. I only thought how trim he had kept his figure and that it was perhaps the crew rowing he had had at college that had given him those good shoulders. Perhaps the overtraining was what had given him that slight heart weakness, too.

I watched him take out his gray spring suit and close the door of the wardrobe, turning the key so it would not swing open again. But he did not say good night and go out. He laid the suit over a chair by the door and came toward me. I moved one arm so that it lay across my book. With the other hand I drew the covers higher across my breast. He stood beside the bed looking down at me, his eyes dark and intent. Could he see why I wore the yellow gown? Could he see that it was not for him that I had brushed my hair? So often he had seen what was not. But now the thing he feared was closer than it had ever been before, and how blind he was!

For he only said, "You are very lovely tonight." His voice was low and gentle, the voice he kept for me alone. He lifted one hand and pushed the hair from my forehead, holding it back, studying me.

But he could see only the surface, I thought, no matter how deep he seemed to probe. Had he never seen anything more? Was that why, searching me with this same look, he had found me often guilty when I was innocent? He let his fingers move over my hair, stroking it away from my forehead. It was a familiar gesture and it brought back other times with overpowering vividness. For as in anger one may remember former grievances and hurts that multiply and feed it, so the more tender moment gathers power from the memory of other such times. Something woke in my heart, though it was but the ghost of what had been there, a ghost wrapped in pity and sadness.

He bent lower and his voice was only a whisper. "Have you missed me?"

I drew in my breath sharply. God, but it was I who had been blind! All day I had only meant to cheer him, I had only tried to be kind. I had not meant . . . I had not wanted . . .

The quick movement of my body—or of his as he bent closer —displaced the book I had been reading. It slipped from the bed and fell, striking the bare floor with a sharp bang that made me cry out.

"Damn!" Philip said and stooped to pick it up. He was about to lay it on the table beside the bed when the title caught his eye. "Whose book is this?" he demanded.

"It belongs to Jeff Wheeling." The sound of his name spoken here and now was louder and more sudden than the fall of the book. Or was it only that it sounded so in my ears? As if I had cried out to him. I stiffened against the trembling that went through me. I made my voice low and indifferent. "He gave it to me when Miss Stockbridge and I saw him the other day."

Philip was scowling down at Jeff's name. "Just the sort of thing he would have. I might have known it." He turned on me with swift fury. "And I find you reading it! My wife! I won't have you reading anything belonging to that fellow—a radical, a trouble-

182

maker, probably a Communist." His voice had sharpened, his face was dark and angry.

I looked back at him coldly, without flinching. Some new power was building up within me, so that he could move me no more. He was angry with me and I was not afraid. I did not any longer care. And because I did not care I could speak quietly. "But, Philip," I said, "it is only a book. Anyone may read a book."

"You don't know anything about it. They are fellow travelers if not worse, he and Miss Stockbridge. I wish you had never brought that woman to Cedar Bluff. It was your idea." He began to stride back and forth on the rug before the fire.

"The money has been useful," I reminded him.

Philip was not listening. He was holding the book in one hand, tapping it with an angry finger. "Don't you know who this writer is? Don't you know how he libels the South, stirs up trouble continually with his lies and exaggerations? A Negro who claims to be proud he is one. I won't have this book in my house." He flung it into the fire, scattering ashes over the hearth. Then he whirled on his heel, caught up the gray suit and left the room.

I lay motionless against the pillows, making no move to rescue the book that was smoldering among the embers. I watched it blaze up and burn merrily. I could buy another copy for Jeff and read it before I gave it to him, if I liked. I was not concerned about that. I was intent on a new idea, a new feeling. "I am free of Philip now," I said aloud to the leaping flames. "I cannot be hurt any more. I don't care any more. He cannot make me do anything I do not want to do, or leave off doing what I wish." It was a bitter hard sort of freedom, but I would treasure it, hold it fast. We always have to make do with whatever life has brought us. This had come to me in place of love, and I would make the most of it.

After a while I blew out the lamp and watched the long shadows of the bedposts shift against the wall as the fire sank or flared. But I could not sleep. I got up and looked at my watch. No wonder, I thought. It was still so early. Besides there was too much stirring and throbbing in my mind. At last, more restless and wide-awake than ever, I rose and dressed. I would go out to look at the river, I would walk along the bluff till I was tired beyond thought.

I went through the nursery, stopping to listen to Henry's quiet breathing, then I went on through his door to the ell porch. I stood by the railing, looking down into the black courtyard. The moon was frosting over the tops of the cedars, throwing long shadows. The river would be bright beyond the shelter of the bluff. As I moved noiselessly toward the stairs, I heard a whispering step below me somewhere. I stood, not frightened, only alert and puzzled. Then I thought of Callie and felt the door of Philip's mother's room. The bar was up. I swung the door open and looked in. Moonlight was coming through the eastern window and I could see that Callie's cot bed was empty. From the big bed came the sound of gentle regular breathing. Callie had slipped out—to meet Anse, perhaps. I closed the door and went quickly down the stair, across the ell porch and down into the black courtyard. I was moving between the azaleas when a sound stopped me, a creaking hinge. Was it the door to Philip's room? I stood motionless, my hands pressed tight against my breast.

Then I heard Philip's voice, impatient, petulant. "You've been a long time coming."

Callie giggled. "Thought she'd never get to sleep." The door creaked shut.

I stood frozen. Philip. Callie. I ran, stumbling across the uneven bricks of the courtyard, out under the cedars and past the chicken houses, by the uneven rows of the plowed kitchen garden. Anywhere, anywhere, to get away from that house. I ran, I fell sprawling, and I ran again. I crossed the gravel road and went on into the deep woods.

I paid no heed to darkness or to danger. I did not remember Philip saying, "Don't go out of call. No white woman goes alone in the dark." I had no thought of that or of the rattlers I might tread on in the night. I went like one possessed, my mind racing back, a shaft of light, picking out the things I had seen without seeing, heard without understanding—Callie's manner to me, that dirty satin slipper under Philip's bed, his words to Miss Kate

184

about Anse, "He's been a source of annoyance to me for a long time." I saw it now, Philip hating all Negroes because they reminded him of what he would prefer to forget, but for Anse having a special hatred. "Don't come on this place after dark." What he had meant was "Keep away from Callie." Oh, how blind, how stupidly blind I had been! This was no new thing, just come about. There was no telling how long——

I stopped, breathless, to lean against a tree trunk, all these things crowding in on me while Philip's voice kept on sounding in my ears like a bell that has started ringing and cannot stop: "You've been a long time coming, a long time coming." And only tonight, a little earlier, if it had not been for Jeff's book—— I shivered and clung to the tree while nausea swept through me. "A long time coming"—his voice fretful, unsurprised, expectant. Only tonight I had thought I was free, I had been secure and proud in my new indifference, armored against hurt. But marriage went too deep, it was too much a part of one, it had access to one's most secret and vulnerable self.

In the night silence around me I heard the small silken rustle of some wild thing, and I wished that I too could go into darkness and hiding and never come out. I pressed my forehead against the rough tree bark and wished that I could burrow into it and be closed up forever.

· 20 ·

How long I wandered through the woods, I do not know. It was not until I paused at the edge of a small clearing that I became aware for the first time that I was in a strange place, that I had come far and that the moon was now high in the heavens. I remembered nothing of how I had come except that I had crossed the field and the road.

The trees here stood in a circle, holding in an open space like a bowl to catch the still light of the moon. From the center rose a single stark chimney that lifted a barren grate, reminder of the fire that had once burned brightly there, warming hearth and home. But the fire had played false, it had consumed rafter, room and floor, it had left the chimney bereft and cold.

Suddenly, in the shadows under the trees, a darker shadow moving caught my eye. I stood motionless, unafraid, not even wondering what would happen now. I was numb with too much happening. A man was there. A man was coming toward me. His voice was familiar—and so were the words, "Shore took a long time comin', Callie."

They rang through my head like an echo—took your time . . . a long time comin' . . . Philip, Anse, both of them. Comprehension struck me silly. Oh, that was a good one, that was the funniest thing I ever heard! I began to laugh and the sound burst out harshly on still woods, dead chimney, the cold moon.

Anse came quickly to me. "For Gawd's sake, Callie——" He put out one hand, then fell back with a gasp.

That sobered me. "It's not Callie, Anse." I jerked the words out. "It is Anse, isn't it?"

"Y-yas'm." His darkness merged with the darkness of the trees.

"You—" my voice rose, the words shaken from me, bitter and

186

insistent—"you know why——" I waited, choking, for his answer.

It came faintly, from a distance, like an anguished, dying echo: "Yas'm."

For a moment I saw him between the tree trunks, caught in a shaft of moonlight that set him up like a black cutout, faceless, his long arms uplifted, fists clenched. I moved forward, my eyes on him. I stumbled and fell, crying out as I went down, my head striking something hard. I came out of blankness, hearing Anse. "Gawdsake, Miss Bent! Is you hurt?"

I tried to move, and sky and trees went spinning. "What . . . what did I do?" All my body was bruised and the side of my head felt broken.

"You done fell on the old cave-in, top of the well."

"Bricks . . . hit my head." I felt around me, lifted a hand. "Help me up, Anse."

He caught hold and pulled, but the bricks were uneven under my feet, and with my dizziness too I would have fallen but for him to cling to. "Got to git you out of this mess of bricks," he mumbled, apology in his tone. Half lifting, half dragging me along, he stood me upright on solid ground.

"Steady me a minute more, Anse. I'm dizzy."

At that instant bright, blinding light struck us, like a spotlight on a stage. I was turned partly away, but it fell full on Anse's yellow face. I saw his eyes widen, showing a circle of white around the dark center. His mouth fell open and his breath came hoarsely. "Gawd, lemme go, please, ma'am." I felt him tremble under my hands, slipping from me.

The lights swept from us, across the circle of trees and back to a gravel road again as the car rounded a curve and went on. "It's only a car, Anse," I said. "There's a road. What's the matter?"

His words came in anguished gasps. "They seen me. I'se just holtin' you. I wa'n't doin' nothin', Miss Bent. But they seen me . . . mought be comin' back . . . git me. Is you all right?" He was backing from me into the shadows, bent over in terror. "I wouldn't hurt no white lady, 'fore Gawd I wouldn't!" His voice was a whine, high and trembling.

187

"Of course you wouldn't, Anse," I cried. "Don't——" But his terror went through me, a shiver of evil, and I choked on the word.

"Git on home, Miss Bent. Hadn't ought to——"

"But which way? Where am I?"

His voice came from among the trees now, with a going-away sound, quavery and breathless. "Don't take the gravel. . . . Other way, ma'am, by the colored church. . . . Gawdsakes, hurry!"

I stood a moment, frozen, caught in the contagion of his fear. Then I came to myself. Nonsense to be afraid. If they came back I would just tell them what had happened. But would they believe me—a white woman alone in the night, a Negro with his arms around me? Of course they would have to believe me. I gave myself a shake. Anse, poor, ignorant Anse, was frightened. It was ridiculous for me to be disturbed, save with pity for him, for his fear, for his anguish over Callie.

Callie? For a moment I had forgotten. Philip . . . Callie. It came over me again, and yet with a difference. There was something between now, a small air space. For the pressure of loss, of disaster or hurt, is lightened by any small happening that sets it away from us, even for a moment. So bit by bit the unbearable can be borne.

I went away from the road as Anse had told me. I knew I must go home. Henry was there. I must go back to him. I walked slowly, my head throbbing with the blow, the bitter thoughts. Callie, a Negro girl. Negro? She was as white as Philip, or almost. Wasn't she? O God, it was all horrible, hopeless, sickening. As I went on through the dark woods, more open now and easier for walking, suddenly I lifted my head to listen. There was a sound of voices singing; there was a light between the trees ahead. Mellow and sweet the song came, like something out of another world. One high soprano rose above the rest, clear and pure:

"Shall we gather at the river,
Where bright angel-feet have trod;
With its crystal tide forever
Flowing by the throne of God?"

188

In mighty volume rose the answer:

> "Yes, we'll gather at the river,
> The beautiful, the beautiful river . . .
> That flows by the throne of God."

It was not the words, it was a quality in the voices that drew me, a longing and a hope above race and color, belonging to all lost and wandering human beings, a poignant, universal despair running through the joyful texture of the song. Like someone under a spell I went slowly toward the length of yellow light that lay along the beaten dirt path. I went up the single step and stood in the door.

Against the walls open oil lamps flared in the night breeze, their smoke a cloud above dark heads. An old woman, alone on the back seat, rose and came toward me. "Yes, we shall gather at the river," she sang with the rest, one black hand making a gesture of welcome, offering me her place. Why not? Wasn't I human too, lost and cast out and seeking? I took two steps and sank down on the hard board bench, leaning my back against the wall. I was in shadow here, alone. I was like the bleak, stripped chimney in an empty space with the sound of singing pure as moonlight pouring over me. No one turned, no one had seen. Only the old woman, and now she was merged with the others, lost among them.

The service went on, the preacher's rich voice filling the room. My ears were stopped to the meaning of his words. I heard without hearing, and only afterward it came back to me, brokenly. "I like it, what it say here. . . . Let the enemy rage. God will make a way somehow. . . . You know what it mean? Mean you don't have to worry about no hows and whys. . . . Now you say, Why do the righteous suffer? You feel it don't pay to be good. . . . There was a woman come to my door, say, 'Closer I gets to God, looks like the more I got to bear. . . .' But I tell you the righteous and the onrighteous, they both suffer, the bond and the free, the just and the unjust. . . . I almost gave over. . . . My foot almost slipped. . . . But I rested in the Lord and my strength took on wings like the morning."

That phrase kept sounding in my mind as if spoken again and again by someone walking from me in a vast echoing hall: "wings like the morning, wings like the morning."

The singing began again, but was muted now so that the preacher's voice could rise above and prevail over it.

"Oh, sometimes the shadows are deep,"

they sang;

> "And rough seems the path to the goal,
> And sorrows, sometimes how they sweep
> Like tempests down over the soul."

"Come one, come all," the preacher pleaded. "That's right, sister. That's right, brother. Come to the mourners' bench."

> "Oh, then, to the Rock let me fly,
> To the Rock that is higher than I. . . ."

"Yes, Lord, come to the Rock. Down on your knees, confess your sins and praise the Lord."

A movement went over the congregation, like wind in the pines. They were bowed low now, all the dark heads. I leaned over, resting my forehead on the back of the seat before me.

> "Oh, sometimes how long seems the day,
> And sometimes how weary the feet . . ."

Voice and song, antiphonal, mounting, one striving with the other, beat out a rhythm, hypnotic, soothing. "Rise, brother, and the Lord bless you, brother. Rise, sister, go in peace."

"Rise, sister, go in peace." The words came as if spoken for me. I got up and stole out into the night, eased, I knew not how.

The moon was high, a lopsided, waning moon to light my way. I went by the road, knowing the turns, a silver road edged with black-lace shadows. My body was weary, my feet dragged. It was not till I was almost at the plantation gate that I heard the step behind me. I knew then that I had been hearing it for a long time, slowing and quickening as I changed my pace. At the gate, lifting the chain, I looked back and saw a lean black shape behind a sassafras bush, silver with new leaves. "Minerva?" I said.

She came on now, followed me through the gate, put the chain around again. "You all right, Miss Bent?"

"I'm all right."

She grunted, took a step away on the path that would take her across the field to her cabin. Then she said, almost too low for hearing, "Miss Bent, we's all God's chillen."

I said, "Thank you, Minerva," and went on by the plantation road, seeing the house loom up far ahead, dark and still and shut in by the secret cedars.

· 21 ·

OUTWARDLY, in the days that followed, there was little difference in our lives. I drove with Miss Stockbridge in the mornings, and if she found me silent and unresponsive, she made no comment. If she saw that I came alive only when we stopped at the school and Jeff came out to speak to us, if she saw that my eyes lingered on his house as we drove by, for once she held her tongue. Philip perhaps thought me sulking over his throwing Jeff's book into the fire. I paid no heed to what he thought. I tended the baby as usual and saw with satisfaction that he was growing and developing as he should, yet even that touched me only superficially. As I had once tried to escape into a blankness of mind, into a withdrawal from all reality, so now I fled into a dream.

Almost every afternoon I met Jeff at the sand bar. In his dugout we explored the island down the river; we went far into the deep swamp to places which had known no human being since Indian days; we went inland by ways made newly navigable by the high waters of spring. The rest of my waking hours I was remembering just how he swung the paddle and the manner in which his hands held it, I was seeing the quick changes in his face as he talked, I was thinking of how the light came into his eyes when he smiled, I was feeling again the firm clasp of his hand as he helped me in or out of the dugout.

No longer did I chide myself for having him too much in my thoughts. No more did I struggle to put him from my mind. Why should I? I needed someone to think about. I needed to know that someone liked me. Did this new freedom of thought and feeling arise out of something as small as spite, a desire to get back at Philip? I do not like to think so. Yet if one is honest, one must see that all human motives and feelings are infinitely complex, and that even the purest is a combination of many emotions.

I only know that I had a great hunger for companionship. I

192

had a terrible need of comfort and reassurance such as I found in him, for he alone could make me relax and laugh and be my natural self. Was it wicked of me to turn to him so? Is it a sin for a plant to climb toward the sun? In our relationship there seemed to be only a friendly ease and pleasure, simple, uncomplicated. If Jeff felt any change in me, if he wondered at the open eagerness with which I came to meet him, he gave no sign and took no advantage of it.

It must have been a kind of madness that was upon me then, reckless of consequence. Perhaps love is always a madness in which all else is unimportant, disregarded, so that one moves in the midst of it unmindful of danger or of the day of awakening. I was even blind to the forces that were growing underneath Jeff's casual-seeming friendship, and when, like some underground stream released from pressure, they broke through at last in a mighty torrent, I was taken unaware.

We had been deep into the swamp where gray moss hung down as delicate as rain arrested in mid-air, where day was muted and a leafy twilight was on the afternoon. We came down the bayou and upstream to the sandbank to find the sky red with sunset and river red as sky. "You will be late," Jeff said, nosing the dugout in, springing ashore and holding out his hand to help me.

"That doesn't matter any more."

There was something in my voice, some finality or indifference that told more than the words. He did not let go my hand but drew me nearer. "You must tell me what you mean." Then when I was silent still, he added, "Haven't I the right to know?" He must have read the answer in my face.

Even as he took me in his arms my eyes were opened to what I had done in my selfishness. Even in the mad release, the warm delight of his lips on mine, even then remorse and bitterness came stinging sharp, like the aftertaste of the wild red grape. I drew away, holding him from me, my head turned away in shame. Why had I not thought of him? He would be hurt now. I . . . I was calloused, toughened against it, but he—— Oh, was there no loving without hurt? Was there no pure essence of love unpoisoned by pain and heartbreak?

193

"Tell me," he said and his voice went through me like the deep, stirring sound of a bell. "Why do you turn away?"

"I've done wrong to let you—just because of my need—to let you——"

"You couldn't have stopped me from loving you, Bentley. Not since that first day when I found you lying on the sand."

I looked up at him then. Was it true that I had not driven him into love, or beguiled him to it? Had it just come, like the rain or the flood or the sun in the morning? He must have sensed the easing in me, the swift yielding as he took me again in his arms. And now the sun that had fired the sky and turned the river blood-red had no fiercer flame than that which swept through me.

Is it just an illusion, the conviction that all one's life has been lived in order that this moment may be? That the years have been but the long, low hollow of a wave, gathering strength and piling up to break at last in splendor? Perhaps it is only on looking back after the lapse of time and event that one may see clearly and know whether this was a brief spark in the night or the rising sun of a lifelong day. No matter how it then appears in that after-knowledge, the wonder and exaltation of the moment cannot be diminished. For always to discover that another shares the love and longing one has cherished in secret is to escape, however briefly, from that great loneliness in which all human beings live.

When I left Jeff in the gray of evening, the earth filling up with first dark and only the river holding light, we had spoken just a few broken phrases. But the warmth of his love went with me along the familiar path, and, like one who moves under a spell, I came into the shadow of the cedars.

I had never stayed out so late. Minerva was serving dinner, and a quick glance at Philip, as he rose to place my chair, told me that he had been both worried and annoyed. "I was about to go out and look for you, Bentley," he said.

"There was a beautiful sunset." I did not meet his eyes. I wondered if all I had felt was written on my face for him to read.

"The sun has been down for nearly an hour."

"There was an afterglow."

194

"Yes, quite lovely. I saw it from my window," Miss Stockbridge said.

But Philip went on as if neither of us had spoken: "I mention this on your account, Miss Stockbridge, as well as Bentley's. As a Northerner you do not realize, and Bentley seems to disregard it too often, that it is not safe in this part of the country for a white woman to be out alone after dark."

"Ah," Miss Stockbridge said with satisfaction, "the psychopathic bugaboo of the region. Pray continue." She regarded Philip with her bright, speculative gaze.

"Call it what you will, the danger is not imaginary. Here we have a large population of ignorant, irresponsible Negroes. The majority, I admit, are harmless, but there are occasional vicious individuals whose criminal tendencies are unrestrained by the veneer of civilization which some of their race have acquired."

"Well," said Miss Stockbridge, cutting a bite of pork roast and eying it with relish, "I have no fear of man or beast and I certainly do not mean to be frightened by the local rape myth. Um, delicious meat!"

Miss Kate had let out a little gasp, and I saw with surprise that Philip seemed to be less angry than contemptuous, as if he were thinking what a fool this woman was. "This is no myth, Miss Stockbridge. I had not meant to mention it because I did not want to alarm any of you unnecessarily, but I see that I shall have to. In this very neighborhood just recently there has been a shocking . . . er . . . incident."

"Why, what do you mean, Philippe? I have heard of nothing."

"It is not generally known, Aunt Kate. The people involved have not been identified yet as the details are rather vague. But——"

"I believe the details are usually vague in these cases, are they not?" Miss Stockbridge murmured.

Philip gave her an annoyed glance. "The facts are clear enough. Our neighbor across the road tells me that a friend of his was driving home late at night and his headlights showed up a couple in the woods. A Negro man with a white woman."

I caught my breath and felt the blood drain from my face. That car—Anse and me—I had not thought of it again. "God!" I whispered.

Philip nodded his satisfaction. "That shows you, Bentley, how real this danger is. Until the man is caught——"

"But, Mr. Churston," Miss Stockbridge cried, "how could a person in a car at night, driving fast no doubt, perhaps drunk, be sure of anything, much less of identifying——"

"He was not drunk," Philip said. "There is a sharp curve in the road at that point, and you may have observed, Miss Stockbridge, that in such circumstances the headlights are thrown off the road to light up the adjacent woods with great vividness. No, there was no mistake, I regret to say. It was definitely a white woman, and the Negro will be identified sooner or later."

Miss Kate cried, "Oh, dear me, what a terrible thing! Why didn't this man stop the car and do something about it, save her?"

"He did, of course, Aunt Kate. As soon as it was possible. He was going rather fast and I know the stretch he means—there is no place to turn around for half a mile or more."

"There," Miss Stockbridge said with satisfaction, "he himself admits that he was going fast. Did he find anything when he did go back?"

"Of course not," Philip said. "The fiend had escaped."

"And the white woman?" Miss Stockbridge persisted.

"She was gone, too. But we have not heard the last of this, I assure you," Philip said and added with satisfaction, "So you see that I am not inventing a mythical danger to frighten you in before dark."

I sat with bowed head, my heart pounding furiously. What could I do? What could I say? What would Philip think if I told the truth about it? Would he believe Anse innocent? Would anyone believe it? No, better to keep still and hope that Anse would never be identified.

"Very interesting indeed," Miss Stockbridge said and continued her dinner now with unabated relish.

I tried to eat but I could not swallow. Even Miss Kate noticed it. "Dear me—" she sighed—"I wish the lock on the front door was more secure. I suppose it is best to know about these terrible things, but see, Philippe, Bentley is too upset to eat."

"I . . . I have a headache," I said. "If you will excuse me——" I got up and left the room, hearing Philip as I left, hearing him say that it was a good thing for me to take it seriously. Conditions were bad and rapidly getting worse in this part of the country.

In my room I walked back and forth trying to think what I could do, deciding in the end that there was nothing. Not for a long while was I able to put aside my fears for Anse and think again of Jeff. But I could not go back under the spell which had been on me. My own life and its realities had intervened.

It was the next morning at breakfast that Miss Stockbridge spoke for the first time of her plans. She had about finished writing up her field work now, she said, and must be leaving soon. She wanted first to go to Natchez to see some of the old houses and then to New Orleans. She would keep her room, come back here to pack and take final leave.

Philip, perhaps thinking of her weekly check, said, "We shall miss you, Miss Stockbridge. And if you want to come back another winter——"

"I never repeat, thank you. One cannot, at my time of life. But it has been an enlightening experience and I am grateful. You have all been most co-operative."

"I'd certainly like to read your paper, your book or whatever it is," Miss Kate said. "You're so clever to write it."

"My thesis. But no, I'm not clever in the real sense, only persistent." Her eyes lighted up as they did when she was contemplating some deviltry. "Since I don't plan to return, maybe I will send you a copy."

Later, as we were jogging down the plantation road, she suddenly let out her high, sharp cackle, startling Ergo into a trot.

"What is it?" I asked.

"Just imagine Miss Churston reading my thesis! I wouldn't dare come back."

"Have you been so hard on us?" I asked, not smiling. For always when she began to look at us as specimens, as examples of this or that attitude, I fell into a defensive stiffness.

"I have not spared the indifference, the blindness, the prejudice that I have met with. I have told the truth as I see it—no one could do less. Miss Churston will not like that, nor your husband either. By the way—" she turned on me with the quick pouncing movement that always caught me off guard—"by the way; I'm an old woman and not used to beating about the bush so I'll come right out with it. How much longer do you propose to continue this sort of life?"

I caught my breath. Then I hedged. "Wh-what sort of life?"

"Now don't be proud and stupid. I have eyes in my head and I'm no fool either. I know very well that you and he are estranged —quite hopelessly so, I should say. Also, I know how things are with you and Jeff. Life's too short to keep on like this. Don't you know that?" She pulled up Ergo with a loud "Whoa there!"

I got out to open the gate, saying, "There's nothing I can do."

"Nothing you can do!" Miss Stockbridge snorted, as I climbed in beside her. She slapped Ergo viciously with the reins. "What nonsense, what utter damn nonsense! You can divorce your husband and marry Jeff and lead a reasonable, happy life."

I stared straight before me, my lips tight set.

"Now don't get huffy. Honestly, when I see how people mess up their lives, the only lives they've got——"

"Miss Stockbridge, there are reasons why it is impossible. One is my child."

"The devilish things that are laid onto an innocent child, the sacrifices, the . . . the tomfoolery! Really—" she gave me a severe glance—"you make me almost lose my temper."

I gave her a twisted smile. "You are an outsider, Miss Stockbridge. You could not possibly understand how I am bound——"

"Bound, my foot! And you needn't be so mysterious about it. I can guess your scruples, your incredible, emotional slavery to an outmoded idea. Slavery—that's rather good, the masters now the slaves. I must remember that." She turned on me. "I could always put two and two together."

"What do you mean?" Was she a devil seeing into everything?"

Miss Stockbridge laughed, then sobered abruptly and her voice for once was gentle, though crisp as always. "Wasn't it written plain on all your faces that morning at breakfast when I put the question about miscegenation? I thought Miss Churston would never speak to me again—except to order me out of the house—and as for your husband, if I were a man, I'd be swinging in the breeze from a cedar limb. And you white as a sheet—much as I dislike that trite expression!"

I stared at her openmouthed.

"I put the question on purpose, of course, to get the reaction. And did I get it!" She laughed. Then with a glance at my face, she added, "Sorry, but I just can't seem to take pure nonsense seriously. Matter of fact, I've always thought that most Southern families have Negro blood. That's why they're so touchy about the whole thing, and——"

"It's not true!" I cried. "They haven't. I don't know any other. Mine hasn't, and——"

"It has now," she said dryly.

I covered my face with my hands.

"There you go, making a mountain out of a molehill as usual. Don't you see it doesn't make the least difference in the world? It's only this stupid feeling about it."

I let my hands fall to my lap and drew a long breath. "I reckon there is nobody else in the world that thinks the way you do."

"Nonsense. There are many parts of the world where such things are taken as a matter of course. Even in some parts of this country, there is no stigma. How utterly provincial this great tragic attitude is!"

"But how can it help us here that people feel differently else-where? If they do."

"Well, it ought to make you think twice before you make a mess of your life. You could do any number of things—move out of this part of the country, for instance. Though Jeff would think that cowardly. He believes——"

"Jeff!" I cried. "You haven't talked——"

Miss Stockbridge gave me a disgusted glance. "Do you think I go around talking about what I learn when I am a guest—of a sort—in anyone's home?"

"I hope not. But in your thesis——"

"That's a very different matter. Oh, I name no names, of course. I change the nonessentials so there's no identifying people."

We drove in silence for a little, the only sound the creak of the carriage and the sound of old Ergo's hoofs in the gravel. I felt outraged and exposed, and yet it had done me good to hear it spoken out—what had never been spoken before. And then I thought that there might not ever be anyone again to whom I could speak. "Miss Stockbridge," I said, my voice barely audible above the noise of the carriage, "the one thing I can't see my way around is this: I cannot let Jeff bear my problem—my child's. I can't let him get involved with . . . with unhappiness and fear, such as this has already caused."

Miss Stockbridge gave a loud sniff. "He's involved with anything that concerns you, willy-nilly, and there's no getting away from it."

How simple it all seemed to her! But she was wrong. She came from the outside; she was not involved. She did not know how deep the feeling was in the South, or how dark and terrible the burden of such knowledge as I had. I could never share it with Jeff. I loved him too much to be willing to let him suffer under it. "It's hopeless," I said. "There's no way——"

"Change it, then!" she snapped. "Start with yourself. This is an age of transition. That's why it's so uncomfortable. Anything can change these days."

"Not in time to help me—or my child."

"Then hurry it up, for heaven's sake! Do something. That's what I keep telling Jeff. That's what all our arguments are about. He holds back, waiting for a natural development, as he says. Oh, I get so cross with him sometimes, I could—I could spit." She pulled Ergo up sharply. "There, see? I almost went past the house where I must stop, just because you are so stupid!" She gave me the reins and went scrambling up the road bank to knock at a cabin door.

200

She stayed a long time, but I was glad to sit alone. At last I was facing things as they were. I had to gather courage for what I knew I must do.

I did not go to the river that day. I worked about the house and wheeled the baby under the cedars. All the while, and far into the night, I wrestled with my resolution, rebelling against it, trying to see some way out, some other way than the hard one. There was none. Bleakly my life arranged itself before me, fixed and inescapable as a picture hung on the wall. Yet as I looked at it, another picture, the bright impossible one, was superimposed on it. Two exposures on one negative in crazy juxtaposition.

The next morning Miss Stockbridge said she would not need the carriage. She would finish typing her notes, and this afternoon she would walk wherever she wanted to go. "I need the exercise," she said. "All this good food. Can't let my figure go entirely. At my age all a woman has left to hang onto is her figure."

As I helped Minerva with the window washing, for Miss Kate had set her to spring housecleaning—today, of all days—I could hear the busy tapping of Miss Stockbridge's typewriter. I envied her the sureness with which she thought and worked, even when she was wrong. I wished I could be as detached as she, as uninvolved.

It was still early in the afternoon when I brought the baby down to the courtyard and called to Minerva through the kitchen window. "If I should be late, just roll him along when you go to milk Peggy," I said. "And tuck him in bed after his supper."

Minerva leaned out, resting her crossed arms on the window sill. Perhaps she saw the eager, the desperately eager light in my eyes, perhaps she knew why I went to the river. Perhaps she thought I had been too often. It was impossible to know what she thought. "Humph," she said, " 'lowed as how I'd set an' rest my back." She looked down at me, dark and unyielding.

"But he's asleep—good for two hours, and——" I moved closer to the window. "You've got to help me. Please, Minerva. I'll never ask you again. I . . . I'm not going walking by the river any more, not after today. Just this once."

Minerva said, "Reckon we can make out, him and me."

I turned and ran across the courtyard and out to the bluff, down the familiar path to the sand bar. It was early still. Jeff could not be there yet but I wanted to have a little time to think out exactly what I had to say, and to savor his coming. I lay on the sand in the shade of the green willow tree, looking up through the shifting leaves to the blue sky. It was like that first time. I rolled over and hid my face on my arm. So it was that Jeff found me when he came—the first time and the last, alike, making a circle, finishing the round.

I had thought it all out, I had planned what I would say, how I would begin, at once, before Jeff could speak or touch me, lest my resolution waver. But he took me by surprise, and once I was in his arms I could not think; I could only feel.

So I put it off and let myself dream a little while, and Jeff with me. We sat on the warm sand, leaning against the willow log, the water lapping at the shore, the sun going down beyond the green-gold other shore. Jeff said we should be practical now and arrange things. He said I might go with the baby to Fayette where his mother lived and stay there with her till everything was settled and the way was clear. It was cruel to let him go on. I must stop him, I must tell him. I took up a handful of sand and let it run through my fingers slowly, reluctantly, thinking that when it was all gone, I would stop him. But he was going too far and too quickly with his plans, making them too real and immediate. I clenched my fist and sat up, leaning forward so that his arm was no longer around me, facing him with resolution. "No, Jeff. It can't be like that." My voice was so low he had to bend nearer to hear me. "I shouldn't have let you go on planning. It was cruel of me, knowing all the time——" I choked.

"What do you mean, Bentley?" His eyes held mine, concerned, yet kind as always.

"Just this." I turned my head so my hair made a curtain for my face. "I cannot leave Cedar Bluff. I am bound forever. I have to go back now and not see you again—like this. I have to live out my life the way I have taken, without you."

Jeff sat silent till I lifted my head. He must have heard the

202

finality in my voice, and now he saw it in my face. He looked at me steadily for a long time, a terrible, anguished time. Then he leaned over and rested his head in his hands.

That was the worst moment. I reached out my hands. They almost touched his head. Then I drew them back. "I should have told you the minute I came, but I was weak. I wanted a little while, pretending it could be." My courage wavered when he turned his eyes on me, but I held his gaze without flinching.

"But you do love me?"

"Yes," I said with sadness, "I love you." It was the only time I spoke those words.

"Do you want to tell me why we cannot be together?" He was not demanding, just quietly asking. It moved me more than if he had raged and cried out against me.

His arm was behind me, along the willow log. I could lean back and lose myself. But I would not. "No. I cannot tell you." I was on my knees in the sand before him now and I spoke quickly, to finish, to be gone. "It has to end, here, now. Don't ask me to change. Now, right now, I must go." I stood up. "I must go—like this." I turned from him and ran, bowed over, letting the tears come. At the top of the bluff I had to look back. He was standing as I had so often left him, arms folded, his eyes holding me, drawing me back. I waited for a long moment, caught in the spell of his loving. Then I broke it deliberately and walked away.

At the foot of the steps that led up the bluff, I sat down on a stump, bent over, my head in my hands. I sat there a long time. Then I went to the water's edge and washed my face and let the evening breeze dry it as I climbed the bluff. Of long habit, my eyes went to the end of the gallery. The car was there. Philip was home. But it was not for him that I had left Jeff, hurt and bewildered. It was only for Henry that I could have done that.

203

· 22 ·

I CAME slowly through the dusk-filled hall to the library. Philip was not there, only Miss Kate at the window, her back to the room. The lamp was turned too high, the flame smoking one side of the chimney. Mechanically I moved across the carpeted floor to turn it down. Then I saw the pistol lying on the brown-covered table under the lamp, its mother-of-pearl handle opalescent in the light.

Miss Kate whirled around with a little startled scream. "Oh, Bentley, it's you. Oh, dear, oh, dear!"

"What's the matter? What's happened?" My lips were stiff. "Where's Philip?"

"Gone with Mr. Johnson. Philip had just driven in when Mr. Johnson drove up and they went right off. I begged him—" she pointed a small shaky finger at the pistol—" but he wouldn't and——"

I went to her swiftly. "What was it? Where did they go?"

Miss Kate shook her head. "These things . . . so terrible . . . all due to the Communists. I just don't know what we're coming to."

"But what——" I whirled around at a sound from the hall.

Miss Stockbridge stood in the doorway, her bright eyes missing nothing. "Well! Dinner ready? I'm starved. Had quite a walk." She crossed to the center table and Miss Kate let out a small scream as she picked up the pistol. "Ah," Miss Stockbridge said, breaking it open and peering into the barrel, "one of the early Smith and Wesson's. But it needs oil. Shame to let such a gun go rusty. What's this?" She took up a small brocaded purse.

"That's where I keep the bullets. But do be careful." Miss Kate was more breathless than usual. "I never load it. I——"

"Miss Kate," I broke in, "can't you tell me exactly what——"

She made a little gesture in Miss Stockbridge's direction with

204

a faint *sh-sh*-ing of her lips. Miss Stockbridge laid the gun down and gave Miss Kate her wickedest glance. "Well, aren't you going to tell me what the trouble is? Haven't I given you enough time to make up a likely tale in case you don't want me to know the truth?" She let out her high cackle. "Any fool could see there's something up."

"Never mind her, Miss Kate," I cried. "Just tell me, for God's sake, where did they go? What is going on?"

"By all means, out with it, my good woman! Out with it!" Miss Stockbridge said.

Even in her distress Miss Kate bristled at being called anybody's good woman. "I really know nothing about it. I didn't hear all Mr. Johnson said. The Johnsons, our neighbors across the road—" she turned to Miss Stockbridge—"good plain people, but one does not meet them socially. The grandfather was our overseer, and——"

"Miss Kate!" I broke in, for this was the sort of nonsense she could keep up all night long, and there was no telling what was happening this minute. I caught her by the arm. "Can't you for once just tell me what it's all about?"

"Well, it was at the overall factory. They caught him handing out pamphlets. You know he's been stirring up these meetings and——"

"Who?" My fingers dug into her flabby arm so that she cried out.

"Why, Anse, of course."

I let go her arm. It wasn't Jeff. What a fool I was! It couldn't have been Jeff. But Anse? Meetings? I turned on Miss Stockbridge. "You're back of this. You went to his cabin, to see how the meeting went. I heard you say so. I took you there. And now ——" I bit my lip. It wasn't just that Anse was arrested. He might be recognized, that man might see him, know——

"My dear child," Miss Stockbridge said, snapping off each word, "I had offered to give some play equipment to the Negro school and I went to ask what action the P.T.A. had taken. I didn't even know Mr. Vickers boarded there till I got there."

"Oh," I said blankly.

"Now, Miss Churston," Miss Stockbridge said with firmness, "I must insist that you tell me what has happened to Mr. Vickers."

"I told you," Miss Kate said, apparently not even noticing the *mister*. "They caught him handing out pamphlets at the overall factory. So they took him to jail and there's a lot of feeling about it and——"

"A mob?" Miss Stockbridge cried.

"I . . . I'm afraid so." Miss Kate sat down abruptly in her rocking chair. "I didn't want to tell her." She turned to me. "I knew she'd put it down in her notebook and make it sound awful and——"

I interrupted: "Is that the only reason they're after Anse? There must be something else. A mob wouldn't, just for that ——" My breath gave out.

Miss Kate nodded. "He was recognized; it was Anse, the one Philip told us about, in the woods. Oh, I never would have thought it! One of our own Negroes a viper in the bosom! Why, it might have been one of us—worse than murdered . . ." Her hands trembled on the arms of her chair.

"What utter nonsense!" Miss Stockbridge cried.

"Nonsense?" Miss Kate echoed. "He was seen, plain as day. He . . . he had her . . . in a . . . compromising position and——"

"What incredible Victorianism! Why can't you come right out and say it? There's a perfectly good word, Boston to the contrary."

But I was at Philip's desk, pawing through his papers. "The car keys, Miss Kate! Where are they? Philip always——"

"He didn't come into the house, dear. Oh, I'm so upset!"

Then maybe they were in the car. I started for the door. O God, let them be in the car! But Miss Kate somehow got there before me, blocking my way. "Bentley! What are you thinking of? You can't go!"

I thrust her aside and ran through the hall, down the front steps. I heard Miss Stockbridge tearing after me, calling "Wait, wait! I'm coming with you," and Miss Kate behind her, incoherent, exclamatory.

But I would not wait for anyone. If the keys were not in the car, I would run to the highway, hitchhike, get there somehow, stop them. I flung open the car door and felt for the keys. Yes, thank God!

While I was stepping on the starter, Miss Stockbridge climbed in and slammed the door. "Hurry, hurry, get it going!" The engine sputtered and died and while I struggled with it, swearing under my breath, I heard Miss Kate on the other side of the car, panting, puffing, expostulating, her voice a wail.

"But you can't—a white woman, on such a night! Oh, dear, it's not safe. Headstrong girl!" She thrust pistol and brocaded bag into Miss Stockbridge's hands. "If you will go, take this and defend your honor. Oh——"

Just then the engine caught and we were off, bouncing over the cedar roots, gathering speed. At the plantation gate Miss Stockbridge was out and running to open it before the car had come to a full stop. Once on the gravel road, I drove faster. Loose gravel flew up, striking the underside of the fenders. The lights flung a yellow, green-fringed carpet before us and the car ate it up faster and faster. All my attention was concentrated on getting to town as soon as possible. What I would do when I got there I did not know, but I would do something. Philip—I caught my breath in a sob—how could Philip be a part of this shameful, this horrible thing? But he hated Anse. That was why he had gone with Johnson, that must be why he could range himself on the side of a mob. I would find him, I would make him tell them—— But would he?

"Might be just as well to get there alive," Miss Stockbridge's dry voice informed me.

I brought the car back from the shoulder of the road. We were on the paved highway now. I passed one shabby rattling car, a truck, another, all going the same way. In town the main street was deserted. Saturday night and not a black face to be seen. By some grapevine underground whisper they knew and had taken cover. I turned to the right and came abruptly into sight of the courthouse square. My hands tightened on the wheel and I slowed the car. Flaming torches illuminated the scene. A crowd

207

milled about the open space within the hollow square formed by the live oak trees. Men stood in a close-packed group before the small barred building at one side.

There was no parking space left, for cars lined the curb, close-packed. I switched off my lights, swung into the driveway that led directly to the jail, then turning at once I came to a stop on the sidewalk between the parked cars and the outskirts of the milling crowd.

"G-good enough," Miss Stockbridge said and I thought I heard her teeth chattering. "What n-now?"

My eyes were searching the crowd. Where was Philip? I saw Johnson leading a small group through the crowd, pressing toward the steps of the jail. But Philip was not with him.

Miss Stockbridge's voice was for once quavery and uncertain. "I d-didn't realize—— Is there no way to . . . to stop it? The police, the National G-guard?"

"Stay here." I opened the car door softly and stepped out. Standing in its protection, shadowed by the hedge, I searched the flarelit faces. Where was Philip? My only hope was to find him. Once he knew the truth, despite his hatred of Anse, he would have to stop them. He could do it—if he would. Hadn't he stilled the panic at the munition plant when the explosion came? Hadn't he prevailed over a fear-mad mob then? He could do it again; I knew he could, if I could only find him, make him see—— I went into the fringe of the crowd, reckless now. They did not see me. All their attention was fixed on the door of the jail.

Miss Stockbridge came alongside me and I thrust her away, not turning. "But I c-could make a speech," she whispered. "I c-could——"

I gave her a quick glance. Her lips were trembling, her firm jaw was loose now and shaking. In that instant while she held my notice, I thought with savage spite, Now you're up against the real thing. Now you know you can't settle anything with a pencil and notebook.

"I c-can testify against them, anyway. At least I can do that. I never forget a face."

208

I turned away with a fierce "Hush!" What good would all the testimony in the world do Anse when this was over? I moved forward.

"Bust the door in!" a voice cried from the crowd. "Come on, boys, what you waiting for?"

Then someone spoke from behind the bars of the dark window beside the door of the jail. The voice rang out, firm and authoritative: "Stand back and I'll open the door. Stand away, I tell you."

"Philip!" I choked on the cry.

Johnson retreated a few paces, his gun ready. The mob moved back and then pressed close again. Slowly the door began to open. Philip's voice came again. "Stand away!"

The crowd stirred, swayed, waited, tense and cautious. One man shouted, "Bring him on. We've got you covered."

Another cried, "No tricks or we'll shoot."

Then Philip appeared in the doorway, his dark thin face lighted by the flaring torches in the courtyard. Behind him he dragged Anse. "Here he is, boys."

"No, no!" I cried out with all my strength but my voice was lost in the angry roar that came from a hundred throats. I ran to the car and snatched up the pistol, broke it and rammed in the shells, six of them, as I came back to Miss Stockbridge. "Listen!" I shouted in her ear above the clamor of the crowd. "When I shoot, yell your head off. The militia—say the militia's coming. Yell it out."

She nodded. "I can yell from here to Boston." I was thankful to see that she had got herself in hand again.

Philip was at the top of the steps now, his head lifted, his face set. Anse a cowering shadow behind him. The men surged forward, silent now, grim and purposeful. They surrounded the steps. "Wait!" There was such a ring of authority in his tone that even the men already starting up the steps held back. Philip looked the crowd over coolly. "Here's your man, and there's nobody to stop your taking him, so what's the rush?" He spoke in a quiet, an almost conversational tone, yet it carried across the courtyard, effortless, calming. There was not a sound now, only

209

the faint breeze stirring the live-oak leaves, only the crackle of flame as a torch flared brighter. My finger was tightening on the trigger.

"Of course," Philip added, his voice hardening, "of course before you take him, you must first kill me."

My smothered cry was lost in the gasp that came from the crowd. A sound like a rising wind went among them, a confused muttering. I shook away the swift proud tears. God, I should have known! He might hate Anse, but he was a Churston. The Churstons had always stood for law and justice. Oh, but the old judge, old Henry, he would have been proud of this moment, for all the alien blood that ran in Philip's veins! I stepped forward, my finger tightening again on the trigger. I would move in shooting when they rushed him. By God, some of them would fall before they touched him!

The men had recovered from their first shock now. One shouted from the rear, "Aw, cut it, Churston. You can't stop us and you know it."

"You bet he can't," another cried.

Philip's thin lip curled. "How could any one man, unarmed, stop you?" He leaned toward them, his dark face earnest now, his gaze steady and clear. "All I ask is a few minutes of your time. And the evening's young yet."

"Yeah, while the militia gets here," several cried. Others shouted impatiently, "Enough of this. Come on, boys, rush him."

I was in the shadow of the shrubbery close to a great live oak, the pistol steadied against the trunk, the bead on Johnson whose foot was on the bottom step. I was quite calm. I would take Johnson first, the man in the blue overalls next, and after him——

Philip lifted his hand. "I give you my word. No militia is coming. I am alone." He jerked a thumb in the direction of the dark jail behind him. "Unless you count the sheriff in there nailing himself up in the john."

There was a loud guffaw from somewhere on the other side of the courtyard. Laughter ran through the crowd, and there was at once an easing of tension, a new tolerance in the atmosphere. Johnson, grinning, spat a stream of brown tobacco juice on the step. "Well, speak up!" someone shouted. Other scattered voices rose.

"Whaddya want?"

"Get on with it!"

"Ain't got all night."

Philip said, "Even a condemned criminal is granted a few minutes to make his peace with man and God. Can't you do as much for me, an old friend and neighbor?"

There was an indistinguishable murmur from the crowd. "Some trick in it," someone said and gave an oath.

Another said, "Aw, what difference'll a few minutes make? Phil Churston's no liar. Go ahead, Churston. What's on your mind?"

Silence settled over the crowd. I kept my eyes on Philip's face, saw the faint triumphant twitch of his thin lips. Then his face relaxed into friendly, almost genial lines. Even his habitual reserve seemed to fall away, yet there was no diminution in his air of authority. O God, I thought, here is the real Philip, the one who should have been, taking his rightful place, commanding, unafraid.

He moved out on the small platform now, dragging Anse behind him. He came slowly down the steps, speaking as he came, his voice easy and cheerful, his words taking on a colloquial flavor, homely, intimate. "Well, boys, I appreciate this, I sure do. You know, we all got to die sometime, and far as I'm concerned this here is as good a time as another. But it's a funny thing, isn't it, Collins—" he nodded to a man in the group around him—"a funny thing. Reckon I've been as decent a fellow as most of the boys here tonight, and now I got to get filled full of buckshot all on account of this good-for-nothing nigger here." He gave Anse a jerk that brought him swaying to his feet. "Stand up, boy," he said roughly. "Take a walk—last one you'll get. Or me either. May as well enjoy it."

I held my breath, one hand still gripping the pistol, my eyes not moving from Philip's face. He was bent over Anse now, shaking him by the scruff of the neck. His lips were twisted, his nostrils flaring, dark eyes blazing. "Stand up, you goddam blasted

211

nigger! Act like a man for once in your life. You're a man if you are a damn nigger, aren't you, you——" He cursed him then with all the pent-up hatred in his heart, with such fury and venom that even the rough rednecks around him fell back, as if afraid of being scorched by his words.

Raising his head, Philip looked at the crowd for a moment as if he had forgotten that he and Anse were not alone. He laughed. "You can see I've got no love for him."

"Whyn't you hand him over, then?" a man shouted from the rear.

Philip's quick glance spotted him. "Just a minute, Wilcox. It's my turn now." Again he was easy in manner, reasonable, almost jovial. Slowly he strolled along, dragging Anse behind him, talking all the while. The crowd opened before him, fell away. He passed close to where I stood in the shadow. If he had turned his head he might have seen me there. But he did not look. He went on with his leisurely walk, addressing first one man then another, calling them by name.

"Look at this boy, will you, Jones? One of the laziest niggers ever born—and that's saying plenty. No real harm in him, when you come right down to it. Just a nigger. Can't really blame him for that, can you, Weaver? You remember him, don't you Linders? Used to drive that truck of yours till he went to sleep one day and ran into the side of the barn. Yes sir, Anse likes to sleep—and he's got sleep aplenty coming to him now, a good long sleep. But I reckon the Lord'll remember he didn't have much sense to start with and less chance to learn. Kind of unlucky, a fellow like that, eh, Withers?

"Say, Ellard, you know who this nigger is, don't you? His mother was Lizzie, used to work for your Aunt Emma. Made the best sweet-potato pies in the county. Remember the day Miss Em caught us in her watermelon patch, gave us hell—and half a pie? I bet this nigger's mother made that pie."

He walked slowly on, hauling Anse behind him, not once glancing at him. "Evening, Simpson," he said. "Seems to me Lizzie cooked for you for a while, didn't she? Funny thing, how come a good colored woman like Lizzie ever had such a child as

212

this Anse here. White or black, his pa must have been an ornery specimen."

Someone snickered knowingly. The man called Simpson moved back. There was a little parting of the crowd as he edged farther and farther away.

So Philip went on, making his leisurely circuit of the court-yard. And where he had passed, I saw with wonder there was a thinning of the crowd. Singly at first and then in groups of three four, without comment or explanation, without even exchanging a glance, they drifted away. First to the sidewalk, then to the street. One car started up and rolled away. Another followed.

By the time Philip was nearing the jail step again, there was but a handful of men standing there. They had a bewildered, uncomfortable air. But Philip did not seem to notice any change. He spoke to these men too, calling some of them by name. Then slowly he began to mount the steps, pulling Anse after him.

His back was to them now. I lifted the pistol, just to be ready. But these men, too, were scattering, disappearing in the shadows, hurrying as if they wanted to get away before he could speak again.

"An act of superb courage," Miss Stockbridge said.

I did not move. My eyes were fastened on Philip. He had done it. All alone, he had done it. And he knew he had triumphed. By the light of the single overhead bulb I could see it in the proud lift of his chin, the set of his shoulders as he stood there still holding Anse by the collar, looking over the empty courtyard.

Then abruptly he turned to Anse. "Was that you in the woods?"

"Yassuh, b-b-but——"

Philip's voice rose. "Don't I know, you fool nigger, she'd look white?" He flung Anse to the floor with a force that sent him head over heels. "Didn't I tell you to leave that girl alone? Get going now before I kill you. And if you ever come back——"

Anse kept on rolling, of his own volition now, striking the ground on all fours. Then he was running, curved over, a dark shadow streaking across the courtyard yard, making for the break in the hedge where Miss Stockbridge stood. Dodging, shying from her, he stumbled and fell. She got to him instantly, thrusting

something into his hand, whispering, "Here—money—take it!
Get a plane north. They'll never guess."

I heard the crackle of paper money, Anse's inarticulate murmur and then he was gone, lost in the shadows beyond. Philip—
I whirled around—Philip was standing as Anse had left him, only
bent over now, both hands pressed to his side, his body swaying,
his face twisted. For a moment so great was the change in him I
could not move.

And as I stood there, frozen, unable to grasp what was happening, a man came cautiously out of the jail door behind him.
"What'd you let him get away for, Churston. I was just fixin' to
come help you when—— Say, what's the matter?"

I got there as Philip sank down on the top step. "Oh, Philip!"
I cried.

The sheriff came quickly down the steps. "I better call the
doctor, Miz Churston. Looks like he's got a heart attack."

Philip straightened up then, his face distorted, white. "What
are you doing here, Bentley?"

Before I could answer he was bowed down again by pain. "Get
the doctor, quick!" I cried.

"No." Philip spoke between clenched teeth. "Help me up. I'll
go home. I've medicine there."

Together we got him into the front seat of the car. "He don't
look too good, Miz Churston," the sheriff said.

"I'm all right now, thanks." Philip leaned back with a sigh.

The sheriff opened the rear door for Miss Stockbridge and
would have helped her in but she was too quick for him. "You
need not trouble yourself, Sheriff." She bit off each word and
spat it at him. "You . . . you scum!" She slammed the door.

I swung the car out on the street and headed home. By the
faint light of the dash I could see Philip's set face. But he was
sitting erect now and his hand was not to his side.

We were out of town on the highway before anyone spoke.
Then Miss Stockbridge said, "Mr. Churston, I must say that I
have never seen anything more magnificent than your handling
of that mob."

Without turning, he said, "Not at all, Miss Stockbridge. As soon as I had won a few minutes, I knew I had them."

"But . . . but how could you know?"

"Simple enough. When you break a mob into individuals, it disintegrates. Give the victim a name and a place, no matter how lowly, in the community, and he is no longer an impersonal menace that must be destroyed."

Miss Stockbridge said, "I must put that down. In fact with your permission I would like to quote it verbatim in my thesis.

"Certainly, Miss Stockbridge."

I had to keep my eyes on the road but I glanced at Philip now and then. His face was drawn and pale, the lines deep around his mouth. Was he really all right now? He did not look it, and I knew very well that if he were himself he would insist on taking the wheel.

We were on the gravel road when Miss Stockbridge said, "I simply cannot understand it. I am so . . . so confused."

"What is bothering you?" Philip asked.

"Why, that you, a perfect reactionary if I ever saw one . . . that you would risk your life to save a Negro. It is unaccountable, it is inconsistent. Until tonight I saw everything so clearly. Now I . . . I just don't know what to say."

"I risked my life for the preservation of law and order, only incidentally for a Negro. There are plenty of people in this part of the country who would die for the preservation of our American ideals—and there have been plenty who have done it. But don't forget there are just as many willing to die for white supremacy. We don't propose to have Negroes ruling over us here. We simply will not take it."

"But that doesn't make sense, Mr. Churston. It's a contradiction, one of the other."

"Only in the copybooks are human beings perfectly consistent, Miss Stockbridge—and in the minds of the theorizers." Then he added sharply, "You're too close to the shoulder, Bentley."

I brought the car back in line and gave my attention to driving. Philip was always a nervous passenger on the rare occasions

215

when he let me drive, and I did not want to upset him in any way tonight.

"Of course," Miss Stockbridge went on, "I have heard, I have read of that attitude—you know, the Dixiecrats, the Talmadge-ites, the rebel yell, that sort of thing. But it seemed too ridiculous to be possible. Buffoonery, romantic play acting, in terms of America today. But now, after looking into those faces to-night——"

"That was no play acting." Philip's voice was grim. "That's where you Northern reformers make a sad mistake. Any emotion powerful enough to break out as it did tonight is something to be reckoned with, whether it is turned into mob violence or into political action."

"Well, I must say, it is most disturbing." She sighed. "I had my thesis so well planned, with all my facts and observations fit-ting neatly under my convictions. And now——"

"Perhaps," Philip said, "perhaps it might be more logical and scientific to draw your convictions from your facts." He gave a little chuckle.

At least I thought it was a chuckle till I saw from the corner of my eye that his hand was pressed to his side. We came through the plantation gate which we had left open as we went. I stopped the car, saying, "I'll close it." But Miss Stockbridge was already out of the car. I looked at Philip. "Are . . . are you all right?"

"Yes, yes," he said with impatience. "I'm just sleepy and tired of talk."

As we came past the pecan grove and drew near the house, I saw through the cedars that every room was lighted. Miss Kate was taking no chances of being raped in the dark. She met us at the top of the steps, her hands twisting together, her voice more breathless than ever. But she only said we'd missed our dinner, and oh, dear, she'd been so nervous about us.

Philip said, "I'm not hungry, thank you, Aunt Kate. I'm going to bed, if you will all excuse me." He went on through the hall.

"Well, frankly, I am starved," Miss Stockbridge said. "But aren't you even going to ask what happened, Miss Churston?"

"Well, I don't like to—such things are not fit for a lady's ears—but——"

I left them in the hall and overtook Philip at the head of the ell steps. "Are you sure you're all right, Philip?"

He turned and faced me then, the dining-room light falling full upon him. He nodded, not speaking. Then he waited, and I thought there was a question in his eyes.

"Philip," I began, and suddenly my eyes were stung with tears. "Philip, I can't tell you—— I was proud, terribly proud tonight."

His lean drawn face softened, the lines of pain faded, and he smiled. "Good night, Bentley . . . dear." Then he went on down into the darkness.

I think he said "dear." I hope he did. It would be a good thing to remember.

· 23 ·

WHEN I came down next morning I found Miss Kate on the ell porch, looking around in a distracted way. "Oh, it's you, Bentley. I can't think where old Humble can be. Do you suppose Philip forgot to let him out?"

"Philip never forgets," I said, looking across at the well platform where Humble always lay in the morning waiting for Philip to come in from his early morning walk to the fields. "But I'll look downstairs."

I went down the steps to the courtyard, whistling for Humble. Then I heard a scratching sound from the direction of Philip's room on the ground floor. My step quickened as I went along the dark corridor to Philip's door. Humble was inside, whining. "Philip?" I called, my hand on the doorknob. There was no answer, only Humble's petulant whine. I flung the door open.

Philip lay across the low cot or bed, dressed as he had been last night, his face turned away, one arm trailing to the floor. There was a fearful stillness on him. For breathing is a stealthy thing; the lack of it is loud as thunder. I crossed the room, knowing, even before I touched his hand and felt its coldness spread through me. "Philip?" My voice was a trembling whisper. There was no faintest stirring, no flicker of the eyelash, only the terrible indifference of the dead. "Philip!" I cried. Then I just stood there, my hands pressed to my cheeks.

Always there comes first a selfish sense of injury, that what has responded with love, with hate, with something, no matter what, is silent, forever withdrawn. After that comes the feel of a life finished. So now, standing there with old Humble whining at my side, I said, "Is this all? Is this all that his life is to be? Finished, set aside, like this, all done and over?" I saw it in a flash then, as a whole thing: his boyhood here on the plantation, the time at college of which I knew so little, the Sunday mornings at church where I had first seen him, the dull small duties at the court-

218

house, the release of the war years, my coming—and always the knowledge, the fear, the pride and the abilities unrealized save in moments of crisis when his true self emerged, courageous, triumphant. Now here, in this dark room, the finish of it all. Oh, was it always like this with all lives—that so much was left still undone, that so much that might have been was lacking? If only I could have been better, could have helped him to more happiness, to greater fulfillment! He had had so terribly little.

I stood there a long time, looking down at him. Then I went through the corridor and up to the ell porch. In the dining room Miss Stockbridge was in her place, Miss Kate was pouring coffee. "I can't imagine where Philippe can be. He is never late. He didn't look well last night."

I stood beside my chair, both hands gripping the back of it. "Miss Kate?" My voice was cracked and strange.

She turned her gray-green eyes on me and slowly they widened till there was a circle of white around the pupils. The cup dropped from her hand, the thin china breaking as it struck the saucer, coffee spreading in a slow brown stain. "Philippe?" Her lips shaped his name but no sound came.

I bowed my head. Then I watched her small white hands moving among the coffee cups, mopping up the coffee with her napkin. She lifted the soaked linen square, folded it daintily, carefully, laid it down on the white cloth. Then she rose slowly, stiffly, unbreaking, but all at once terribly old. "If you will excuse me, please." She went across the porch and down, her step dragging, heavy and slow.

I went then to Philip's mother. She was alone, sitting as always in the little chair, looking out through the barred window. She was in her nightgown still, her body lost in its folds. I laid my hand on her arm. "Philip is dead."

I had thought, downstairs in his room, that all was finished, complete and forever. But this was really the end, when the words were spoken. Now it was true and set in the finality of speech and sound.

"Philip?" She looked up at me with her vague eyes. "Is it someone I should know?"

219

"Your son."

She shook her head and turned back to the window. "I have no son."

That was true, too. Now. I looked around the room. Callie's bed had not been slept in; her clothes were gone from the rack in the corner where they should be hanging. "Where is Callie? The nurse—where is she?"

The old woman shook her head. "But there is a nurse. There is always a nurse."

I went out quietly and closed and barred the door.

Philip was buried in the plantation graveyard at the top of the bluff. There were flowers from Miss Kate's clubs, from the men in Philip's office, from many of the prominent families of Sherrysburg and the county. For no one stood higher than the Churstons. Many came to the service and followed the coffin to the grave.

The warm sun shone bright on the river below us. It shot dazzling shafts through the branches of the trees beyond the iron-fenced enclosure. But here under the thick, broadleaved magnolias it was dark. The Negroes, standing all to one side, kept close together, their voices mellowing the one hymn that was sung. I saw Jeff, at a distance, among people I did not know. Our eyes met in the silence as the minister stooped for a handful of earth before he began the lines, "Dust to dust . . ." For a moment I rested in the love and pity in Jeff's face, and in that brief moment, like a warning, I heard the crackle of dead magnolia leaves on the path outside—Philip's Grandfather Carrol, walking, reminding me of the secret shame that could not be buried, that had warped the lives of all who were laid here, that reached out to me now, relentless, unescapable. I bowed my head, my grief dark and unrelieved.

For some, grief is pure, self-healing, cleanly cut with a sterile blade. But mine was a two-way wound, cutting back into the festering past, slashing into the future. As the days went by, I saw my life ahead, fixed and unalterable. I thought things through. First, the practical—I must begin at once to make as many smocked dresses as Miss Ida would sell. No matter what Miss Kate said I must let it be known that I would do dressmaking for anyone who would pay cash money for it. I was already caring for Philip's mother in place of Callie, gone the night of Philip's death. "Hear tell she lit out for Nyahleens," Minerva said. Miss Stockbridge, away since the day of the funeral, would pay only a little more rent at most. This year's crop would be the last, and of course there would no longer be Philip's salary to count on. There was his insurance, but I meant to save that for Henry's education.

We would manage somehow. The hard thing was to give up all thought of Jeff. I had already put him out of my life, but now I would not let myself even think of him. He had no place in this life of mine, or in my child's. If he felt as Miss Stockbridge did, then I might risk telling him, I might count on his saying, "What difference does that make?" But I remembered too well her discussions with him and his words, "Not in my time . . . and I am glad of it." So I went no more to the sand bar. Once as I rolled the carriage under the cedars, out to the edge of the bluff, I saw Jeff paddling by. I moved quickly back out of sight, though all that day I was shaken. Again on a clear still afternoon I thought I heard the willow whistle, but I stopped my ears.

One letter came from him. "When may I see you?" he wrote. I answered as briefly, "It is impossible, now or ever. It is my wish never to see you again." That was the end. Life stretched ahead, dull and monotonous. Miss Kate began going again to her club meetings. "We must carry on," she said. I drove her to the bus when she asked me, and met her in the late afternoon. She had to get her own murder mysteries and historical novels from the library now, but in them she could lose herself half her waking hours. Only in her face did she show her grief. There were deep, sagging lines around her mouth, her tight small lips had a downward curve. She closed the piano, put away her music. "I shall never sing again," she said.

Unexpectedly, early one morning, Miss Stockbridge arrived

by taxi from Sherrysburg. She had to leave that same day, she said. She must get the noon train from Sherrysburg to Jackson, her plane passage being engaged for that night. She got her things together in short order, and Old Sam carried them out to the car.

Miss Kate, following us to the head of the steps, said, "It's been a real pleasure to have you, Miss Stockbridge, and if you don't plan to come down again, I do wish you would recommend Cedar Bluff to some nice friend. We shall be lonely here now."

"And we shall need the money," I said, going on down the steps.

Miss Stockbridge was doubtful. "It's been perfect for me, of course. I'm used to roughing it. Put in a bathroom, central heating and——"

"Roughing it!" Miss Kate cried. "A bathroom—— Why, the . . . the atmosphere would be ruined."

Miss Stockbridge laughed. "The atmosphere would be definitely improved, to my mind. More sanitary. But I'll do what I can. The food I can recommend without reservation."

As we drove down the plantation road between the fields of corn and sweet potatoes, she said, "You going to run the plantation yourself now?"

"I'll do what I can, with Sam to help me. But I don't know enough about it really, and it's such a gamble at best that I——"

"Well, luckily you won't have very long to worry with it."

"What do you mean?"

"You'll be moving down the road before long or I miss my guess. Say good-by to him for me, will you?"

"You will have to say your own good-bys." I slowed the car before the plantation gate, added as I got out, "I shall be staying at Cedar Bluff."

We had gone perhaps half a mile on the gravel road before she spoke again. "I am disappointed in you, Bentley. There is no real reason why you can't marry him tomorrow. I'm not one to consider appearances. Ridiculous! Oh, wait six months if you must," she said in answer to my shocked glance. "But do it. You're a fool if you don't, a supersensitive fool. Sorry, but you ought to be used to my plain-spokenness by now. He's a fine man.

222

I've a good mind to—— If I didn't have my passage engaged——"

"No," I said with such decision that she subsided for a little. I drove quickly along the paved road, resentment and anger mounting. "I know what my life must be and I am ready to face it."

"Life is long, my proud little simpleton, and you'd better do something about it while you can. A man as attractive as Jeff is not going to be hanging around forever."

I kept my eyes on the road and said nothing.

"You should at least see him once and tell him what the fool reason is, why you won't——"

"No, no!" I cried. "That is not my secret. It belongs to the Churston family. I'll spend my life guarding it, fighting it, for my baby's sake. Never will I——"

She snorted. "Dramatics, pure and simple. Sacrifice!" she said with scorn. "Nothing more foolish and shortsighted and futile. Your child will find out, he'll get your exaggerated notion of the seriousness of the thing and——"

"He will not find out."

"You did."

I caught my breath. Those letters. I would get them tonight and burn them, every one.

"Yes," Miss Stockbridge repeated, "he's as smart as you are. He'll find out, go into an emotional tailspin over it and pass on his hang-over to the next generation."

"To the third and fourth generation," I said. "Only I won't let him find out. I'll——" I was silent. We were on the main street now, turning for the railroad station. "Miss Stockbridge," I said, for I did not want to part from her in anger, "I don't doubt that you know a lot of sociology and that you will write a good acceptable thesis, but you will never understand the feeling here about these things."

"Humph! I've got eyes in my head, haven't I? I may be old but I'm not in my dotage. Not yet. Oh, my dear child, use your head about this. If you won't take Jeff, then move to South America where there's no stigma attached to mixed blood and you can acknowledge it openly. Even just to move away, to any new place

223

somewhere in the North, would be better than doing nothing. But of course the best way of all——"

She broke off abruptly as we came to the cindered parking place alongside the depot. She opened her pocketbook, took out an envelope. "Here is a check for my last month and enough over to pay the express on my box of books. I would appreciate your getting it off as soon as possible." She snapped her handbag shut, took hold of her brief case that was bulging with notes. She thrust her head out the window, called, "Sst—sst—porter, please!" to the trainman lounging against the dingy brown wall of the station. "Good-by, my dear. Don't hold it against me for speaking my mind, and good luck to you in any case!" She flung open the car door.

My hands slid from the wheel. She was going. There never again would be anyone with whom I could talk freely, anyone who would know, even without understanding. And what was it she had begun to say, before she gave me the check, about the best way of all? "Miss Stockbridge," I stopped her as she was about to step down from the car. "You said, just now . . . the best way of all—— What is the best way?" My breath caught in a noisy gulp, and she must have seen the despair in my eyes.

But she gave me no sympathy, even now in this last moment. "Why, simple enough," she snapped. "Just come right out with it, tell everybody your child's got Negro blood, laugh, keep your chin up and show them. Show them! Is your child's father the only parent who has any guts?" She slammed the door shut in my horror-struck face, jerked a thumb toward the rear of the car as a porter came running, and went on into the station without looking back.

• 24 •

CHANGE in the great social scene, in the individual life, comes less often through a single mighty upheaval than through the cumulative power of small, often unnoticed, happenings. Certain it is that during the dull days of that summer when the hot sun wilted and dried the earth and the muggy air enervated body and spirit alike, the small things in my dreary life began to mount up and gather strength.

Philip had been a bridge between Miss Kate and me. With that gone, the distance widened and deepened. The smooth outer covering fell away, the rough-edged stone emerged. She spoke to me sharply and I replied with unconcealed irritation. It was my turn to worry now and I understood better Philip's continual anxiety about money matters. Now it was I who shouldered all the responsibilities of the place. Looking ahead I could see the bleak years before me—how Miss Kate would become more and more of a care as her health failed. Already, since Philip's death, she showed her age in many small ways. And Philip's mother was another burden. These things had been laid on me and there was no escape. For Philip's sake I must bear them. I had done so little for him while he lived, I must do this now. It seemed to me that Philip's life had been doomed from the beginning, and as I thought on it, I was filled with pity and sadness. Not that I forgot the ways in which he had hurt me, but the hurt was softened by its inevitability.

I was now earning all the cash money that came into the house and I felt the right to have some say about how it was spent. When I found a library book three weeks overdue, I spoke out bluntly.

"Please remember, Bentley," Miss Kate said, "that the plantation belongs to me. Little Henry will be my heir. But meanwhile there is no reason why I should not manage my own business affairs."

223

Her business affairs! What business did she have except to pay out money for club dues and book fines! I was knitting wool socks —Miss Ida said people might buy them for Christmas—and the yarn stuck to my sweaty fingers. I bit my lip to keep from blazing out at her.

We could no longer afford to pay Old Sam regularly. He got a part-time job near town in the overall factory and worked in the field on a share basis. I suggested to Miss Kate that we let Minerva go, but she said, "I'd sooner be dead than have no servant in the house. We haven't sunk that low yet."

Even with Minerva I had plenty to do, caring for Philip's mother, tending the baby, who was teething and fretful now, doing my sewing and knitting. I worked feverishly, going from one thing to another. Yet of a sudden sometimes in the midst of it I would be struck still. Sharp and fierce, my longing for Jeff came over me. I felt his arms around me, his lips on mine. I saw his deep-set eyes, his smile. I heard the very tones of his voice. Then blinking, looking around me, seeing my life as it was, I would flare out at Miss Kate, answer her bitterly.

She criticized me for walking over the fields with Old Sam, trying to salvage something of the year's planting. "Suppose someone should be driving by and see you," she said.

"Who am I to be ashamed of being seen with a Negro?" I said with bitterness.

Again, about my sewing, she said, "The ladies of the Churston family have never worked for pay. If you insist on doing this sort of thing, at least send Sam in with the bundle. It doesn't look well for you to be seen——"

"Philip took my things in for me sometimes," I reminded her.

"Philippe was a Churston," she said in the tone of one remarking that the king can do no wrong. "You are one by marriage only."

"I'm not likely to forget it," I said. Yet I knew why she was trying to make a Churston of me. I knew why there must be no talk, no whisperings. We had that one thing in common: our determination to make things right for Henry, and little by little I was molded to the pattern. For I knew no other way. I even forced myself to go to church again, following Miss Kate down the aisle, stiff-necked and haughty, and afterward as we came out, bowing coldly when she smiled and greeted friends. Once I overheard one of them say to Miss Kate, with a nod in my direction, "She really has quite an air—a look of real distinction. Must have good blood somewhere."

Good blood! God, how I hated the woman—and Miss Kate, so sweet and deprecatory and yet managing to imply that anything I had was due to her tutelage.

Another Sunday morning, as I sat in the Churston pew, the purple shaft of light from the stained-glass window falling now across my shoulders like a royal scarf, I looked over to where my mother and I used to sit. Usually I did not look that way. The eager child, the young girl I had been, gay and clear-eyed and warm, reproached me for what I was becoming. But this time something more powerful than my will drew me, forced me to look.

Then it was that I saw Jeff, his arms folded, his eyes fastened on me. For a moment it was as if we were alone together, my blood pounding in tune with his. Then slowly I hardened my heart against him, against my love. I wrenched my gaze from his, turned away. After the service, coming out, I saw him again in the vestibule, standing to one side where I must pass him. I I pressed my lips tight together. I looked through him, past him and went on. It was the only way.

At the car Miss Kate said, "I was glad to see you cut that Wheeling person. Philippe never liked him. He would have quite approved of the way you passed him without recognition. Just as well to keep such people in their place."

I said nothing, my heart leaden and dead. Yes, I was cruel and hard and bitter then. Even now when I look back on that time, a blankness of spirit falls on me and I feel old and worn, remembering. For bitterness is stony-cold while it lasts and leaves a chill when one thinks on it afterward.

At home I was sharper-tongued than ever with Miss Kate. Strangely enough she took no offense, not even when I interrupted a tale of the great old days and the Churstons' thousand

227

slaves. "I've already heard that a thousand times," I said, "once for each slave."

"I know," she said, "but this is a part of Henry's heritage, and if I repeat often enough, you will remember and pass it on to him. And don't forget he must go to Virginia to school."

I said I would remember, and knitted the faster. Many pennies, one by one and set aside, would do it. But when she began to question me about my own family, especially the Bentleys who had come from South Carolina, I could see no point in it. I knew nothing except a few family names like Abijah and Thatcher Bentley. "My grandfather Carr was a wheelwright and floated down the Mississippi from Cairo on a flatboat," I said with malice.

"It is not necessary to mention that. There are many things in the past that are better left undisturbed."

"I am sure of that," I told her, careless of how I might hurt with seemingly innocent words.

One week in midsummer she had me take her every morning to the bus and meet her in the late afternoon. She was tracing a branch line, she said, looking it up in the library records. She wrote thick letters to various state archives of history and sent money to some firm whose advertisement she had seen. She was elated when they replied that they could trace the line back through the kings and queens of England to Adam and Eve, not to mention the Revolution and the Norman Conquest on the way. But I would give her no money for that. "You know enough, you know too much, about your ancestors already."

Surprisingly she agreed. "Yes, I think I have enough. We'll see."

One day when I was in town for some necessary purchases, I went into the small bookstore on the main street and ordered a copy of Jeff's book that Philip had burned. I had it sent direct to him with no word from me. He would know where it came from. I took a grim satisfaction in sending it like this. It was a period set at the end of a little . . . a little parenthesis in my life. For I knew now that those weeks when I let myself love him, not thinking of him but only of my own need, that brief mad time had no place in the pattern of my days. My love for him had been like a curl of mist over the river, vanishing with the dawn. It was no more than the brief rosy fall of petals when the azaleas were going by their blooming. It was the pure clean call of a night bird in the dark, quickly hushed.

I came out of the bookshop and stopped by Miss Ida's shop to see how my little dresses and knitted socks looked in her window. She had the space jammed with trinkets and toys and trays and fussy gift-shop stuff. My things were to one side, and crowded. Some ladies passed me, going into the shop and, as always, feeling eyes on me, I stiffened, holding my head high. Then from inside I heard one of them, shouting so that deaf Miss Ida could hear, "Isn't that Philip Churston's widow?"

I stood motionless, staring down at a cluster of pink and blue rattles. Philip Churston's widow—it had a strange sound in my ears. It was like a tombstone at my head, my life carved and set down for time and eternity.

"Yes, Bentley Carr that was," Miss Ida said in her strident monotone. "What say?"

The customer laughed. "I said she's only a Churston by marriage but it must be catching; she's got that stiff-necked, you're-dirt-under-my-feet look."

Moving away, I saw myself reflected in the window. It was true, what that woman had said. I was a Churston now, armored with coldness, with pride and reserve, shut away from everyone in my terrible aloneness. I shivered as I went on down the street toward the parked car. Couldn't I ever again be easy and gay as I used to be long ago? As I had been even in the first years of my marriage? Couldn't I ever be honest again before the world? Or face it unafraid?

Driving home, my bundles beside me on the car seat, I kept hearing that laughing, careless voice: "stiff-necked, you're-dirt-under-my-feet . . ." Deep within me something stirred. It was not ready yet to break out in open rebellion, my will was too strong. But slowly, as the days went by, my own secret, hidden self began to wake again.

For one may not deny oneself forever. The essential *me* is too strong, too persistent. Thrust down, no matter how deep, by the pressure of outer force and circumstance, it will not die while life lasts, but waits, biding the time, gathering strength. So it had been with Philip, his true self emerging in time of crisis. So it was with me. Not through any great single event but through the piling up of many small things, so that at last one more, like the proverbial last straw, broke through my resistance.

The heat of summer was still on the land, September heat, the worst of the year. All day the air was still and oppressive, the moss hung motionless on the cedars. Henry was fretful and missed his nap. In the late afternoon I brought him downstairs and fed him and rolled him in his carriage under the trees. He dozed in the soothing motion, though the heat was unrelenting and even the river had no coolness, only reflecting the heat of the sky, doubling it.

Miss Kate came to the gallery with a tray. "I'll watch him while you take this up," she called. For now, to economize, we had our dinner in the middle of the day and let Minerva go home right after. Miss Kate prepared the tray for Philip's mother and I took it up. She did that much to help me.

"He's asleep at last," I said, taking the tray from her.

Upstairs I waited, setting the room in order while the old woman ate in her usual slow, listless way. I helped her to bed, then I came out and let down the bar across the door. I might as well be barred in a room myself, I thought with bitterness. What was the difference between her and me? Both barred in, only my cell was a little larger than hers. "I'm in prison," I said aloud to the silent shadowy courtyard. "I'm caught, caught, and I can't get out." My voice, rising, was thrown back and echoed by the empty gallery walls. I wiped the sweat from my forehead and took the tray on down to the kitchen. It must be the heat, I told myself. There was a distant roll of thunder. Perhaps a shower would clear the air.

Miss Kate and I sat side by side on the front gallery while the baby slept in the yard below us. Her chair squeaked as she rocked slowly back and forth, fanning herself with a palmetto fan. The sound set my teeth on edge—*squeeuck, squeeuck*. It went through my head like a hot knife. There was a yellow light in the western sky, for it was just after sundown, a strange, metallic coppery light that altered the green of brush and shrub, rusted over the cedars and seemed to set us on a stage in an unreal, theatrical world.

Miss Kate said, with a wave of her fan in little Henry's direction, "You must trim his hair—a boy has no business with curls."

I just looked at her. Must everything remind me? Could I never be allowed to forget for a moment that straight hair was better? I said, "It's going to rain; his hair is always curly when the air is muggy like this. Besides, I like curly hair."

"No need to be so vicious about it, dear," Miss Kate said, her chair squeaking as she rocked. "I may as well tell you now—perhaps it will cheer you up. I've had your tree looked into."

"My tree?"

"Yes, your family tree. I was just waiting for a quiet moment to tell you. I had Abijah Bentley traced back through the South Carolina records."

"Oh? I suppose he was hanged for murder or something." I leaned back in my chair and tried to relax.

"On the contrary. I got the complete records in the morning's mail. Abijah's father was Captain Thatcher Bentley who served in the Revolution!"

"Does it matter?" He could have been the King of Siam for all the good it would do me. I would still be right here.

"Of course it does. Now you are eligible to the D.A.R. and I have just filled out your application. I will sponsor you and——"

I straightened up slowly in my chair. "Thank you just the same, Miss Kate, but I'm the same person I was yesterday and the day before too, no matter who Abijah's father was. I'm still me. If I wasn't good enough before, I'm not now. I don't want to join anything."

"Don't want to!" Miss Kate cried. "You . . . you just don't know enough to know what it means, in this county, anyway. You don't——"

"Yes, I do. It means going to meetings, seeing people, putting on——"

"But that is what you need. It will make little Henry's position secure. I won't be here always and people forget so quickly. Besides, it will be good for you. I don't know what my life would have been without my clubs—the associations, the educational and social advantages——"

"I don't want them. It's all foreign to me. I won't fill up my life with them."

"It doesn't matter what you want, you little fool," Miss Kate burst out. "It's your duty. You must think of the family standing. For your child's sake you must carry on. Oh, must I see all I have worked for all my life wiped out by a little know-nothing?"

"It won't do my child any good. Nothing will, but himself. He's got to stand on his own merits. He——"

"What nonsense! Now you listen to me, Bentley Carr!" She pounded on the arm of her chair with one small fist. "The Churston family has always taken a prominent place in the county. Just because you don't care for social life is no reason—— I tell you you must keep up appearances. Oh, if only Philippe were here he would make you! He was always so careful, so meticulous in every way, never missing church service, always doing the right thing, even to giving his life for law and order."

"Yes, he did that." Then suddenly the whole bitter tragedy of his life rose up before me—and the reason for it. "What ruined his life was the . . . the pretending, the fear!" I shouted. "Oh, I know. He was always afraid. Well, I tell you, I'll have no more of it. I'm through." I sprang to my feet. "It's time there was an end to it and I'm the one to do it."

"What on earth are you talking about?" Miss Kate cried. "And who are you to say what you will do and what you won't do? You, a seamstress' daughter, a . . . a nobody! I took you in, I did everything for you, opposed as I was—and you had your own way, you had your child. Well, you won't have your own way about this."

I faced her, furious now beyond all reason. "Maybe I am a nobody. Maybe my mother was a seamstress. But she was honest. She didn't live a lie. She didn't pretend to be what she wasn't."

Miss Kate drew in her breath with a hissing sound. Her face took on a mottled look.

But I was past stopping now. "So you think I don't know? Oh,

232

yes, I know why Philip was warped and bitter and madly jealous, hurting me—me whom he loved." I caught my breath in a sob. "It was fear that drove him so he had to be always proving himself —to the world, to me, even to a Negro girl—proving that he was at least a man. Negro! She was as white as he."

Miss Kate was shrunken down in her chair. "You . . . you know," she whispered.

"Know? Of course I know," I cried. "I know why you hated me. You were afraid I would find out. You were afraid for me to have a child. You would have killed him before he was born. I know, oh, I know, how it has warped and twisted all your lives—that poor broken one upstairs, too. And it wasn't the truth that did it, the truth you were trying to hide; it was the hiding of it, the horrible pretense, the false front before the world, the terrible soul-breaking strain of it! That's why Hollis Churston killed himself. And now you expect me to keep it up, to go on forever—to the third and fourth generation. Well, I won't, I tell you!"

Miss Kate staggered to her feet. "Stop, stop, you . . . you. . . ."

I paid her no heed. The words poured out, there was no stopping me For I saw it all now, clear as never before. "I won't and my child won't. He shall know the truth from the time he knows anything. And I shall teach him to tell it to all the world without shame. She was right—Miss Stockbridge. The best way of all, she said, and that's the way I'm taking now, me and my child, and we shall be free, free of fear and free of lies." Just speaking the words gave me release. The long tension eased. I stood before her, head up, defiant, feeling the burden roll from me.

Miss Kate crossed the distance between us, her face twisted with fury, her voice hoarse. "You . . . you devil! You shan't do this. I won't let you. You are insane. I'll have you shut up. I've done it once and I can do it again. I'll have you committed to the asylum where nobody will hear your ravings. I'll——"

I shook my head. "You can't do that. People will believe me." My voice was almost quiet now. "They will believe because there are those who know it is true."

Miss Kate shrank back, her lips shaping words but no sound coming.

"You can't keep a thing like that altogether secret. You——"

"Stop, stop!" she broke in. "You lie, you lie to torment me. Oh, what a . . . a viper I have cherished in my bosom! I've done everything, even offered to sponsor you, to make you worthy of the Churston name and this is all the thanks I get—these insults, these lies. They are lies, all lies. Get out of here!" Her voice rose. She beat me across the face and shoulders with her fan. "My house . . . Get out, filthy-mouthed Jezebel! Out, now, this instant!"

I held her at arm's length, her arm flabby under my firm grasp. "Stop striking me and listen," I said so quietly that she was shocked into stillness. "I will go. I will take my child with me. I would rather go and live among Negroes and bring him up among them, knowing the truth, than live this lie among white people."

I let go her arm, turned and went down the steps, not looking back. I wheeled the carriage across the yard under the cedars, out past the chicken house and along the path to the field. It was not till the baby began to cry that I realized the rain had come. I pulled the carriage top over him and went on, finding my way across the field by flashes of lightning.

Where was I going? Alone in the night and the rain with my child. Where could I go? Who would take me in? Then off to the right I saw yellow light streaming out through an open window—Minerva's cabin. "All right," I said aloud, lifting my face to the rain." I said I would rather go and live among Negroes, and I will."

Minerva opened the door, her bony, gaunt figure outlined against the yellow light. She blinked at me standing there on the little porch, the rain splashing about my feet and ankles, the whimpering baby held tight in my arms. "Reckon you want to git in out of the rain." She stepped aside, holding the door against the wind.

I stood just inside the door, my breath still coming fast from my hurrying. I looked into her dark, closed face. What did I know of her, really? Perhaps she hated me, hated all white people. "I want more than to get out of the rain, Minerva."

There was no change in her face. She waited with a terrible dignity, saying no word.

234

"I want shelter for the night—and until I know what I am going to do."

There was a faint quiver at the corner of her lips. Was it scorn, amusement? "She turn you out?"

I nodded, my lips trembling. If Minerva would not let me stay, what would I do?

Minerva went to the fireplace, threw on some pine knots from the box in the chimney corner. Then she straightened up. "You is welcome."

I let out my breath. Then I shook my wet hair out of my face. "I must tell you something first." For I was going to begin now, being honest, concealing nothing. "You may not want me."

Minerva said, "Been lookin' for a blowup. Come dry yourself."

"But I have to tell you. I'm through with hiding anything— anything, I tell you."

She stared at me, dark eyes widening. "You mean you ain't goin' hide nothin'? Nothin' at all?" Her voice sank to a whisper.

"You know what I mean."

Her eyes shifted to the baby in my arms. "You got grief ahead."

"I know it, oh, I know it. But there's less grief this way than the other. Oh, Minerva, don't you see? You've known them all, you've seen how it was."

Minerva nodded. "I seen what I seen."

"Well, it's not going to be that way any more. Not for me or my child."

Minerva leaned forward and her black eyes seemed to pierce through to my very brain. "You done made your choice?"

"I have made my choice, come what may!" My words rang out, they filled the room and hung suspended, vibrating on the air."

Minerva's nostrils widened. "I never thought to see the day."

"Now, will you let me stay?"

"I is proud," she said, and she looked it.

235

I WOKE in the little shed room, feeling the narrow cot bed hard beneath me, the baby warm beside me. Stiff and cramped from my narrow quarters, I lay staring up at the dark stained boards of the ceiling, and my first thought was one of thankfulness. The fear, the terrible tension was lifted. Then, as I watched the spears of sunlight that found their way between the boards of the window shutter, a thought came to me as bright and splendid as they. Now I could see Jeff. I could see him once more, just once. I was free now to tell him why we could never be together, ask him to forgive my cruel letter and my coldness. Surely he would understand and know I must do what I felt was right. Even if he tried to change me, I was strong enough to hold out against him and go my way alone.

Quietly I slipped from under the threadbare sheet, and found my clothes, dried and ironed by Minerva while I slept. The front room was empty. The white iron bed where Minerva had wanted me to sleep last night was neatly made. On the hearth before the fire were the baby's bottle and his cereal. Minerva must have gone early to milk. How good she was! In the skillet close to the live embers were side meat and corn pone, and coffee was simmering in a black pot that sat on a trivet over the fire.

When I had eaten, the baby wakened, so I bathed him before the fire, fed him and laid him in the carriage with a tin spoon and stewpan lid to play with. Now what? I looked around the room. I had never before been in a Negro cabin. The floor was bare; the walls were pasted over with newspapers to keep out the cold in winter, the heat in summer. There was a golden-oak rocking chair, a straight chair with a broken seat and a ten-cent-store wooden bottom nailed over it. There was a little old washstand in one corner and above it a brightly colored calendar showing a golden-haired little girl standing on a flowered hilltop, looking up into the sky. Underneath in large letters: JONES AND GREEN UNDER-

TAKING PARLORS, COMPLETE SERVICE. Bleak and bare the room was, but clean.

I finished my breakfast and sat on for a while in the quiet room. What now, what now? I kept saying to myself. I could not stay on and on here with Minerva. I must be earning money. But who would take me in? Would I be denied lodging in Sherrysburg, turned away, the door closed in my face? For it would be quickly known that I had left Cedar Bluff, and I meant to make no secret of the reason why. Then what? Well, I thought, staring into the fire, if white people would not take me in, perhaps Negroes would. I would go to the shabby section beyond my old home. A room would be cheap there.

But I could not spend the time here in idleness, just waiting for afternoon when I could see Jeff. See Jeff? At the thought such a mad, wild feeling came over me that I sprang up. I must do something, anything, to make the time go by quickly. I found a broom and set to work sweeping, taking up the ashes, dusting. I was shaking the one rag rug on the porch when I saw Minerva coming along the path across the field, a bundle in her arms. "My clothes and the baby's!" I cried as she came under the chinaberry tree. "Bless you, Minerva."

" 'Lowed she didn't have no right to them, no need neither," Minerva said, mounting the single step. In the doorway she stopped and looked around, seeing now the rug in my hands, the swept and dusted room. "Hadn't ought to done that," she said gruffly. She set the bundle down on the bed and faced me.

Under her dark gaze I grew uneasy. "It wasn't that the room was dirty, Minerva—only I had to be doing something."

With a little gesture she dismissed the room and set it from us. "Somethin' else," she said.

"What? Tell me quickly." I caught her by the arm. "What is it?"

"Miss Kate."

I fell back, seeing again Miss Kate's darkly mottled face, her terrible vehemence, her anger. "What about her?" I asked through stiff lips.

"Carryin' on somethin' awful. Couldn't make out what ailed her. Say call the doctor, an' I done that."

237

"Has he come?"

"He come."

"What did he say? What's the matter with her?" As if I didn't know—the shock, the upheaval, the threat to all the structure of her life—that was enough to strike her down.

"Doctor, he scratch his haid. He don't know. I knowed but I wasn't tellin'. So he say it's her age, excusin' himself."

"Miss Kate isn't so old, is she?"

"Pushin' seventy."

"I didn't realize she was that old." I went and sat down, bowed over in the little rocker, my eyes on the floor. I saw now what I had done to her. It was a terrible thing I had done. "If she dies, I will have killed her." I looked up at Minerva.

Minerva turned away, but not before I had seen the sudden bleakness in her face. "Ain't no use sayin' what is ain't."

I covered my face with my hands. Miss Kate, broken, old, her whole life, her standing, her prestige which she valued above life, shattered in an instant—by me. Philip's Aunt Kate. Could I be so ruthless, so cruel, to an old woman? But I had to, I had to break free, for Henry's sake. He was more important than she, or I, or anything else in the world. Then all at once I saw what I must do. I stood up, staring straight before me. "I'll have to wait. I cannot go ahead with this. Not while she is living. It is too unkind. No good could come of such unkindness. I'll have to go and tell her that not while she lives will I——" Then my eyes fell on Minerva.

She was standing there, her long bony arms hanging limp at her sides, her nostrils wide, her face set as if carved out of black rock in lines of scorn and bitterness.

"You don't believe I'll ever do it!" I cried. "You don't believe. But I will. I swear it—by God, by the dead Churstons, by my own child, I swear it!" I caught her by the shoulders and shook her, crying out, begging her to believe me. She was rigid under my hands, her dark face changeless, fixed. "Speak, speak! You wouldn't have me kill Miss Kate, would you?"

She let her words out slowly, one by one. "The way's full of people. Can't move on without giving grief to somebody."

238

I fell back from her. I stood there twisting my hands together. It was true. Oh, yes, it was true. Someone must be hurt. "But you . . . you are used to being hurt," I cried. O God, what had I said? What sort of reason was that?

"Humph!" She turned her back on me and went and stood looking down into the fire. I waited a long time for her to speak. "Comes a time folks used to bein' hurt done had enough."

"But you could wait. Please—" my voice broke—"please, you could wait."

"Been waitin' a long time."

"But don't you see," I cried, "don't you see that I am not free? I am bound—by loyalty to Philip, to all the Churstons, to all the past, to . . . to my own kind . . . bound . . ." I caught my breath and looked down at the baby asleep now in his carriage. Wasn't I bound to him, and to the future as much as the past? God, I was right in the middle, torn between the two!

Minerva had turned slowly, and, as I looked up at her now, I saw that she was looking past and beyond me When she spoke, her voice came as if from a distance, like the voice of doom. "I see you is bound." She lifted her head in pride and a terrible dignity. "I see them that was bond is free." She turned her dark gaze on me now. "And them that was free is bond."

I stared at her for a long moment. Then I hid my face in my hands and wept.

After a while Minerva spoke, grudgingly, as she used to speak. "Better git on up yonder and tell her. I'll stay with the baby."

I wiped my face with my hands and went, bowed over, stumbling from the fresh tears that came. I left the cabin and set out across the field. As I came up the front steps, I heard Miss Kate calling Minerva, her deep husky voice cracked and desperate. I went into the hallway and stopped short at the foot of the stairs. Miss Kate stood on the landing, her faded brown bathrobe open over her long white gown—a monstrous flabby figure, she was, her ravaged face unpowdered and yellow, her wig awry, showing the white woolly mat underneath.

"You," she said, "come crawling back——"

239

"No," I cut through her rising voice. "I came to tell you something."

"You can tell me nothing." Her little hand tightened on the railing.

"But I am going to. There is one person who must know, but except for him—" I flung the words at her, at all the Churstons, stiff and fixed in their rigid pose, gold-framed against the walls— "I will keep silent as long as you live. I give you my word, in solemn promise."

She lifted her head, standing proud in a dignity as terrible as Minerva's had been, her eyes fastened on the fanlight over my head, as if I were too low-down to be looked at. "Get . . . out . . . out . . . of my house!" she cried, her voice ringing out deep and echoing, multiplied by the empty hall as if all the Churstons ranged along the walls cried out with her against me.

I turned and went through the open door, down the front steps and out under the cedars for the last time. They were still in shadow, for the sun had not yet reached above the high peaked roof of the house. They were dark and secret as if night still slept among them.

As I went through the kitchen garden I saw the car in the carriage house. The car belonged to Philip. Surely I had a right to it, and I would need it. For now I knew what I had to do. I could trespass no longer on Minerva's kindness. I must go to town and find a room with someone who would care for the baby while I worked. I could sell the car for enough to tide me over and to put away for emergencies. I drove it out by the plantation road, down the gravel highway till I was opposite Minerva's cabin. There I parked it and went in across the field. I told Minerva I would like to stay this one more night, then I would go.

She said, "You is welcome." Then as she went down the steps on her way to the house and Miss Kate, she paused, not looking back at me as I stood humble, uncertain, in the doorway. She spoke gruffly, with reluctance, as always. "Reckon you kin stay as long as you needs."

I watched her go with her long stride across the field, and my

240

eyes blurred. What had I done to her? I had given her hope and withdrawn it. And still she was good. Oh, goodness had nothing to do with the color of one's skin or the bood in one's veins! "I'll make little Henry be good," I said aloud. "Nothing else matters."

Then I sat down on the step under the shade of the umbrella China tree and let the morning pass, and noon. I waited for Minerva to come back from Miss Kate's so I could leave the baby and go down to the sand bar, my sand bar, and find Jeff for the last time.

At the top of the bluff I looked down, then cried out in dismay. The big willow was down, blown over by the storm last night, its branches flung out across the yellow sand, its roots naked to the air. Was it a sign, a symbol of what was ahead of me? And the whistle, where was it? Lost, buried in the sand? I ran down the path, flung myself down, crawled in under the green branches till I reached the heart of the tree. It was split wide at the crotch. My fingers dug through the leaves and sand, searching desperately.

I found it at last and I lay there, panting, holding it to my lips with no breath to blow. When the sound rang out at last, it was high and clear and imperative. It went out across the water and through the swamp and far back along the distant reaches of the bayou. Again and again I blew, the bluff adding its echo to the high, shrill call.

Now for the first time I thought, Suppose he hears and will not come? Why should he come, after my letter, after that cruel day at church? I was still standing there among the fallen willow branches when the dugout nosed the sand and Jeff sprang ashore. I stumbled out to meet him as he came toward me. We looked at each other dumbly, unsmiling, intent. Then before I knew what I was doing I was in his arms. Wordless, I pressed close against him, forgetting everything except that he had come, that he had not turned from me in anger, that he loved me still. For there are times when words come secondhand and poor, and the speech of the body is eloquent beyond the power of language.

When I drew away from him at last, though he kept my hands in his as though he would never let me go, I said, "There's some-

241

thing I must tell you, Jeff. It's what has kept me from you." Then I told him, I told him what the Churstons had kept hidden and how the hiding of it had warped all their lives.

"Yes," he said with no surprise. "I've had an idea of that."

"You mean you knew?"

"I've heard rumors, that's all. But, darling, let's forget that now and——"

"But this isn't just a rumor I'm telling you. It's true, it's true!" I searched his face, steeling myself to see him turn from me.

But he only said, his voice gentle and low, "For just that you kept me away?"

"It isn't just that," I cried. "You don't know what it's like or you wouldn't call it 'just that.' You'd understand that I couldn't let you be drawn into all that grief and shame. Oh, after I found out, I thought everyone was staring at me. Wherever I went, except here with you, I felt their eyes on me, curious, horrible, prying."

"No, never that. The evil was not there. It was in the hiding and the fear of being found out."

"But it's not going to be that way any more! I'm going to stop it now and forever, for me and my child. He is going to know from the first and tell it without shame or fear. And—" I stiffened against what he would think now—"and when Miss Kate is gone, I shall not keep it from anyone!"

He nodded slowly, his eyes steady on mine, and I could see no change in their bright gaze.

I thought he had not understood, and I said it again, hurrying on then, lest he speak and I should hear dismay or coldness in his voice, lest he have to search for some way to escape from me. "I just came to tell you, so you'd know, so you'd understand why I have to . . . go on alone." Now he could let me go. Now he could say, "I understand, yes." I had made it easy, so easy for him.

But he shook his head. "Not alone."

I turned my face away. Would he even go along with me in this? Against all his belief, his feeling? "But I won't let you. Enough people have suffered for this already. I cannot let you be another.

242

But I thank you—oh Jeff, I do thank you for being willing to get involved."

"But, Bentley, don't you know that we are all involved, everybody, black and white and mixed, whether we like it or not? We are born into it."

I shook my head, my eyes on the water rippling past the sand bar. "Not so intimately, Jeff, so . . . so nearly. No, this is my life and I have to go it alone." I would have drawn my hands from his but he held them too tightly. "Let me go now," I whispered, my voice failing. "It will be easier."

"But I won't let you go, not ever. We'll do this thing together."

I was near to the end of my strength. "No, no, Jeff! I was selfish too long, letting you love me, not thinking of you, only of myself and my need of you. I love you too much, darling, to let you have any part in what's ahead of me."

"Have I nothing to say about it? Look at me, Bentley."

I faced him, desperate now. "No, you haven't. I won't let you. Why, you'd lose your job. You would be an outcast, too. God knows what it will involve. Oh, let me go, let me go!" I struggled to free my hands.

But he held me, his voice quiet, his eyes steady. "I could farm my land. I could teach in the Negro school."

"Don't—don't tempt me. It's more than I can bear, Jeff. I know how you feel, really." I flung back my head and I threw the words at him: "I know what you said that day at your house. 'Not in my time,' you said, and you were thankful. Oh, I can still hear you!"

"Wait. It's true I said that. But I said something else, too."

"What?"

"Miss Stockbridge had said the world must be changed all in a moment, by force of will and edict. I told her that any real and lasting change in human relations must come slowly and naturally, not from the outside, but from within. Remember?"

I nodded, waiting, holding my breath.

"This stand that you mean to take, that we will take together, facing the truth and doing something about it—this is something that comes ready to hand, natural, unforced, out of the general

243

situation. I'd be proud to be a part of it. Oh, my darling, don't you see? It's what I believe in with all my heart."

Trembling, I searched his face. It was true. God, it was true! "Then I . . . you . . . we . . ."

"Yes." He smiled and took me in his arms.

So now the time has come to turn from the past and look forward, as do we who wait on a promise, with hope and courage. We go in bondage still, for we were born to it and change comes slow and hard. There will be grief before the morning of our freedom, but has the morning ever failed to come?

THE END